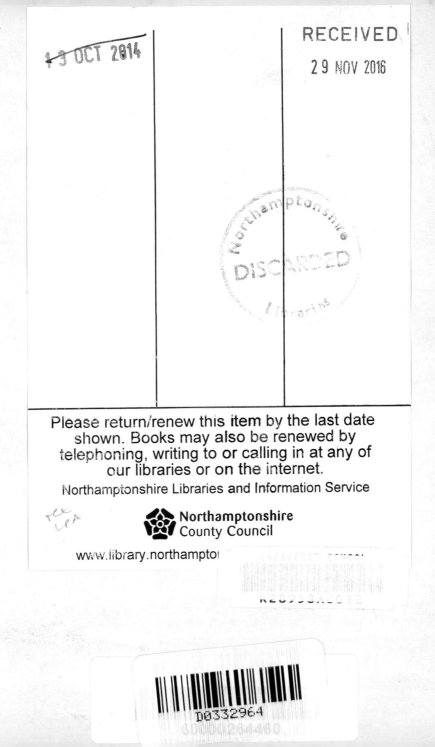

BRIGHTLING

REBECCA LISLE

HOT
KEY
BOOKS

First published in Great Britain in 2014 by Hot Key Books
Northburgh House, 10 Northburgh Street, London EC1V 0AT

Copyright © Rebecca Lisle 2014

A CIP catalogue record for this book is available from the British Library.

ISBN: 978-1-4714-0057-5

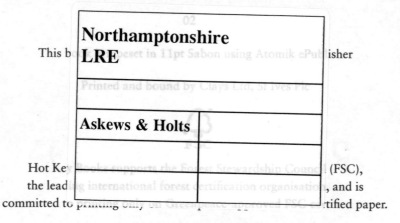

This book is typeset in 11pt Sabon using Atomik ePublisher

Printed and bound by Clays Ltd, St Ives Plc

Hot Key Books supports the Forest Stewardship Council (FSC),
the leading international forest certification organisation, and is
committed to printing only on Greenpeace approved FSC-certified paper.

www.hotkeybooks.com

Hot Key Books is part of the Bonnier Publishing Group
www.bonnierpublishing.com

for Toby Lisle

1

Sparrow

'I can't find him! I *must* find him!' Sparrow cried, looking around wildly.

She ducked under Mr Pynch's outstretched, grabbing arm and raced past him towards the stone stairs.

'Come here!' Mr Pynch roared.

'Where is he?' Sparrow cried, racing up the stairs two at a time. 'I can't go without saying goodbye! I can't!'

In the hall below, the other orphanage girls watched her anxiously.

Miss Knip was standing on the landing blocking her way. She tapped her cane against her palm. 'Sparrow, you have one minute to leave this establishment.' She pointed to the clock high up on the wall. It was nearly six. 'One minute!'

'You'd better go.' One of the girls took Sparrow's hand gently. 'It's now or never.'

Little Jean took her other hand and they guided her back down the stairs.

'You've no choice,' Mary whispered.

'None,' Little Jean added.

'But Scaramouch . . .' Sparrow said, pulling away from them.

Mr Pynch was holding the big black door open. Before she knew it, Sparrow was being helped out. She was on the doorstep. She was outside.

'Goodbye, dear Sparrow!' she heard Mary call, before the heavy door slammed shut behind her.

'And good riddance!' Miss Knip's voice trilled sharply from behind it. She rammed the long iron bolts into their sockets as though she had a grudge against them.

'Go and boil your heads!' Sparrow muttered, then loudly, 'Go and boil your horrible old heads!' And, picking up her bag, she thundered down the path.

The gatekeeper shuffled out of his cosy little room to meet her.

'Sparrow, are you really leaving us?' He looked up at the sky. 'It's not long until dark, lassie,' he said. 'Are you sure you want to go now?'

Sparrow nodded. 'I've no choice, Barton. You know the rules. I'm an evening babe. Come at six o'clock, must leave at six – and if I don't, I stay for ever.'

Barton nodded. 'You wouldn't want that.'

Sparrow looked up at the bleak building and its unlit windows. Each room housed a cold, empty grate, curtainless windows, and hard, bone-bruising furniture. 'I wouldn't want that,' she echoed.

'Which way are you going, Sparrow?' Barton asked.

'Towards Dragon Mountain, to Stollenback. I have to!' she added, as Barton scowled. 'Don't look at me like that. I know it's dangerous, but, Barton, what else can I do?'

'Aye, well, both ways is as bad as the other . . .' Barton sniffed. He took a heavy key from a chain on his belt and slid it into the lock on the big, wrought-iron gate. It turned with a well-oiled click. 'Sorry to see you go,' he muttered, pushing the gate open.

'Miss Knip won't be sorry to see the back of me.'

'Or the back of that cat, that Scaramouch . . . But surely you're taking him?' he added, looking round for the cat.

'Oh, don't!' she cried, her voice catching. 'I never said goodbye. I couldn't find him. I'll miss him so badly.'

Scaramouch was Sparrow's shadow.

He was a cat; a big cat. He stood as tall as her knees. His fur was short and the colour of barley or dry grass. Tawny-coloured stripes, running down his back and wrapping round his legs were just visible if you looked closely. When the light changed, his fur changed colour too. Sometimes it was the colour of mink, gleaming light gold and even silver. The tips of his ears and tail were tinted dark chocolate and his beautiful eyes were rimmed with black. His paws were like small padded plates.

Sparrow saved him titbits from her own meagre meals. She combed burrs from his fur and knew how to rub the bridge of his nose just the way he loved until he fell into a daze. Even though Miss Knip tried to keep him out of the dormitory, he slept on her bed every night.

Barton swung open the gate a little wider and peered at

the gloomy trees looming around the orphanage. 'I don't like to let you out into this,' he said. 'Hey, Sparrow, why not sleep here? I don't mind sleeping in the stable with Horace –' He stopped abruptly. '*Knip!*' he said, pointing to an upper window of the Knip and Pynch Home for Waifs and Strays.

Miss Knip was staring down at them with an expression of malevolence. She waved her hand in a shooing action, as if Sparrow were a stray dog.

Suddenly the unmistakable silhouette of Scaramouch appeared on the windowsill beside her.

'Oh! There he is!' Sparrow cried.

Scaramouch looked fixedly down at Sparrow with his yellow, saucer eyes. His tail twitched angrily.

'Knip has him! The old witch!' Sparrow said. 'I hate her! Dear puss, dear, dear Scaramouch . . . Goodbye . . .' She waved at him weakly.

'Old bat,' Barton muttered. 'Here, lass,' he added and thrust a bottle into her hand. 'Take this. It's not much, but . . .' Sparrow shook the bottle of pink-coloured liquid. 'Pop-pear juice,' he said. 'Gives you strength. Helps you see in the dark.'

She grinned and stowed the bottle in her bag along with the pop-apples and lumps of bread and cheese wrapped up in her special shawl. 'Thanks, Barton.'

'And Sparrow, if you ever come across any of that Brightling stuff, send some back for me, hey?' He rubbed his bent back. 'It'd mend this back of mine, I'm sure.'

Sparrow nodded. She didn't know what Brightling was,

only that it had a reputation for curing every ailment under the sun. 'I will.'

She went out through the gates and headed down the path.

Scaramouch, dear Scaramouch, she thought. Miss Knip must have had him locked up in her room all the time. How typical of the evil old bat! She hadn't had a chance to give him a last stroke and hear his deep, wonderful purr. To think she'd never see him again . . . it was terrible!

She took a deep breath – here it was, the start of her new life. Stollenback. A large town, far away at the foot of Dragon Mountain.

The name *Dragon Mountain* conjured up fairy-tales and times of mystery and danger – but she'd heard that there weren't any dragons on the mountain these days, only some sort of school or academy.

She was heading to Stollenback because although most baby girls brought to the orphanage came with nothing – no name, no clothes except perhaps a scrap of blanket – Sparrow had arrived wrapped up in a fine, white shawl. The maker's name, *Sampson's of Stollenback* was woven into one corner of the square. It was all she had to go on. She didn't expect to find her parents – they wouldn't have left her at the orphanage if they'd wanted her – but maybe someone in Stollenback would know something about her true identity. Maybe someone there would be kind and give her work and a place to live. She had no other reason to go anywhere in the world.

If she went in the opposite direction, north, she would have passed the Bleek and Barr Home for orphaned boys and come eventually to Nollenback, and trolls lived there.

Sparrow swung her bag over her shoulder and dug her hands into the pockets of her small jacket, which pulled tightly across her shoulders. It wasn't long since she'd made herself the thick wool jacket and already it was too small for her.

Where the lane rounded a corner, she stopped and looked back for a final sight of the Knip and Pynch Home. She was too late; it had already disappeared behind the trees.

Now she was alone, really and truly. She jutted out her chin and squared her shoulders. She began to whistle softly. She hoped if she hurried she'd reach somewhere safe before total darkness fell because she had no tinderbox, no light of any sort.

The path soon brought her out of the trees and into open land with scrubby thorn bushes and tall cactus plants. She felt better here, having a wider, broader view, and as she walked she swung her arms and looked from side to side. Wild things lived here; the orphans had heard them crying and barking at night.

She walked for a long time and her feet began to hurt. Although she was used to hard work, she wasn't used to walking and her boots were rubbing against her heels. At the top of the next rise in the track her heart lifted and she suddenly felt brighter and stronger. She was free of the orphanage; all she had to do was head towards that mountain . . . If only she had Scaramouch with her. How could she ever, ever live without him?

She set off again down the steep path and into the valley below, telling herself that now she was eleven she didn't need a cat. She didn't need anyone.

Then she came to the marshes.

Squelchy bogs of weed and mud stretched for miles and miles. There were two problems here, she knew – she could fall in, or something could jump out.

Dead trees stood up from the marsh like weird, black, cardboard cut-outs; it was hard to believe that they had ever lived. They were ironwoods, their wood so hard that even when they died they stayed standing for years and years. Once Mr Pynch had given out blocks of ironwood in carpentry class. After a week of trying to make a cut in it, they gave up. Only Mr Pynch thought it was funny.

Sparrow paused, ate a pop-apple from her bag and then went on, carefully picking her way along the narrow, raised paths that crossed the marshes.

The dusky sky was now purple and grey and pink; the sun was still showing above the distant hills but it would tip over the edge any moment now. She sped up, telling herself that it would be all right and nothing would get her. Then she heard the first splash and slither beside her in the water. She stopped dead and looked over to where the noise had come from. Something long and dark and fast slipped between the reeds. She saw a row of horny ribs along its back and a long tail flick and slap the water, then it was gone.

A krackodyle.

She threw the pop-apple core in its direction and ran.

Krackodyles can run too, but she was determined to run faster and to run for ever if she had to. 'I'm faster than you, you old scabby thing!' she cried.

The marshes seemed endless. She ran and ran, only stopping when she had to, to draw breath and look around again. Now there were rustling and slithering noises from all directions. She looked left and right and saw the bending reeds and whirling muddy water as krackodyles weaved their way purposefully through the swamp towards her.

She swallowed; took a deep breath, and ran again. It was getting darker, objects were becoming less distinct, and she couldn't run like this for ever, no matter what.

Suddenly she tripped.

She came crashing down on the path and rolled right to the edge of the bog – one hand in the foul water. She screamed, snatched it back before anything could snap at it, got to her knees and stayed there, breathing heavily.

They were there, the krackodyles; they were everywhere. She could hear them creeping in closer. There were five or six of them, because everywhere she looked the black water stirred and rippled. There was the slap of a tail and there, the blink of red eyes, watching her.

Sparrow slowly got to her feet. She had the strength for one last burst, she thought, one last effort. She would rather die running than have the krackodyles come and get her while she sat.

Her feet throbbed and burned in her boots. Her heart boomed and thundered in her chest; she could barely stand, let alone run, but run she must.

She steadied herself, took one step forward . . . immediately something rose up from the water beside her in a shower of stinking mud. She saw snapping jaws and the inside of a large, pink mouth and so many teeth and then, just as she thought it would get her, just as she thought she was dead, there was a piercing cry, the most terrible, heart-stopping cry she'd ever heard. A mink-coloured ball of fur rocketed past her and flew through the air, locking itself over the krackodyle's head. The ball yowled again. It had a tail and claws, and the claws were in the krackodyle's eyes, gouging and scratching.

The krackodyle roared in pain. One of its eyes was gone; its skin was ripped and torn. It grunted and roared, thrashing from side to side. It flung the thing from its face and splattered backwards into the swamp.

Sparrow was safe.

2

Miss Knip

Miss Knip had watched Sparrow until she was sucked up by the darkness beneath the trees and had disappeared into the woods. That was one orphan she was very glad to be rid of: a tiresome, springy girl; unsinkable, like some nasty beetle that, no matter how many times you plunge it under the water, bobs back up. She had stayed at the window for some considerable time, listening to the mewling cat at the closed door behind her and the sound of a child crying somewhere in the dismal depths of the Home. She had smiled, contented.

She ignored the knocking that sounded on her door a little later, because she wanted to savour Sparrow leaving. Such an insolent girl, she thought, tapping her long fingers on the windowsill. Such a sharp little minx! The place was going to be much quieter now, and run more smoothly, without *her* stirring things up and making trouble.

She sat down at her desk to go through some paperwork.

'Be quiet, cat!' she shouted as Scaramouch scratched at the closed door. 'Keep your claws to yourself!' Miss Knip snapped. 'Or use them to catch mice, you big useless lump!'

She would have had the cat drowned years ago, but her associate, Mr Pynch, said that would have brought bad luck to the Home. 'When a cat makes a place his home as Scaramouch has,' he'd said, 'nothing should get in his way.'

Miss Knip struck a fire from her tinderbox and lit the two glass lanterns. The room gradually glowed with a dull greenish light. She began to go through the papers on her desk.

Time slipped by.

When the knocking sounded again later, Miss Knip called out, 'I'm too busy! Go away!'

The door opened a chink and Annie the maid peeped in, looking scared. As she inched the door open, Scaramouch squeezed out. Annie felt his fur against her bare legs and shivered.

'Miss Knip, Miss Knip, *please*!' Annie cried. 'There's a person to see you and this person says it's urgent!' The candle she was holding wobbled and hot wax burned her hand.

'Who is here to see me?' Miss Knip asked.

'This person.' Annie jigged up and down in pain as more wax fell on her. 'She came here on the food wagon. She said she must see you and it's urgent and she's been waiting for ages. I don't think she's all that well . . .'

'Oh for goodness' sake!' Miss Knip snapped. 'Let her come in!'

Later, when she heard what it was that her visitor had to say, Miss Knip would bitterly regret not opening the door at the first knock.

She was completely unaware that Scaramouch had escaped and was at that moment streaking across the marshes to Sparrow.

3

Krackodyles

'*Scaramouch!*' Sparrow cried to the flying ball of claws and gleaming yellow eyes. 'You!'

She wiped the spattering of mud from her face and gazed at him in amazement and delight. 'You found me! You saved me!'

Her heart thumped and galloped crazily. She was crouching on the path, staring at the big cat beside her who was still bristling, his fur standing on end, his whiskers twanging. The end of his tail twitched furiously. They watched the injured krackodyle slowly sink below the muddy water, bubbling blood. When it had vanished, Scaramouch wound around her legs, purring: but only for a moment.

He turned his blazing wild eyes to her and never had those dear eyes said so clearly, wordlessly, *Follow me!*

'I'm coming!' Sparrow called. 'Anything you say. You're the boss!'

Scaramouch didn't follow the main path, but turned straight into the swamp. He leaped from tussock to tussock and stone to stone with Sparrow struggling to keep up. Suddenly a krackodyle shot up in front of them, flat and hard as an ironing board, but Scaramouch was on it in an instant, spitting and clawing at its eyes. Sparrow bit back a scream and dodged out of its way. Her legs felt like jelly, her heavy, wet boots were dragging her down and it was hard to move quickly. All she focused on was following the cat as he hopped and leaped across the swamp.

He was heading towards an isolated, dead tree.

Scaramouch made a final leap right onto the back of a krackodyle and, without daring to think, Sparrow did the same, closing her eyes and jumping blindly, bouncing off the creature's back as if it were a springboard, and from there into the black skeleton of the ironwood. The creature swirled round angrily, snapping at her. More krackodyles were slithering towards them. The muddy water heaved and swirled as they came.

Scaramouch was up the tree and quickly scrambling higher, digging in his claws and running vertically upwards. Sparrow wrapped her tired arms around the lowest branch.

'Wait!' She hauled up her leaden legs. 'Wait!'

Snap! Snap! Krackodyles were biting at her toes.

That made her yank up her legs quickly. Fear helped Sparrow to drag herself onto a higher branch, then up onto another, until she was clear of the fearful open mouths below.

The krackodyles gathered around the base of the tree, clacking their teeth as if they were taking part in a strange chorus, opening and closing their jaws like a nest of gigantic, ravenous baby birds. Sparrow edged her way over to Scaramouch, who was sitting in a wide hollow where five branches grew out from the tree trunk and where there was enough room for them both to snuggle safely.

Scaramouch lay on her, pushing his forehead against her chin and purring loudly. His long whiskers tickled her chin. His massive paws kneaded her stomach as if it were a lump of bread dough.

'Yes, we're safe, we're safe, Scaramouch – you dear, wonderful thing,' Sparrow murmured, rubbing his head and his ears. 'You found me. You saved my life!'

Scaramouch's purr rumbled on like a giant bee, and his eyes closed.

'I know, I missed you too. I wanted to take you, but that nasty Miss Knip locked you up.'

'Meow.'

'She is evil, isn't she? But we'll never see her again. Ever.'

Sparrow lay back against the branches. The sky above her darkened and darkened and she watched the stars come out until the night was alight with thousands and thousands of brilliant twinkling dots. She did not look down at the krackodyles, preferring to pretend they didn't exist, and at last she closed her eyes and slept.

All night the krackodyles slithered around the base of the tree and occasionally Sparrow woke as one of them thumped against the trunk and set the ironwood ringing, or snapped its horrible chops more loudly than the rest.

The cat, butting Sparrow under the chin with his head, woke her.

She sat up quickly and looked around, remembering where she was. It was not quite sunrise; it was that moment when the air is silent of birdsong, strangely colourless; the sky, the reeds, stones and grass, grey and toneless. The air was very cold and still.

Sparrow looked down to the ground. It was as if the land was made of a patchwork of leathery, knobbly logs and not an inch of grassy swamp or water was visible – everywhere were krackodyles; hundreds of them.

Their path looked very far away.

Sparrow took a big, shuddering breath. 'What now, Scaramouch?' she said. 'We can't stay up here for ever.'

The cat was motionless as he stared across the marshes. His whiskers were on alert, his ears pricked up, his eyes narrow. He was thinking.

She turned and followed his gaze. He was facing the east. Watching. Waiting. Sparrow waited too. The sun, a shapeless, brilliant orange light, inched upwards over the hill and began to flood its warmth across the sky. And even before it came over the hill, the grass began to show a little green, the leaves a touch of emerald, the water glistening gold and brown and black.

It was the signal to move.

'Meow!'

Scaramouch slipped away from her, leaving her chilled where he had rested against her. He walked daintily but quickly along a black branch out above the water. The krackodyles didn't move. He glanced back over his shoulder at her, came back, and began to climb down the trunk.

'Scaramouch!' she whispered loudly. 'Don't! Is that your only plan? To run again? Please don't!'

On the lowest branch the cat stopped and looked at her; then at the ground; then back at her.

The sun glowed orange and pink behind the horizon.

'I can't!' she whispered. Tears filled her eyes. 'I can't go down there again. Don't make me!'

Scaramouch flicked his tail dismissively. He didn't look at her again, but jumped down from the tree, as lightly as a cloud on his four soft paws, and landed like thistledown on the broad back of a sleeping krackodyle.

Sparrow held her breath.

The krackodyle didn't stir.

Scaramouch tiptoed along, stepping delicately between the rows of protruding knobbly ridges on the creature's spine. He walked right along its length, stopped on its rocky forehead and looked back at Sparrow.

Her heart seemed to fill her chest, stop up her throat and throb so loudly in her ears she couldn't hear anything but its boom boom boom. 'No, Scaramouch. I can't. They'll wake! They'll get me!'

Scaramouch, motionless as a dead thing, stood his ground, waiting. He was a whisker away from the krackodyle's teeth, from certain death. 'Go! Leave me, Scaramouch. I'll be OK. Run! Go!'

But Scaramouch sat down delicately on the krackodyle's broad head and fixed his eyes on her. He yawned a fresh, pink, bored yawn.

'Oh all right, all right! I'm coming.'

She moved slowly, inching down the rough sides of the tree, gripping the bark with trembling fingers. How had she got up here so quickly the night before? Now it seemed to take a lifetime to come down.

She lowered herself very gently to the squelchy, boggy ground. Still the krackodyles slept on. She clung to the tree, never wanting to let go, though she knew she had to. Trying to calm her painful breathing, she put a hand to her chest and pressed hard. Still her heart boomed on.

She fixed her eyes on Scaramouch's round, yellow ones.

'I'm coming, I am, I really am!'

She moved as lightly as she could, stepping onto the long, narrow tail of the first krackodyle, one hand against the tree. She waited, swallowed, and moved gently onto its back. Her weight sank the krackodyle an inch further below the surface of the muddy water, which now swirled over her feet. She paused, holding her breath. She wanted to run, she wanted to shout and run as fast as she could. But she didn't. She waited, searched out her route. The path to get to was just five – or was it six? – sleeping krackodyles distant.

Almost one done; four – please let it be only four – to go.

She pushed away from the tree, eased one foot off the animal and gently set it down again, between its back legs – heel, ball of the foot, toes – gently, gently all along the length of the krackodyle's broad back.

Scaramouch had already leaped nimbly onto the next krackodyle and was waiting, watching her movements carefully, tail low and thrashing backwards and forwards.

'I can't be as light as you!' she whispered to Scaramouch. 'I'm trying.'

She trod tentatively along the ribbed and leathery skin, staring fixedly at the animal's head, alert to any shift in it, to any hint that those jaws might open.

Nothing happened. It was safe. She could do it. She crossed to the neighbouring krackodyle, walked along it, and then the third, the fourth and – just one more krackodyle between her and the path where Scaramouch was. If she could touch Scaramouch, she told herself, feel his fur, then she would be safe.

The orange and yellow rays of the sun were beginning to inch over the treetops and a bird had started singing far away.

The final krackodyle was so submerged only the rounds of its eyes and nostrils broke the surface of the water, and it was hard to see exactly where its body began and ended. She lost her footing, slipped and landed on its head with a thud and a splash.

'Help!'

Immediately the krackodyle woke, its red eyes flicked open and its jaws snapped at the air, first to this side then to that. She stumbled away, clambering onto the bank, never taking her eyes from the krackodyle as it bit at the air, its teeth clashing hard, jaws juddering as they banged against each other with an empty, hungry *clonk*.

She flew the remaining few feet and dropped on the path beside Scaramouch with a wallop.

The krackodyle snapped blindly behind her. It missed her completely. Bit at nothing. The sun had risen and was in its eyes and it couldn't see. It was completely blind!

'Thank you!' Sparrow cried, giving Scaramouch a quick, light stroke.

She spun round just as the unseeing krackodyle launched itself towards her – sensing her smell? Hearing her voice? – she didn't stop to wonder but grabbed a stone and hurled it at the beast.

The rock hit the krackodyle square between the eyes and sent it toppling backwards, setting the others flapping and splashing, but they only railed for a few minutes before they settled again with their eyes closed, and all went quiet.

'Oh, Scaramouch!' she whispered. 'We did it, we –'

But Scaramouch was already off, bounding lightly down the path.

'Oh blimey, Scaramouch! Here we go!' She hurried after him.

They ran along the path, passing many other sleeping krackodyles, but none stirred – they slept on, immobile as dead things, hiding from the light of the brilliant, morning sun.

4

Nanny Porrit

Miss Knip sat down at her vast desk and put on her spectacles, which she thought made her look clever and stern. Who could be coming to see her on the weekly bread wagon? She pushed a few bits of paper around and checked her pale face in her desk mirror in case she'd got ink on it or a strand of hair was out of place. Whoever was here couldn't be important, not arriving like this.

'Here we are, Miss Porrit,' Annie could be heard saying in the corridor. 'Mind your step, dear. In you go. Careful.'

The old woman whom Annie showed into the room was as small as a child and as bent and crooked as a hairpin. Her face was all nose and pointed chin beneath a black bonnet and wispy white hair.

'Who are you and what do you want?' Miss Knip snapped at her, without moving from her desk.

It took a few moments for the old lady to get the strength to speak. 'Nanny Porrit at your service, miss,' the old woman piped. Her neck was so bent that she spoke all twisted, addressing the floor. 'I'm old, so old,' she added.

'No need to state the obvious,' Miss Knip said. 'Well, Nanny Porrit, whoever you are, why have you come here bothering me?'

'May I sit down? May I sit?' she trilled in her squeaky voice. 'I'm so old.'

'Oh for goodness' sake! Yes, sit.'

Nanny Porrit sank into a deep chair. 'I've come. I pray not too late. I pray she's still here. Oh, my old bones.'

'Who's still here? What are you talking about?' Miss Knip asked.

The old woman started sobbing. Miss Knip rolled her eyes in disgust. She loathed any display of emotion, sure it was done for show. She took out her smelling salts and quickly took a sniff of them to sharpen her wits.

'I was working for a lady in Stollenback,' the old woman said at last. 'Sampson was her name, Mrs Sampson. I was old then, but not as old as I am now. Mrs Sampson was a nurse, a keeper of babies. We put them in cradles and rocked them with our feet. Tap, tap, tap, rocking on the stone floor . . . I can hear it now . . .'

'And? And?' Miss Knip asked. 'What's the relevance of this to me?'

'We rocked them to sleep, the babies.'

'I don't care about that! Tell me why you are here!'

The old nanny tried swivelling round to face Miss Knip but only managed to twist her head inside the wings of her bonnet, so she couldn't see at all. 'I'm blinded. It's all gone dark!' she whimpered.

22

Miss Knip got up, went over and yanked off the offending bonnet.

'There. Now, old thing, get on with your tale.'

Nanny Porrit looked startled and blinked several times, but at last continued her story. 'Her husband – Mortimer Sampson – got the Swamp Fever. He was a fine man. He died.' She sobbed, gathered herself and went on. 'Mrs Sampson was, was . . . never . . . She couldn't work any more. She gave them back, those babies, to their parents. She had no strength . . . no strength at all, like me. So old I might crumble.'

'But no fever I hope?' Miss Knip asked her anxiously, scanning the old lady's face for signs of rashes. 'Just old, are you? Can't catch *that*! Very well, go on, what next? And? *And?*' She returned to her desk and drummed her fingers on the desktop.

Nanny Porrit drew breath and started again. 'Mortimer Sampson was good, a warm heart. A weaver. She couldn't go on without him.'

Miss Knip let out a sigh like a bicycle tyre going down and stood up. 'You are wasting my time,' she said. 'I have no idea what you're rambling about. You're deranged, woman!'

'I'm not, I'm not wasting time,' the old nanny cried. 'But when you're as old as me, when your brain's unravelling like a ball of string . . .' She hit her knee with her hand. 'Listen! Listen to what I've got to say. We must put right what's been wronged.'

'This is your last chance. Get on with it.'

'Mrs Sampson gave the babies back –'

23

'You've just said that!' Miss Knip yelled at her.

Nanny Porrit shrank back in her seat. 'How can you shout at a poor old thing like me? How can you? You make me shrivel up like a salted snail with that voice of yours. Oh, you mean thing.' But she collected herself and went on. 'All the babies went back except one, a girl. Her mother had paid regularly, had seen her daughter as often as she could. She was a dancer or something. Lovely costumes. Glittery. She loved her baby, and hoped to marry the baby's father – so she said. But then she stopped coming. There was no money for baby's keep, not for weeks and weeks. Mrs Sampson treated that child like her own . . . Still the mother never came. She promised she'd come back and take the baby just as soon as she'd got married.' She sighed. 'Lovely girl, lovely.'

'And?'

'And,' went on Nanny Porrit quickly, 'and, when she never came back, we worried. But Mrs Sampson said money'd always be paid, 'cos she knew the family. Knew baby was from a good family in Stollenback. She didn't want to go to them for fear of getting the young lady in trouble, do you see, for having a baby out of wedlock.'

'I'm not sure,' Miss Knip said, although she *was* beginning to see and she was beginning to suspect that there could be money involved and that she might get some of it. She rubbed her hands together.

Nanny Porrit started weeping again. 'Dear Mrs Sampson died,' Nanny Porrit told her, with a sob. 'I had nothing, no wages, nothing except a baby girl to feed and clothe and . . .

What was I to do?'

'I think you're going to tell me,' Miss Knip said to the ceiling.

'I brought her here.' Nanny Porrit squinted round and turned her pale eyes on Miss Knip. 'So's the orphanage would look after her. I wrapped her up in her lovely *Sampson's of Stollenback* shawl and gave her up, but I never –'

Miss Knip perked up. She knew of one child in her care who'd had such a shawl.

'Go on,' she ordered.

'I gave her to old Miss Knip, that was before you, and I never did tell old Miss Knip that I knew the baby's family. This little Sparrow –'

'*Sparrow!*'

'That's it, that's the name her mother gave her. Old Miss Knip said I should come and collect her as soon as ever her mother appeared. But she *never* appeared. So I never picked her up.'

'And why are you here now?'

Nanny Porrit crumbled again, rubbing at her eyes with her fists. 'She's eleven, isn't she? I want to give her what's hers, the name of her family. I want to give it back to her . . .'

Miss Knip guessed the old woman was hiding more. 'Nanny Porrit,' she said slyly, 'what a kind-hearted old thing you are. Travelling all this way, just to tell us Sparrow's family name. Sparrow will be so glad to see you . . . But why didn't you come sooner?'

'I've been . . . wondering. Meaning to . . . I'm old and . . .'

'Ready to die?' Miss Knip said. 'You wouldn't want to die with a guilty conscience, would you?'

She had hit on something. She saw it immediately the way the old nanny flinched and went pale. Her hand shot to the pocket of her greasy black coat and held whatever was there, tightly.

'I should have, but . . .' the old nanny mumbled. 'I'm here now. God forgive me, I'm here at last.' She brought something out of her cavernous coat pocket. 'Here it is. I never sold it, did I? I could have done, but I never did. I pawned it once but I got it back and saved it for little Sparrow. She'll have it now, won't she? Can I see the little mite? Can I put it – Oi!'

Seeing the flash of gold, Miss Knip had shot round the desk and grabbed the thing from her hands.

'Oi, oi!' screamed Nanny Porrit. 'You can't take that! I say you can't!'

'*You* did. *You* took it to sell it, didn't you?' Miss Knip said, dangling the gold locket on its chain in front of the old woman.

'But, but I didn't never sell it!' Nanny Porrit wailed.

Miss Knip sneered at her. She opened the locket. On one side was a tiny painting of a pretty young woman with messy blonde hair like Sparrow, with Sparrow's flighty green eyes and dark, straight brows. On the other was a name.

Miss Knip smiled. She snapped the locket shut and slipped it into her pocket.

'It's worthless,' she said, 'but I will give it to Sparrow, as you wish.'

'But can't I see her? Before she goes out? Please?' Nanny Porrit began to cry.

26

Miss Knip took no notice of her. She walked briskly to the door and opened it. 'Good day to you, Porrit. I hope the bread wagon hasn't left to return to Nollenback yet. You'll be able to get a lift back home. Goodbye.'

'But –'

'Goodbye.'

Miss Knip rang for Annie who came and helped Nanny Porrit as she hobbled out. Miss Knip closed the door firmly behind them. She rubbed the locket between her bony fingers and smelled the metallic scent of the gold on her fingers. A smile creased her cruel face. She went quickly to the window and looked out, almost expecting to see Sparrow still there.

She cursed the empty road.

'How shall I make the most from this very interesting situation?' she wondered.

5

Betty Nash

Sparrow knew that amongst the rows of mountain peaks that rose up like sharp, spiked teeth on the hazy horizon, Dragon Mountain was the tallest. As long as she kept it in sight, she knew she was on the right track.

They had walked all morning, leaving the swamp far behind, and the sun was high in the sky when at last she spotted the first houses and farms in the surrounding countryside and hoped she was getting nearer to Stollenback.

Scaramouch had fed himself on mice and voles and other small creatures, but the few morsels of food Sparrow had put in her bag were gone. She had set her heart on reaching Stollenback before stopping, but maybe Stollenback was days and days away. She had no idea and now she was very hungry and thirsty.

The first dwelling they came to on the road was an old stone cottage beside a murgberry tree. The cottage had an enormous, shabby, thatched roof that reached over the windows like heavy eyebrows. There were holes in the thatch, and moss and frothy ferns sprouting from it. The paint was peeling from the door and tiny daisies and dandelions grew around the doorstep.

'Doesn't look as if anyone lives here,' Sparrow said to Scaramouch, 'but let's see. Perhaps there's a pump round the back – I'm desperate for a drink.' She was about to push the gate at the side when suddenly the door of the cottage opened.

A short, square woman with very black, beady eyes appeared. She looked at Sparrow through gold-rimmed, round spectacles, looked again, and must have liked what she saw, as a smile spread over her plain, wide face.

'What a lovely, *lovely* day,' she said, looking keenly at Sparrow. 'How can I help you, my lamb?' She had an upturned, pig-like nose, and thinning hair pulled into two long, shoelace plaits. Her bare feet were thrust into misshapen leather slippers. 'I *can* help you, I'm sure,' she added.

'I'm Sparrow and I didn't mean to . . .' Sparrow began. 'I thought the house was empty and I need a drink of water.'

The woman flapped the ends of her plaits against her shoulders as she looked Sparrow up and down, up and down. Her smile grew bigger and broader. 'Well, well,' she said. 'Orphanage, isn't it?'

'Yes, I was eleven yesterday. I came right through the krackodyles,' Sparrow added proudly.

'Made it through the swamps, eh? You must be strong, though you don't look it.'

Again those black button eyes looked Sparrow up and down, appraising her.

'Could I just have a drink, please?' Sparrow said. 'I haven't had a drink for so long.'

'Miss Knip your matron, was she?'

'Yes,' Sparrow said.

'She's a baggage, she is. Is that your cat?' the woman added. 'A fine specimen; worth a penny or two, is that cat.'

Sparrow nodded. Scaramouch belonged to the orphanage if he belonged to anyone, and Miss Knip was just the sort of person who might accuse her of stealing him. 'He's a stray,' she said brightly. 'He's lovely, isn't he? He just appeared and joined me on the road. Come here, puss, come and say hello.' But Scaramouch had wandered off and was sitting on a tree stump cleaning his paws. He looked at Sparrow as if he barely recognised her.

'He does just as he likes, doesn't he?' the woman said. 'That's a cat all over, that is.'

'Er, yes, isn't it? Just water, a drink of water, that's all I want,' Sparrow repeated. 'Then I'll go. I'm going to Stollenback. I've walked all morning and I'm so thirsty.'

But it was like talking to a brick wall.

The woman bit on her plait and smiled thoughtfully. 'I can't take my peepers off those little stitches in your jacket,' she said, after a few minutes of staring hard at Sparrow's sleeve. 'Tiny, neat little stitches. That's not done by a sewing machine, is it?'

'No. I made it at the Home. We all had to sew.'

'I know – I mean, so I've heard. But not many are any good at it.'

Sparrow's mouth was so dry now; she could hardly speak.

She licked her parched lips. She wanted to get on, but she couldn't without first quenching her thirst. 'If I could just –' she tried again.

'Of course!' The woman suddenly brightened up, as if she'd just heard some good news. 'Come into our humble abode, Sparrow, dear – and you are as dainty as a little sparrow, aren't you? Come in and have some refreshment: a drink and something to eat.'

'Thank you. I won't stay; I don't want to disturb you.'

'Come in, that's right, come in and sit down, have a rest. My name's Betty, Betty Nash,' she said.

Betty slopped into the cottage in her loose slippers and Sparrow followed. The cottage was dark and gloomy; the overhanging thatch cut out most of the natural light. 'Sit. Sit down. Rest, my little lambkin. I'll get you a drink.' Betty Nash hobbled off into a room at the back.

Sparrow sat tentatively on a chair and looked around. A jumble of brightly coloured fabric on the table, all pinks and fiery orange, turquoise and emerald green, caught her eye. The colours stood out in the dingy room where everything else was brown or grey or black. She wondered what the material was for.

'Here I am, lambkin, here I come,' Betty cried, shuffling back in with a thick glass tumbler and a jug. 'And this is my little boy, Tapper.'

Tapper was not a little boy, but a young man. Sparrow couldn't suppress a shiver as he came in; it was as if a block of ice had entered the room. Sparrow inched away from him instinctively.

Tapper was dark and thin, with a long, narrow, straight nose. His hair was shaved close around his head except on top where it was very long and straight and kept back by constant swipes and smoothings. He came in and settled himself against the wall, folding his arms and crossing his legs as if erecting a personal scaffolding to keep him upright.

'So you're an orphan, Sparrow,' he said, sweeping a hand over his hair and fixing his unfriendly eyes on her. 'You don't have no parents, no one in the world who cares for you, so,' he said.

Sparrow would have spoken but he went on too quickly.

'Ah, don't look ashamed!' he said. 'Not your fault your parents didn't want you,' he added with a nasty grin.

Sparrow felt herself stiffen with anger. 'I only stopped for a drink of water,' she said, running her tongue over her dry lips and eyeing the jug in Betty's hand. 'That's all.' She glared at Tapper. Horrid. Horrid young man.

'So give her a drink, Ma,' said Tapper. He came over and leaned his grubby hands on the back of her chair; it seemed he preferred to prop himself up on something . . . or some*one*, than to stand alone. 'Poor little lonely thing,' he added. The lids of his eyes hung, half-closed over his pale-grey eyes, which made him look sleepy and yet sneaky at the same time.

Sparrow turned to stare straight back at him. She was so thirsty. She must have a drink and then she'd give this Tapper something to think about.

'Here you are, my lamb!' Betty handed her the heavy glass of water and set the jug on the table.

Sparrow grabbed it and gulped down the water gratefully. She quickly refilled it from the jug and drank a second. Mother and son watched her, mother chewing on her plaits and Tapper gnawing methodically around his nails.

Sparrow grinned at them as she wiped her mouth. 'Told you I was thirsty,' she said and calmly poured out a third glass of water and drank it slowly, savouring the cool liquid as it trickled down her throat. Tapper took the empty glass from her. He was grinning stupidly as if he had a secret.

'What's the matter?' Sparrow said. 'Do I look funny? Thank you, Betty,' she added as she got up. 'Now I must go.'

'Oh no,' Betty said quickly. 'You mustn't hurry off. We hardly have any visitors, my lamb, we want to keep you with us for as long as we possibly can.'

'But –'

'I've just made a lovely stew,' Betty went on, shuffling over and lifting the lid from the pot on the fire, 'and I so want you to stay and share it with us. We're only poor folk, but we can't let you go hungry.' Her glasses misted up from the steam as she leaned over and stirred the gravy, but Sparrow could still see a greedy glint in her eyes. 'Good bit of meat it is, Sparrow, dear,' she said. 'Carrots and parsnips too.'

'That's kind, but I couldn't. Really.' Sparrow didn't want to stay, even though now that Betty had opened the pot, the delicious aroma of beef stew was seeping into the room. She was hungry, but she didn't want to eat their food or stay a moment longer with them in this dingy house than was absolutely necessary.

And what about Scaramouch? she thought. Where was he?

'So, think we can't afford to share our food?' Tapper said, looking offended. He sleeked back his long fringe of hair. 'Think we're poor?'

'No. Yes. Well, I don't want to take from you when I can't pay –'

'Can't pay? Who said anything about reimbursing, my pretty little lambkin?' Betty said. 'We just want to send you off well fed and ready for the next stage of your long journey.'

Feeling awkward, Sparrow got up and made for the door again, but Tapper was in the way.

'Now, what's the hurry, lamb?' Betty Nash took her hand in her own broad one and held her back. 'If you must go, you must. But first I want to show you something. Do wait so I can show you our little spitfyres. We're so proud of them and I think you'll appreciate them, being such a good needleworker yourself.'

'All right.' The fear of being rude or seeming ungrateful was somehow worse than the fear of staying longer with these awful people.

Sparrow allowed Mrs Nash to sit her down again. Tapper brought over an old canvas bag and opened it. Kneeling beside her like a dark grasshopper, she could smell his greasy hair and a whiff of cheesy, dirty clothes, which consisted of a strange patchwork of dark blue and black scraps of fabric, sewn randomly over each other. Sparrow tried not to shrink from him as he lifted a fabric toy out of the bag and placed it in her lap.

'So, it's a spitfyre,' he said. 'We make 'em.'

Sparrow forgot how badly she wanted to leave when she

34

picked it up. 'It's a winged horse,' she cried, delighted. 'It's so beautiful! How clever of you!'

Betty beamed with pleasure. 'It's a cracker, isn't it? Tapper takes a big bag of them to town and sells them. Makes a tidy profit. He's a sweetheart, is my boy Tapper,' she added, beaming at her son.

How could something so charming, so delicate and pretty, come from the hands of two such unlovely people? Sparrow wondered.

The body of each flying horse was made from panels of different coloured, fine cloth. Each hoof was ringed with a semi-circle of gold or silver wire. The manes and tails were made of coloured thread, turquoise, green and yellow. Their see-through wings, held up by a network of finest wire thread, sprang out of their shoulders like exquisite, strange leaves. 'I think they're gorgeous,' she said, quite truthfully. 'Do they really exist, these winged horses? Or is that just in fairy-tales?' she asked. 'We were never sure in the orphanage.'

'Exist? They do so exist, all right,' Tapper said. 'Up on Dragon Mountain there's a school where they keep 'em. The hoity toity Academy,' he added in a posh voice. 'For snotty rich kids, so.'

'I'd like to see a real spitfyre,' Sparrow said dreamily.

'You might,' Betty said. 'They do fly over sometimes, poppet.'

'They drop out of the sky too,' Tapper said with a short laugh. 'Vanish.'

'*Drop out of the sky?*' Sparrow said. 'What d'you mean?'

'He doesn't mean a thing,' Betty said, '. . . only, this year one or two did sort of vanish. Just disappeared off the face of the earth!' She laughed. 'It's in the newspapers. Everyone wonders who and how . . . There aren't many of them around – only those at the Academy. Now, look here, look at this little pink and purple fellow. Isn't he lovely?'

Betty lifted another spitfyre toy up for Sparrow to admire. Each one was different, with its own expression and character, with fiery eyes or gentle, secretive ones, an angry mouth or a soft one. They were pink or red or green or a mixture of all colours.

'The finishing-off is hardest. You need sharp eyes for that,' Betty said, squinting through her glasses.

'And nimble little fingers,' Tapper added.

Which neither of them has, Sparrow thought, so how did they manage?

'Now do stay and have some grub, won't you?' Betty said.

Although she'd tried, Sparrow couldn't ignore the smell of the food any longer. Now she felt too hungry and weary to refuse it. 'All right. Thank you, that's kind. Then I must go. I want to get to Stollenback before dark.'

'No, dear. Even on a horse you wouldn't make Stollenback today. It's a long way off,' Betty said.

'Well, at least I need to get started,' Sparrow added lamely.

Betty shrugged and smiled. 'We'll see.'

Soon they were sitting at the table and Betty was spooning the stew onto Sparrow's plate. There had never been such delicious food at the orphanage and despite herself she ate two platefuls.

Tapper carried the dirty dishes out himself. That's good of him, Sparrow thought. Had she misjudged him? she wondered.

Two seconds later there was a cry of pain and Tapper stumbled back into the room, clutching his right hand to his chest.

'I'm in agony!' he yelled, rolling against the wall. 'Aw! I burned my hand, Ma!' He jumped around and paced up and down. 'Aw, it's hurting bad!'

'You need to put it in cold water,' Sparrow suggested, getting up. 'Let me see, I could –'

'No, no, don't touch it!' Tapper yelled. 'I'll go put it under the pump. Oh, my hand! The pain!'

Betty did nothing to help him, but remained at the table, mopping up the gravy on her plate with a wodge of bread. Sparrow sighed. She couldn't leave now, she'd have to help with the clearing and washing up. She glanced at the window, wondering about the time and how Scaramouch was doing outside.

'Oh well, dear, you'd better come and help me in the scullery,' Betty Nash said, finishing her food at last. 'Tapper won't be any use, will he?'

There was a deep stone sink in the narrow scullery and it was already filled with murky water. Sparrow rolled up her sleeves and began to wash the plates and forks. Through the window she thought she saw Scaramouch creeping along the wall beneath the trees. She longed to join him.

'. . . The thing is, Sparrow,' Betty was saying, 'I've got to finish sewing the spitfyres tonight. There's a travelling salesman coming along first thing in the morning to collect them. Fifteen he wants, and that's what I've promised, but now Tapper's hurt he won't be able to sew. What can I do?'

Sparrow clamped her mouth shut. No, no, no! She would not stay and help. She wanted to leave. She went quickly to the other room and opened the front door. Scaramouch was there, thank goodness, his tail curled neatly around his front legs as he watched her from his perch on the wall.

'I'm sorry, but I must go,' she told Betty.

Tapper came back in, with his hand wrapped up in a grubby bandage.

'There, there, poor little boy,' Betty said. 'You go and sit down, dear. Does it hurt an awful lot, your poor hand?'

Tapper nodded. 'So, what shall we do, Ma? What can we say to that travelling man when he comes in the morning? Fifteen spitfyres to finish and we've only done three, so?'

Betty Nash began to cry. 'We'll manage somehow. We have to.' She adjusted her spectacles and dabbed at her eyes with the ends of her plaits. 'I'll just have to try and do the sewing myself, even though I can hardly see a thing, I'm so blind. Perhaps I can manage one or two. Heavens above! We'll starve; we'll have nothing to eat all week. Not a crumb. Not a morsel.'

Sparrow stood on the doorstep, the sun on her face, her back cold. She felt herself being sucked back into the cottage, into the arms of the Nashes . . .

'Don't cry, Ma, please don't take on so!' Tapper said. 'We'll get by.'

'I'll do it!' Sparrow spoke quickly, stepping back into the room and shutting the door. 'Of course I will. Please don't cry, Mrs Nash. Please don't.'

They were all thanks and praise. Within a minute they had lit the oil lamp beside her, striking a real match so there was no messing around with a tinderbox, and supplied her with needles and thread and scissors. They piled fabric and some half-finished spitfyres onto the table beside her.

'What a lambkin of a girl,' Betty said. 'How big-hearted she is to help poor old Betty.'

Sparrow gritted her teeth. 'It's nothing,' she managed to say. 'Nothing.'

She set about the work with Betty on one side and Tapper on the other, watching every stitch.

The spitfyres were in various stages of completion. Some still needed stuffing and Tapper began to rip up some flowered cotton into small strips for the wadding.

'That's pretty, that stuff,' Betty Nash said, idly fingering the fabric. 'Tiny little daisies.'

Sparrow looked up and glanced at it. 'There was a girl at the orphanage with a dress made of that,' she said.

Betty stiffened. Tapper paused in his ripping.

'What's the matter?' Sparrow said. 'I just said, it's like her dress. Caroline Creevy, she had a dress made of that. She left last winter.'

'Oh, really? Did she, dear, that's nice,' Betty Nash said. 'Common stuff, that daisy pattern is. Very common.' She pushed it away, deep into a bag. 'You're doing grand there, Sparrow, my lamb. Such nice stitches; such lovely, neat knots and you're really good with their eyes.'

'Thank you.' Sparrow couldn't help enjoying the sewing; her nimble fingers were expert at making tiny, neat stitches.

She loved the way the spitfyres came to life in her hands; she knew she was good. Her spitfyres were so lifelike it wouldn't be hard to imagine them flying.

On and on she worked, until her wrists and neck ached and the tips of her fingers were sore from being pricked by the needle. She was sure that she'd done more than enough spitfyres but still the unfinished ones kept coming. The next time she glanced at the window it was getting dark. 'Oh! It's late. I must go,' she cried, standing up. 'Have I done enough?'

'You can't leave, lambkin. You must stay the night,' Betty Nash said quickly. 'The road isn't safe at night. There are robbers and all sorts on the Stollenback road.'

'No, I – I must go. I must get on. Scara— that old cat will be waiting for me.' Sparrow piled the scraps of fabric and half-done spitfyres on the table. 'I'll be fine. Don't worry about me.'

But now Tapper was standing too and he had his hand on her arm. Holding her.

'It's too dangerous, Sparrow,' Betty Nash said. 'Too risky. You really should stay.'

Tapper moved quickly and drew the bolt across the door with a rumbling crash. 'It's dangerous out there,' he said. ''Specially for little girls all alone, so.'

'We couldn't let you go, little lambkin poppet, not when it's so late and so dark,' Betty said. 'We'd never forgive ourselves if anything happened to you.'

'But –'

'There's a room for you upstairs. Here's a candle, and the bed's made up all neat and clean again,' she said, smiling.

'You need a good rest.'

Sparrow stood her ground. 'I want to leave,' she said. 'You can't keep me here. Unlock the door, please.'

Tapper was at her side and his hand was cold and heavy in the small of her back, like a stone. 'So, now now, orphanage girl,' he said. 'Don't be flighty. Course you want to leave, but trust us. Safer here than out there.' She recoiled from him, hating his smell, hating him touching her, and moved away. But despite her attempt to go towards the door, Tapper guided her firmly up the narrow stairs.

Sparrow was amazed at how strong he was. It was like pushing against a bar of iron.

'No, please, please!' Sparrow called back to Mrs Nash. 'Don't let him!'

Betty plonked herself down in an armchair, grinning. 'It's for the best,' she said, waving her grey plait at her and nodding. 'Good night, my precious lambkin. Sleep well.'

There was nothing Sparrow could do and, somehow, seconds later, she was pushed into a little room under the thatch and the door was being firmly shut behind her.

Sparrow sank onto the bed beneath the low, sloping ceiling and stared around in horror. They had trapped her! Horrible, horrible people! They were forcing her to stay!

She could hear Tapper and Betty muttering together downstairs. What did they want with her? She glanced at the bed. Who had slept here before? Feeling afraid, she got up and went to the small closet in the corner. Inside were two faded dresses. Small dresses, about her size. A shabby pair of badly worn-down shoes were tucked in below. She closed the cupboard and went back to perch on the edge of the hard, narrow bed. Next to the bed was a bucket to catch drips; there was a hole in the ceiling – the plaster was stained brown and looked soft from years of leaking. The bedside table had a drawer. Inside the drawer she found a thimble and a felt bundle of needles with spots of rust on the material. Or was it blood?

She looked down at her own fingers – pricked and sore from all the sewing.

Her mind was racing and her heart booming loudly in her ears.

Whose room had this been? Who had slept here before? Had Caroline Creevy been here? Where was she now?

She heard mother and son creak up the stairs and doors open and close. The house grew silent around her. The candle was nearly finished; it was beginning to splutter, sending scary shadows over the walls. The thatch above her seemed to tick and breathe.

How exactly had Tapper burned his hand so badly? Sparrow wondered. There was no fire in the scullery, no boiling water, nothing hot. She felt her pulse race suddenly.

It had all been a lie.

It had been a trap.

She looked around desperately; she had to get out. Now!

6

Escape

The door was locked; of course it was!

Sparrow twisted the handle a few times quietly, gave up and sank back on the bed. Idiot! She was a stupid girl, really stupid. They had kidnapped her. They wanted to keep her here for ever, making those little spitfyres . . . But the travelling salesman was due to come tomorrow – he'd help her . . .

No! She hit the bed. Of course he wouldn't come! That had been another lie to make her work, to make her feel sorry for them. Mrs Nash had said it was Tapper who took the spitfyres to Stollenback to sell, anyway, not a salesman. They planned to keep her prisoner and make her sew for them for ever and ever until, like her predecessor, her fingers broke and bled and she . . . died?

There was no window, no way of looking out. No means of escape.

Sudden small, scuttling noises above her head made her

catch her breath; and she slid into the corner against the wall, listening. It was a scratching, rustling sort of noise in the ceiling. Was it mice? Squirrels? A few crumbs of grey plaster trickled out from the stained and cracked patch on the ceiling. The scratching noise grew louder. It had to be a mighty big squirrel up there, she thought . . .

Unless . . .

'Meow!'

Sparrow leaped forward. 'Scaramouch!' she whispered at the ceiling. 'Puss? Is that you?' Another soft meow told her it was. He was right above her. He must have got in through one of the holes in the thatch and now he was digging away at the soggy lathe and plaster in the ceiling, trying to get to her. She reached up to the gaping hole and began to pull at the soft, crumbling stuff. It must have been rained on for years, because it broke up in her hands, showering horsehair, thin strips of lathe, dust, twigs and cobwebs down on her head and the bed. She shook out her hair.

'I'm OK,' she whispered, shaking off the dust. 'I'm fine. I'm here!'

Scaramouch was just above her; she could almost feel his paws and claws as they dug overhead, but she couldn't see him. Every time she stopped pulling at the ceiling, he called to her, encouraging her to go on. It didn't take long to drag out all the soft, wet plaster and strips of old wood – then there was Scaramouch; his glittering eyes shining down at her with affection and mischief.

'Meow!'

He disappeared again and Sparrow felt the cold night air on her cheeks and caught a glimpse of the moon far above.

'Meow!' He was calling for her to join him.

Very quietly, she pulled the bedside table over so it was beneath the ragged hole in the ceiling. She climbed onto it and pushed her way up into the cool, dark cavity of the roof. Moonlight flooded in through the hole. She couldn't stand up because the twiggy thatch was too low. She knelt and began to dig and scrape at it, widening the hole where Scaramouch had come in. Seconds later she pulled herself through and was sitting on top of the cottage roof.

Her heart was beating hard. She had to catch her breath. Listen. Make sure no one was stirring in the house. Scaramouch flowed alongside her, already on the move.

'Wait! Hold on!' But he wouldn't.

Wide branches of the large old murgberry tree lay over the roof and Scaramouch immediately bounded into the leaves and headed for the ground.

Sparrow clambered down the tree more slowly. The plump, red murgberry fruit burst against her skin, leaving a bitter smell. Typical that the Nashes would have a tree of poisonous, smelly fruit by their house, she thought.

At last she was on the ground, her legs wobbling and turned to jelly from the climb. She glanced at the cottage; the windows were all dark and it was quiet.

'Meow!' Scaramouch was already on the move again.

'Blimey, Scaramouch,' Sparrow said, readying herself to follow him, 'Stollenback won't be going anywhere, you know. Here I come!'

The night sky was awash with stars. The moon hung like a yellow hook, low and gleaming. It was cold, and sparkles of frost glittered on stones and blades of grass. They walked for hours.

'Mustn't stop yet,' Sparrow said. 'Keep going, keep going as long as we can. They might be coming after us, those two.' And the thought of the menacing Tapper creeping up behind her and catching hold of her collar with his filthy, cold fingers made her hurry, even though she was exhausted and all she wanted to do was sleep. She began to dream about getting into a bed with a soft, fresh pillow and closing her eyes.

Although she couldn't see very clearly, she sensed the countryside changing around her and the fact that hedges and woods and sometimes buildings now surrounded her. Still she didn't dare stop and find shelter, not yet.

Suddenly she paused. 'What was that?' she whispered.

They both stood still.

She was frozen, staring backwards into the blackness of the path behind them. 'Oh, no! Scaramouch, is that them? Is Tapper coming?'

But it wasn't footsteps she could hear. No, it was something swishy, sighing, like the beating wings of a giant bat. Sparrow knelt down beside Scaramouch and they both stared up into the sky.

The sound grew louder and louder, as if great sheets of card were beating the air. A burst of golden orange and yellow, high above, was so surprising that Sparrow gasped out loud. In the splash of brilliant light she saw –

Spitfyres!

Two magnificent flying horses were in the air above her and Scaramouch, gusting out clouds of fiery breath. Their vast, leathery wings moved in unison, creaking gently, flapping lazily, effortlessly, as they flew over the treetops and came towards her. The spitfyres were ridden by sky-riders wearing goggles and tight-fitting clothes.

Hoooosh! One spitfyre blew out again and the air was alight with dots of gold and silver and red-hot sparks, which dazzled and glittered, hanging in the dark. The sky-riders must have spied her crouching there because they waved and, even from this distance, Sparrow could see they looked exhilarated and happy. She waved back.

The spitfyres flew round in a circle above them. They tipped their wings so they were almost flying on their sides and then righted themselves, breathing out clouds of gold as they flew. Slowly they spiralled up into the air, gaining height with every turn until they were nothing but bright specks in the sky, like stars, and disappeared.

Sparrow sighed. She felt she'd seen the most wonderful thing ever and was very sad and very content at the same time. She glanced at Scaramouch. His eyes shone and his fur seemed to sparkle. It made her feel sure the spitfyres had thrilled him too.

'How far to Stollenback?' Sparrow asked Scaramouch as they walked on. 'I hope not far. When we get there, I'm going to find some work and lodgings and some kind people to live with. Then we can write to Mary and Little Jean and all the other girls and they can come and live with us too. It will be wonderful. And we'll find Sampson's of Stollenback, won't we? Sparrow Sampson. That sounds good.'

'Meow.'

'Exactly.'

7

Pynch

Miss Knip sat at her desk, her long fingers pointed in a steeple shape, thinking. Two days had gone by since Sparrow left and still she had not hatched a plan that suited her. Every time her eyes closed, she saw a large heap of shining, golden coins; so many coins that they were slithering over each other and tumbling down, sliding over the edge of the table and rolling on the floor. Her vision was so real she almost bent down to pick them up.

Sparrow must be connected to the family whose name was in the locket. There could be no doubt at all; her likeness to the woman in the portrait was so strong. But now Sparrow had vanished. She had to find her. How was she going to do it? Miss Knip imagined herself too fragile to go traipsing off across the country, then searching the streets of Stollenback. She was certain that Sparrow would have gone there. Miss Knip knew how important that stupid shawl had been to the orphan. A few words with snivelling Little Jean and her suspicions were confirmed. Stollenback it was. And then, once Sparrow was found, she'd put the second part of her plan into action – to extract as much money from Sparrow's family as she could! But first, who could she send to find the girl?

Her door opened and Mr Pynch came in.

Mr Pynch was large in belly and head, both body parts being fat and pale and blobby. He had stringy hair and a wet mouth that tended to hang open like a forgotten drawer. For a few moments Miss Knip considered him as a possible candidate to send to Stollenback, but rejected the idea swiftly.

'Knip, guess what?' Pynch said, coming in and dumping himself down by the fire, oblivious to the cold look Miss Knip gave him.

Miss Knip's thoughts were elsewhere and she ignored him.

'That big old cat's gone. Barton said it snuck out. Said it hared off like a, like a hare, I suppose.' He chuckled. 'Without the long ears.'

Miss Knip stood up as though a spring had unsprung beneath her and let out a little scream. 'The cat!'

'What's the matter? Knip? You've gone white as a blancmange, you have.'

Miss Knip had forgotten about Scaramouch. How had she not noticed the cat's disappearance? she wondered. Because she'd been so busy thinking about her plans and the money she might make, of course. 'I meant to keep it in for a couple of days,' she said. 'I thought it might go after Sparrow.'

'It has.'

'Sparrow would have been lost without it,' she said, 'which would have made me happy.'

Pynch laughed. 'Naughty, naughty, Knip!'

'But if it caught up with her,' Miss Knip went on, thinking aloud, 'it will make her easier to trace. People will remember having seen a girl with a cat, especially such a big cat.'

'That cat was a weird old thing anyway,' Mr Pynch said, helping himself to a bun from a plate on the table. 'You know it came here with Sparrow?'

'Did it? I didn't know that.'

'You weren't here then, were you?' He crossed his podgy legs and leaned back in his chair. 'See, you don't know everything, Knip, old girl, though you think you do. Yes, the cat came into the Home the same day as the baby and sat by its cradle day and night. We could hardly shift it to get near the little thing . . . Ah, squidgy little Sparrow . . . She wasn't scrawny like most of them, but fat as butter, and clean. They aren't usually clean, are they?'

'No.' Miss Knip was hardly listening.

'It smelled good enough to eat, did that baby,' Pynch went on dreamily, stuffing another bun into his mouth. 'Ah, me. Eleven years ago. They don't make babies like that any more.'

'I want you to take over here tomorrow. I'm going on a little journey,' Miss Knip said suddenly, coming to a decision.

'You what?'

'Journey. Someone I need to see. Business.'

'Leaving me on my own?' Pynch looked worried. 'What am I going to do? What'll I do with all those girls?'

'Just wallop them, like you usually do,' she said.

8

Pies

Sparrow and Scaramouch walked for three days, scavenging fruit from orchards and hedges, and sleeping where they could; once in a ruined cottage and once in a scratchy haystack.

As they walked on, the lane grew wider and was well worn now by carts and horses and people. They passed farms, barns and sheds, and soon they came to clusters of cottages and then houses and busy streets. They were near the town at last. Stollenback.

Sampson's of Stollenback, Sampson's of Stollenback. Sparrow repeated the name as if it were some sort of spell. She must find Sampson's.

'You can't imagine what it's like,' she told Scaramouch, 'not knowing who you are, where you come from. It puts you at an unfair disadvantage. It leaves you dangling, like something on a string.'

'Meow.'

'No, well, I don't suppose you know who your mother and father are either,' she said, 'but you don't care, do you?'

'Meow.'

'No, I didn't think so. But I *do* care. I want to know who I am. I can't be me unless I know where I come from, who my parents were. I hope I was wanted, Scaramouch. I'd like to know that; I'd like to know anything, anything about the real me.'

Scaramouch flicked his tail and tipped his ears backwards and forwards.

Sparrow had managed to convince herself that *knowing* something about her parents was all she needed, but what if she discovered that they had never loved her and never wanted her at all? How could she cope with that? Best not to think about it, she told herself, looking around. Chin up, Sparrow.

The houses of Stollenback were ancient. Their walls were timbered in black, criss-crossed over the white-painted stonework. The roofs were steeply pitched. The buildings were crammed in, this way and that, along the roads. Their wooden shutters were painted bright colours and decorated with cut-out shapes of flowers, stars, diamonds and even spitfyres. The balconies were crammed with faded plants and doorways were surrounded with tubs of greenery now tinged with red and brown. Horses and carts, fine carriages and bicycles competed for space on the road.

Sparrow was amazed at it all, dazed by the colours and the things that she saw. How would she ever find Sampson's?

She followed the streets and the flow of people until she came to a square where a busy market was set up. So many people and such a lot of noise! It was both exciting and scary, she thought, as she wandered around, looking at the stalls. People stared at her curiously, pointing at Scaramouch beside her. Feeling awkward, Sparrow turned to the wall and began to read a poster advertising a circus, and another plastered over it with a picture of a spitfyre on it.

BRIGHTLING IS ILLEGAL AND CAUSES HARM TO SPITFYRES . . .

She remembered old Barton asking her to send him some Brightling to cure his aches and pains. *Illegal?* Oh dear, and how could it *harm* spitfyres? She was just about to read the small print at the bottom, when someone bumped into her and she spun round.

'Mamma, Mamma!' It was a little girl, tugging at her mother's coat. She didn't even notice Sparrow. Sparrow shrank into herself even more, ashamed of her grey dress and little tight jacket, her grubby hands and messy hair.

'I want a cake! I want a cake!' the little girl cried.

'Of course, sweetheart,' her mother said. 'Which one?' She took out a leather purse from her bag while the girl pointed at the biggest chocolate bun on the counter. 'How much is that?' the mother asked the stallholder.

Sparrow's mouth watered. She followed the bun with her eyes as it was dropped into a bag and then into the girl's waiting hands. The mother smoothed her daughter's hair off her forehead and gave her a fond, indulgent look. 'Little pet,' she crooned. 'You can have whatever makes you happy.'

Sparrow could not take her eyes off them. That could have been me, she was thinking. That could have been me with a mother and a cake and . . .

Now the little girl was biting into the bun, smearing chocolate icing round her mouth. She was laughing. Her mother was laughing. It was extraordinary.

Maybe, Sparrow thought, maybe that woman there was *her* mother and if Sparrow spoke to her now, she'd immediately recognise her and explain what had gone wrong. But as Sparrow looked longingly at the woman and girl, she realised that they were staring back at her, and not in a friendly way, either.

The child was eyeing Sparrow's clothes and a look of distaste spoiled her pretty face.

'Why's that girl so dirty?' she asked her mother.

'Hush dear. You, there, orphanage beggar – don't stare at us!' she snapped at Sparrow. 'I'll call the guards if you keep staring!' She held her bag protectively against her chest as if Sparrow was going to snatch it from her.

'*Sorree!*' Sparrow said, as rudely as she could. The woman's words had cut her to the core. 'There's no law to say I can't stare at you – a cat can look at a king!'

She forced herself to grin as she picked Scaramouch up and rubbed her face against his. 'Can't we, Scaramouch, dear? We can look at anyone and anything, can't we?'

She stalked off, letting Scaramouch settle into her arms with a contented sigh.

'You poor thing, you're tired,' Sparrow said. 'All that walking, you poor dear,' and she rubbed his swollen pads.

'Your feet must hurt. You have a rest, don't mind me,' she added as he closed his eyes.

A young lady with a happy face smiled at them. 'Are you lost, dear? Looking for somewhere particular?'

Sparrow shook her head; but of course she *was* looking for somewhere particular – *Sampson's*. At the same time she dreaded finding it; dreaded finding out something that she didn't want to discover at all.

She wandered round and round the market square. She'd never seen so much stuff: there were stalls selling clothes, books, food and pots, pans and knives. She wished Mary were with her, she'd love it – she loved *things*.

Sparrow was getting very hungry. She stopped beside Bert's Pie Counter, where a pyramid of hot, golden-crusted pies and pastries steamed. A warm, oven smell oozed from the freshly-baked crusts, making her mouth water. She stood there for so long that the man behind the counter finally shooed her away. A notice on the wall behind him said BEGGING IS FORBIDDEN.

Sparrow leaned against the wall and watched the pies from there.

After a while she got a tickling, prickling feeling in her neck and, looking about, saw that another girl, older than her, was staring at her fixedly. She had a mass of long, scraggly hair and wore a short blue jacket. When Sparrow stared back she immediately looked away and pretended to be preoccupied, pulling at her sleeves and digging in her pockets as if looking for money. Sparrow didn't like being watched. She tossed her hair and moved on, searching for any scraps of food that might have fallen, but there was nothing apart from cabbage leaves, rotten fruit and a sleeping dog. She went back to the pie counter and walked round it three times, breathing in the delicious aromas. Next time she looked up, the same girl in the blue jacket was still watching her intently. Now what? Sparrow stared back. The other girl was just as untidy as she was, so it wasn't her clothes she was staring at. She wouldn't let this girl bully her.

The girl came over. 'All right, love?' she said.

She was taller than Sparrow. Her dark hair fell in tight rolls down her back and in complicated plaits and bows, interwoven with brightly-coloured scarves on top of her head. She had a flat brown face with very dark brown eyes and small, crooked teeth that she licked now and then with the tip of her tongue, as if checking they were still there.

'All right?' she said again, nodding at Scaramouch as well.

'Yes. We're fine,' Sparrow said. She realised suddenly that she was on the verge of falling down in a faint. 'Why? What do you care? It's a free country, isn't it?' she snapped, and was furious to hear that her voice cracked.

'You look like you're from out of town, you do. Where've you come from?'

'Knip and Pynch Home for Waifs and Strays.' Sparrow hadn't the strength to lie.

'Oh, my! *That* place! I see now . . . Over the swamp? Well, I thought you looked like a stray, and you are – both of yous,' she added, pointing at Scaramouch. 'He's a big one, in't he? Cheer up, my dear. Gloriana'll help you.'

Sparrow felt immediately better, then cautioned herself to be careful. Remember Mrs Nash, she thought.

'Now, you just ask the nice pie man something,' said Gloriana. 'Keep him busy for a moment. Go on, and I'll get us some nosh.' She pushed Sparrow back towards the pie stall.

'Excuse me, Mister Bert,' Sparrow said when she got there. 'Have you got any spare, please? A broken bit, a little scrap for the cat and me? We're very hungry. We've walked all day.'

'So you're back again, are you?' Bert pointed to the notice about beggars. 'Can't you read?'

Sparrow glanced at the notice. Out of the corner of her eye, she saw Gloriana near the pyramid of pies.

'I can't read!' Sparrow cried earnestly. 'No, I never learned how. I'm just an orphan, up from the country,' she said. 'It's not my fault I'm all alone,' she went on. 'And I've got to feed my cat, he's not very well. Please mister, please!'

'I don't hold with beggars,' Bert said, 'but your cat does look sick. Here, take this one and get on with you. The guards'll be after you if you don't watch out! Best get off the streets.'

He thrust a squashed and mangled pie into a bag and gave it to her. Then he turned suddenly, with a shout to Gloriana: 'Hey! You! What are you up to, missy?'

Gloriana held out her grubby, empty hands to him. 'Nothing, sir,' she said sweetly. 'Just looking.' And she turned away and wandered off as if she and Sparrow were in no way connected.

Sparrow went in the other direction and sat down on the first bit of low wall she came to. She'd only invented the story of Scaramouch being sick to get sympathy, but now she wondered if perhaps he really was ill. He had been very quiet since they'd arrived in Stollenback. She smoothed his fur and tried to interest him in the food.

A few minutes later Gloriana joined her. 'You're a natural,' Gloriana said, patting Sparrow's knee. She grinned. 'I never even needed my thieving fingers, did I?' And she brought out a steaming, undamaged meat pie from a pocket in her voluminous trousers and placed it beside Sparrow on the wall.

'You didn't need to steal. The pie man gave me this,' Sparrow said.

'You always have to steal,' said Gloriana. 'Because if you don't, they will. There's them that takes and them that gives, and you have to be one or the other. I've got nothing to give so I have to take. It's fair, I reckon.'

'I suppose.' Scaramouch ate a little piece of pie but didn't seem very interested in it. It was a shame Little Jean and Mary weren't here to share the food; they were always hungry.

'Don't he like steak and onions?' Gloriana said, watching Scaramouch. 'Fussy, is he?'

'Just very tired, I think,' said Sparrow.

'Don't you look so worried,' said Gloriana, waving a chunk of pie at her then biting into it. 'Think of it as sharing, sharing with Mr Bert. Can't have you starve, can we?'

The girl was older than Sparrow had first imagined, about seventeen, she guessed. Although she was so slight and not very tall, her face showed some strain and lines that only come with time.

'Amazing cat, that,' said Gloriana. 'Is it friendly, then?'

'He is.' Sparrow stroked Scaramouch's head, smoothing the tiny hairs on the bridge of his nose and gently running her fingers over his head, between his ears. He did purr, but only faintly, which was unusual. 'He's my best friend. His name is Scaramouch.'

'What's a *Skarra-moosh*, then? Or is it like what he does, scares the mouses, eh? He's a Scare-a-mouse?' She gingerly scratched Scaramouch under one ear. 'Big, in't he?'

Sparrow grinned. 'Someone told me his name meant acrobat, and he *can* do all sorts of tricks. You should see him climbing trees and walking along a rope even – it's amazing!'

'Well, well. And where are you going, you and the Scare-a-mouse cat?' Gloriana asked her.

'Here, to Stollenback.'

'So you've somewhere to stay then? Friends?'

'No.'

'You've got some money though, for lodgings?'

'No.'

'I see.' Gloriana stuck her hands into the pockets of her voluminous trousers and made a face. 'I see.'

Silence fell. They finished eating the pies and watched the people milling around. Sparrow went on stroking Scaramouch and waited to hear his purr grow stronger and waited to hear what the other girl might suggest. She was sure she would suggest something; she could almost hear the cogs and wheels working in Gloriana's brain.

'I live in Sto'back – that's what we call it – and I can take you home with me if you like,' Gloriana said at last, as if she'd come to a difficult decision. 'A kind woman I know, a lady she is, she keeps a sort of hostel here, a hostel for young girls like you who might be lost and in need of help. She don't charge nothing, neither.'

'Oh. I see.' Sparrow was immediately suspicious. 'No thanks.'

Gloriana laughed and gave Sparrow a friendly nudge. 'I in't going to kidnap you, if that's your worry.'

Sparrow tried to smile too, but Betty Nash had seemed kind enough to begin with. It wasn't easy being an orphan; it wasn't easy having nothing more in your life than a cat, a shawl and the name of a shop . . . Why would this hostel keeper, this lady, not charge for rent unless she wanted something in return?

'Some ladies are just kind 'cos they're kind,' Gloriana said, reading her thoughts. 'You're angry, in't you? I can see that, but you don't need to be worried about Miss Minter.' She licked her little tongue over her teeth again, probing into a molar, and wincing. 'What would you rather do? Stay out on the streets and get caught by the codgers or by *real* kidnappers, or come back with me safe and sound where you can at least sleep the night in a proper bed, eh? It's tough out here, you know – times is hard in Sto'back.'

'I don't know . . .'

'They call me Glori,' the girl added. 'Gloriana's a right mouthful.'

'I'm Sparrow,' Sparrow said.

'Well, Sparrow, little bird, let's get going, shall we?'

Glori knew every back street and turning. She never hesitated as she went down Cottage Road, Meanwood Lane, Spittle Street, even There And Back Again Lane, which was short and led to a stile they had to climb over, then into a narrow, cobbled square. Sparrow was soon confused. Stollenback was a wild maze of houses and streets, she would never remember her way about. She kept her eyes peeled for Sampson's. She even thought about asking Glori where it was, but didn't, because she didn't want anyone to know about that – at least not yet.

The roads grew narrower and narrower and more and more dirty. Piles of rubbish were heaped up beside the doorways, and lines of washing were strung between the windows above their heads. Dirty, ragged children watched them from their dens and dark corners.

'Nearly there,' Glori said as they turned down yet another lane, a grim, narrow place with dangerous-looking dogs who barked at them. Scaramouch hissed at the dogs, his fur up in a fluff. Sparrow squeezed him comfortingly.

'Here we go.' Glori turned down an almost invisible gap into a tiny, cobbled alley; so narrow that only one person could shuffle down it. 'Old walkway,' Glori told her. 'The city's full of them. *Ginnels*, we call 'em.' Tall, bleak old buildings around it blocked out the light, making the narrow space gloomy and damp. 'I was found in a ginnel when I was a kid. Can't remember how I got there. Think I had a dad once, a dad with big wide hands and a grizzly chin. Maybe he left me there.'

'Oh Glori, that's so cruel!' Sparrow said.

'Least I weren't tossed into the river like some unwanted offspring are, eh?' she chuckled. 'Else I'd be proper dead.'

Sparrow felt her heart beginning to thump harder and harder as they squeezed their way along the ginnel. No one could live down here, she thought. It was a trap!

She got ready to run.

Glori turned round and grinned a toothy grin at her. 'What's your problem? Don't worry. It's nothing bad, I promise.' They went a little way further along the passageway and then Glori stopped suddenly beside a door and whistled. Planks of wood had been roughly nailed over the door and it was daubed with paint and old posters advertising long-ago circuses and fairs; it didn't look as if it had been used in a long, long time. Glori followed her whistle with three loud knocks on the door.

A window was hauled open way above them and a girl looked down at them.

'It's Glori!' the girl shouted. 'And she's got someone with her.'

A mighty key on a length of pink ribbon sailed down towards them. Glori caught it deftly and fitted it into the lock.

'Welcome to our home,' she said, unlocking the door.

9

Plans

Miss Knip rarely left the Knip and Pynch Home for Waifs and Strays. It wasn't the dangerous, swampy krackodyles that lurked in the south, or the trolls in the north that kept her at the Home; she just liked to stay put. She enjoyed her job. She thrived on seeing children quake as she walked past them, and any time spent away from the Knip and Pynch Home meant less time causing misery. But now she had to go on a short journey. The prospect of getting her hands on a fortune – a *fortune*! – was too good to miss.

She set out the next morning. She had Barton take her in the horse and cart; her seat high up behind the gatekeeper was safe even from the largest, bravest krackodyle, he assured her.

Her journey didn't take long. Miss Knip arrived at her destination a little dusty and a little tired. She wiped down her black dress and adjusted her bonnet around her mean, narrow face before knocking on the cottage door. 'You wait there, Barton,' she commanded. 'I shan't be long.'

'Yes, ma'am.'

She turned back, hearing the door open.

'Miss Knip!' cried the woman. 'What a surprise!'

'I should imagine it is, Betty Nash,' Miss Knip said, going towards her. 'You can be sure it's something important that's made me leave the Home.'

Mrs Nash grinned. 'Do come inside, Miss Knip, won't you?'

'Don't mind if I do.' Miss Knip trod carefully, making sure she squashed the daisies growing on the doorstep before she followed Betty Nash inside.

'Sit down, Miss Knip, please,' Betty said. 'How can I help?'

'Have you got a girl here?' Miss Knip asked. 'I'm looking for an eleven-leaver, and I thought you might have got her . . .' she fought to hide the eager anticipation showing in her face. She was already looking for signs of the girl in the room. 'I'm sure she came this way.'

'Ah, now, Miss Knip, a great many of your young castoffs come this way, as you know, and we take them in and nurture them, just as you'd wish us to do,' Betty Nash said with a horrible, leering grin. 'But . . .'

'This one had a cat.'

'Oh, the one with the cat! That stringy little girl?' she said. 'Blondish hair? Such a fine needle-woman she was.' Betty Nash shook her head. 'I wish we did have her, Miss Knip, only she's gone, the little minx.'

Miss Knip bit back a cry of displeasure. 'That's a shame; I thought she might be here. I was hoping . . . Well, I've got a proposition to put to your young Tapper,' she went on.

'Is *he* here?'

Tapper slipped out of the scullery as if he'd been hiding there, listening – which he probably had, Miss Knip thought.

'Where else would I be?' he said, taking up a position propped against the wall, like a length of wood. 'So, how's things at the orphanage, Knips?' he added. 'Beaten anyone this morning?'

'Less of your cheek,' Miss Knip said haughtily. 'And it's *Miss* Knip to you.'

'That cat didn't come inside,' Betty Nash interrupted. 'Biggest cat I've ever seen. Tapper would've trapped it, only he couldn't get close. Shame, 'cos it would've made a beautiful fur cape.'

'And the two of them made a mighty hole in our thatch,' Tapper said. 'She owes us, she does.'

'All the more reason for you to help me then, Tapper. Because I want to find her too,' Miss Knip said, locking her eyes with his. 'I think she went to Stollenback – in fact, I'm sure she did; if she came this way where else would she go? I want you to find her. I want you to find out where she is hiding and keep an eye on her for me. Don't let her know what you're doing. I don't want to alarm her. I just want to know her whereabouts. I want her watched. It's imperative that she doesn't get wind of us, do you understand?'

'Yeah, yeah . . . I can do that, but what's in it for me?' Tapper was picking at his teeth with a sliver of wood as if he was hardly concentrating. 'I can't leave me old ma all alone unless there's a very good reason for it.'

'Money,' Miss Knip said. 'Money to pay for the roof and a whole lot more.'

Tapper flicked the toothpick into the fire. 'How much?' he said, leaning over the chair beside her. 'You got to make it worth my while, Knips.'

'A fortune,' Miss Knip said.

Tapper and his mother exchanged a greedy, happy smile. 'I'm your man,' Tapper said.

10

Gloriana

'Don't look so worried, Birdie,' Glori said, grinning at Sparrow. 'I'm not going to hurt you.'

She pushed open the shabby door.

This was the moment for Sparrow to run if she was going to. But she couldn't. Her legs were too tired and Glori didn't seem like a bad person, not really. And Scaramouch was not jumping out of her arms and running away either, so it had to be all right. He was awake and looking around – but maybe he was too exhausted to give her a sign?

She followed Glori into a hallway paved with large black and white tiles – most of which were broken – and bare walls where the plaster had cracked and fallen off, exposing old red bricks and dust. A steep wooden staircase went up to the floor above. A girl's grinning face peered down at them, her long hair dangling over the banisters. Her clothes seemed to glow with a pale light as she stood there in the dark, so for a second or two Sparrow imagined she was looking at a ghost.

'Who's that with you, Glori?' the ghost, who was not a ghost, called down.

'Wait and see!' Glori called back.

She pulled Sparrow up the wide staircase and then up another flight and another. 'Don't worry!' Glori said, grinning at her. 'It's fine.'

Sparrow tried to smile. Why would they need a hideout, unless they were doing something against the law? Why did I come? Why did I trust her? she thought. But still she followed Glori up the stairs, because the idea of being alone out there in the town was too bleak to contemplate. Glori was kind; she was the only person she knew; she was her only hope.

A strong smell of sulphur, a burning sharpness, caught in her throat as she went up the final flight of stairs, then it was gone. Scaramouch winced at the smell and turned his head this way and that, sniffing the air.

'Here they are!' the ghostly girl with the long hair yelled from the doorway.

Glori led Sparrow into a large attic room that stretched right across the top of the old building. Massive beams joined overhead in a lattice pattern and formed wooden pillars supporting the roof. It was a vast space – hot and smelly, noisy and bright.

The noise was made by girls – about ten of them, Sparrow guessed as she looked around – but not like the girls in the Home who had to remain silent most of the time. These girls were giggling and chatting as they lounged around on their beds and chairs. They wore red, orange, pink and green, not orphanage grey. The Home had always been cold, but here a massive fire burned in the ornate fireplace and it was cosy. And there were mirrors everywhere – none were allowed at the Home except one small one in the bathroom, and that had been cracked – probably by Miss Knip looking in it. Pots of flowers and greenery filled every free shelf. Two giant windows, one at either end of the room, looked out on the surrounding rooftops: all sloping terracotta tiles and tall, black chimneystacks.

The other girls left what they were doing to come and gawp at Sparrow. Glori led her to the fireplace, where a slender woman sat perched on a pink chaise longue, flicking through a magazine. She was in her mid-twenties, Sparrow guessed, and was wearing a bright yellow dress that fitted her tightly. She wore shiny black boots with high heels; Sparrow had never seen anything like them. Rows of silver and gold chains glittered around her neck. Her hair was very blonde – almost white – and with a high gloss, like polished metal. She wore it neatly folded and pinned at the back of her head. She had dangling earrings and her lips were full and glistening, like wet murgberries.

Sparrow fixed on her and stared open-mouthed.

'Who is this? Whom have you brought to see us, Gloriana?' the woman in yellow said, smiling vacantly. 'What delightful creature is this in our midst?' She looked at Sparrow with mild interest, frowning as she took in her grubby clothes, her big old boots, the huge cat. 'A girl? Is it a new girl?'

There was something odd about her. Her manner was offhand and she spoke without seeming to connect to what she said, Sparrow thought.

'Is that what it is, Gloriana?' she went on.

'This is Sparrow, Miss Minter,' Glori said. 'She's an orphan,' she added with a wink, 'and that's her rat catcher, Scare-a-mouse.'

'*Scaramouch*,' Sparrow said, squeezing him gently. She moved him onto her other arm. 'We've walked a lot,' she explained, with a yawn. 'We're both really tired.'

'Come and sit by me, my angel,' Miss Minter said. 'You look all-in. Billie Blue-eyes, darling, will you get her something to drink. Kate, bring some food.'

Two girls jumped up to do her bidding. There was some sort of kitchen off the main room and Sparrow heard pans clattering and dishes being banged against each other as they busied themselves.

Sparrow sat down beside Miss Minter on the hard, velvet chaise longue. Her head was spinning and her legs were weak after all the walking. Her feet were stinging from pounding the roads. She sighed and crumpled on the sofa, overcome with exhaustion.

Miss Minter smelled of flowers. She smiled brightly. 'What a wonderful cat,' she said, her voice clear, each syllable pronounced. 'I like cats. Some cats . . . I *hate* some cats.'

Sparrow was confused. 'Sorry, miss, what did you say? I'm so tired . . .'

'I said I love your cat,' Miss Minter said, reaching out a delicate white hand to stroke him, but Scaramouch flinched.

'He's shy,' Sparrow said. 'Nervous. The pie man said he wasn't very well.'

'He'll get better here,' Miss Minter said. 'With us.'

Glori was leaning over the back of a tall chair and was resting her chin in her hands, watching them. 'Yeah, he'll get better here, he will,' she said. 'In the nest. Hey, Sparrow's the first real bird our nest's ever had!'

The other girls giggled.

'*Nest?*' Sparrow looked from one face to the other.

'This is our nest,' the girl called Billie said. 'Used to be the Crow's Nest like at the top of a ship's mast, now it's just the *nest*. Home.'

'What about you, my angel, are you really a bird?' Miss Minter went on. She stoked Sparrow's cheek, just as she had stroked the cat. 'You're not shy, are you?'

'No. Not at all.' Sparrow met Miss Minter's penetrating gaze. 'I've been brought up tough. Not shy.'

'We need to be strong, we girls,' Miss Minter said, gently. 'We stick together and help each other. Let me introduce you to everyone. This is Agnes and that is gorgeous, red-haired Kate and this is Billie with the blue, blue eyes. Here we have dear little Hettie. Violet is the dark one – oh, darling Violet, don't scowl at me! And Beattie is the blonde. Connie and Dolly are twins; I've no idea which is which. Is that everyone? Oh dear, I forgot my Gloriana. And now there's you, Sparrow, to make a round ten.'

Sparrow said hello to them and immediately forgot their names.

They sat at the big wooden table and shared bread and cheese and drank hot chocolate. The other girls watched Sparrow with interest. They all wanted to ask her questions.

'Where are you from, then?'

'Got a family?'

'Have you run away from home, is it?'

Sparrow said nothing.

'Don't ask her so many questions. Don't stare at her so,' Miss Minter said calmly. 'Show some decorum and leave her alone, please. She is our visitor, our guest. We must be gentle with her.'

'What's decorum?' someone muttered, but the girls backed away and went to their beds, which were tucked in below the low ceiling and between the wooden beams. They began whispering and giggling. Only Glori stayed behind, as if, being the oldest, she had some special rights. Miss Minter picked up a newspaper and started to read it. 'You can relax now, Sparrow, you are amongst friends here,' she murmured, scanning the pages of her paper. 'Goodness, there are some terrible people around in the city . . . two children murdered in Stollenback . . . dreadful. It's such a dangerous place these days, I can't imagine what's to become of us all.'

Sparrow drained her hot chocolate and looked around, wondering what they wanted from her.

'I do hope you will stay with us, Sparrow, angel,' Miss Minter said, smoothing her dress over her elegant knees and thighs. 'I look after all these girls, you see, and we work together. We are one big happy family, aren't we, Gloriana?'

'Yes we are, miss!' Glori said. 'Only family I've got, anyways. We all help each other.'

'We most certainly do,' Miss Minter said. 'And your lovely cat can stay too of course, Sparrow, and catch our revolting, dirty rodents. We have mice. We have rats too.' Miss Minter took a lipstick from her bag and ran the murgberry-red over her plump lips. 'We tried eating the rats one horrible winter, we were so desperately hungry, but they don't taste very good. They *look* quite pleasant, furry and cuddly – well, all except the tail – but they taste like –'

'Rancid cheese!' Glori said. 'They were disgusting!'

'But those were in the bad old days,' Miss Minter went on. 'Now we have work and we make money and we are doing very well, thank you.'

'You're so clever, Miss Minter,' Glori said. 'And good.'

'Yes. You are right, I am.' She took one of Sparrow's hands in her own and turned it over, examining her fingers. She tested the tension in her thumb, stretching it back gently against her wrist. 'Lovely hands, angel. I bet you can do all sorts of very clever things with those.'

'I can sew.'

'I'm sure you can. I'm sure those fingers can make such pretty things.'

The very smallest girl left her bedside to come and sit beside Sparrow. She stroked Scaramouch's head. 'He's a lovely pussycat,' the girl said. 'He's striped like a tiger, only you can hardly see the stripes. They're very pale, they're hiding. Did you know?'

'Yes, I knew. I'm glad you noticed,' Sparrow said, smoothing Scaramouch's fur. 'Not everyone sees those lovely stripes. He's like a cup of creamy pale coffee not all stirred in, isn't he?'

'I love cats,' the little girl said. 'We do want you to stay,' she added, slipping her tiny hand into Sparrow's. 'You're nice. Will you be my big sister?'

'What's your name?' Sparrow asked her.

'Hettie. I'm seven and a half . . . I think.' She snuggled beside her, squashing herself under Sparrow's arm like a puppy might do.

'My big sister went –'

'Hettie!' Miss Minter said sweetly. 'Don't crowd our new guest will you, darling?'

Hettie slipped her arm back from where it had crept around Sparrow's waist and folded her hands neatly in her lap. She looked up at Sparrow with huge, dark eyes. 'You look like my sister,' she said.

'I'd like to stay,' Sparrow said, 'but I –'

'Good, that's settled,' Miss Minter said, without taking her eyes from her newspaper. 'You can relax, Sparrow – no more wandering the streets for you now. Miss Minter and her girls will look after you.'

Glori took Sparrow's hand. 'Come on, I'll show you round. There's not much to see.' She took her to the kitchen and then the bathroom. It was tiled in white and had eight cast-iron baths and eight square basins. There were eight cubicles behind. 'It used to be a school in the olden days,' Glori told her. 'Aren't we lucky, eh? Almost a whole bath each!'

'Oh, Mary would like that – my friend at the Home. She always wanted a hot bath . . . So this isn't a school any longer?' Sparrow asked her.

'No, hasn't been for yonks. No one knows we're here. It's behind everything, you see, hidden, and we've been forgotten. Miss Minter's helper, he keeps up a furnace somewhere that makes the hot water. Will you need a toothbrush?' She waved one in front of Sparrow. 'We've got some spare.'

Sparrow shook her head. She brought her toothbrush out from her bag. Glori felt the bristles.

'That must be like brushing your teeth with a yard broom!' she cried. 'Blimey, Sparrow, it's even got your name scratched on it.'

'We only got one toothbrush every two years,' Sparrow told her, 'so you can imagine . . .'

'Poor you!' Hettie said, creeping up beside her again. 'We have everything we want here. Miss Minter gives us all we need.'

'She's a dear, is Miss Minter,' Glori said. 'A bit contrary, but a dear.'

'There's an empty bed for you,' Hettie told her, 'next to mine. It was –'

'Leave her, Hettie. She's tired.' Glori turned back to Sparrow. 'Bet you sleep good tonight.'

Sparrow yawned. Just the mention of the word 'bed' made her legs go weak.

'You can have a bath. I'll give you clothes. It's all sorted now, Sparrow. You'll see.'

She was shown to a narrow bed next to Hettie. Sparrow put Scaramouch down on it and he turned round three or four times, kneading the bedding, then curled up and closed his eyes again.

'There, *he* thinks it's comfortable and quite perfect for the night,' Sparrow said, which made Hettie giggle.

The sheets were grubby and there even seemed to be the impression of someone's small head left on the pillow, but Sparrow lay down on it gratefully. After hedges and haystacks, this was bliss.

It's just for one night, she told herself. I'll be off tomorrow. I'll find Sampson's . . .

Through the massive window, past the gable ends, pointed roofs and tiny attic windows, she could just make out the silhouette of the castle on Dragon Mountain, the spitfyre Academy. She was thrilled thinking such lovely creatures were so near. She hoped she would see one come swooping down over the rooftops.

Her final wish as she drifted off to sleep was that Scaramouch, who all evening had been so flat and quiet, would be better tomorrow. His nose was hot and his breathing loud and grumbly; he seemed exhausted.

She woke once in the night and looked around the dormitory. Each bed glowed faintly. She sat up and stared. Each girl was gleaming as if they had washed in moonlight.

11

Off

Leaving Miss Knip and his mother sitting by the fire sipping tea, Tapper went upstairs to prepare. He pressed his quivering hands together tightly. *Stollenback!* How much more fun it was there than out here in the sticks! He hardly ever got a chance to be in town for more than a night. Now he'd stay there and go see his girlfriend. Well, she wasn't really a girlfriend . . . They'd met in the park in the summer, both sitting for a quick breather in the sunshine, and had got talking. Now they had this little thing going. Every time he went up to town to sell the toy spitfyres, they met up and shared a drink in one of the coffee houses or a pie in the tavern. She was a great girl, clever – cleverer than him, though he never let her know that. Pretty too, in a wild sort of way. She knew a lot of folk who lived there. She'd find Sparrow for him – and wouldn't he like to get his hands on that little minx, he thought. Slipping out of his fingers like that! Mustn't damage the goods, though. He had to keep her clean and tidy so they got a good price when they ransomed her. We wouldn't need much money, he thought. Then maybe him and his girl could set up together and he could get away from Ma and the cottage, away from the orphanage girls and far, far away from those blasted toy spitfyres.

He dashed off a quick letter to her, not wanting to turn up on her doorstep without warning, thrust some clothes into his pack and ran downstairs again.

'. . . the girl, Sparrow, was always trouble,' Miss Knip was saying. 'Right from when she first opened her mouth and said her first words, she was trouble. Answered back. Uppity.'

'What were her first words then?' Betty Nash asked her.

Miss Knip threw a furious look at her. 'Well, I don't know,' she snapped. 'How can I remember all those years back – and anyway, I wasn't there!'

'Sorry for asking,' Betty shot back. 'We could see she was a spirited lass too. Fancy you finding her family! That makes a change, don't it? Even if they've got family, most times it's not one that wants them.'

'Quite,' Miss Knip said. 'But she has and I know they'll be willing to pay to get her back –'

'I'm ready,' Tapper interrupted. 'I'll need a bit of money to keep me going, Knip.' He held out his hand.

'*Miss* Knip!' Miss Knip said, squinting up at him. Reluctantly, she loosened the laces on her leather purse and, with difficulty, as if the coins were glued to her fingers, she handed him some money. 'Remember, all I want at this moment is to know where she is.'

'Certainly, Knips. Your wish is my command,' Tapper said, slipping the coins into his pocket. He patted them affectionately, relishing the clink they made against his leg. 'Find her and watch her.'

'You're not going before you've had your tea, are you?' his mother asked him. 'Have you got clean underbits? A warm scarf? Aren't you going to wait until – Oh, wait until I've helped you pack and made you some big meat sandwiches . . .'

Tapper pulled on his dark patchwork jacket. 'I'm going now. Make hay while the sun shines and all that. So?'

Betty Nash began to shuffle up to her feet to try to embrace him but he was too fast and was already halfway out of the door.

'Just a moment, young man!' Miss Knip shouted. 'Just a moment. I'm glad you're keen, but there's things to sort out.'

Tapper came back and leaned against the doorframe. He folded his arms.

'Yes?' His eyes were cold.

'You will send a letter every day to me at the orphanage. Every day, Tapper, with a breakdown of your expenses and what you've discovered.'

He leaped up again. 'Got it,' he said. 'Anything else?'

'No, but –'

But Tapper had already gone.

12

Miss Minter

Sparrow was the first of the girls to fall asleep and the first to wake. She opened her eyes a fraction, wondering where she was, and then the strange events of the previous day came flooding back.

She was in the nest.

Grey light was coming in through the large windows. She vaguely remembered the giggling and the whispering of the girls as they had crawled into their beds alongside her, but nothing more of the previous night. Now they were still asleep; Hettie curled up in a ball in her bedclothes and grunting softly, like a little piglet.

It wasn't so different from any morning at the Knip and Pynch Home except it was warm; she could hear the fire crackling in the hearth. What a luxury to feel warm in the morning! Without moving, hardly opening her eyes, Sparrow saw Miss Minter standing in front of the big, gilt mirror, brushing out her long blonde hair.

In her half-asleep, just-woken moment, Sparrow lay and watched her. Miss Minter was the most elegant, lovely woman she had ever seen; her smooth skin, peachy cheeks and bright, round eyes were perfect – and yet somehow she seemed unreal. Sparrow had the odd idea that Miss Minter's blood would be as cold as a mountain stream, and not even red, but clear as crystal.

Befuddled as she was, Sparrow was still highly sensitive to Miss Minter's odd manner, the way she had already glanced several times over to where Sparrow lay, as if checking her. So Sparrow kept her eyes half-closed and gave no hint she was awake.

Miss Minter didn't want her to see what she was doing, and that made Sparrow want to watch her.

Sparrow saw her take down a painting of a tree from the wall. Behind the painting was a tiny door – a safe! She opened it using a key from her bag, glancing round suspiciously as she did so. She took out a tiny, delicate glass bottle. In her hazy, dreamy state, Sparrow imagined Miss Minter had taken out a bottle of sunshine. That's what the substance inside looked like, except it rolled and flowed as if it were a dense, heavy liquid. Whatever it was, it was incredibly brilliant, as if all the lanterns in the whole of Stollenback had been miraculously squashed inside the bottle and now they were trying to break out. Miss Minter looked at the bottle from many different angles. She shook it gently and the light shattered into a thousand fragments. Now it seemed she held a jar of bouncing, golden, shining dots, flying around, bumping against each other and fizzling, popping, exploding with an intensely brilliant light. She eased the stopper off very carefully, anxious not to let too much escape, and tipped a bead of brightness onto her finger. It wavered and danced, balancing on her fingertip, like a tiny, phosphorescent flame.

'Poor old Sparkit,' Miss Minter murmured to the blob of light. 'Sparkit has gone for ever. Or is that you, Diamond Eyes?' She looked at her fingertip from a different angle. 'You were a fine fellow. Bluey? Bluey, you should have been more careful – didn't we warn you, you poor, poor darling?'

Then Miss Minter licked the bead of light from her finger, dreamily closing her eyes as she rolled it around in her mouth.

Sparrow was enthralled. What *was* that stuff? She was just about to speak when Scaramouch nudged against her chin and stopped her. She closed her eyes and reached out to stroke him dreamily.

'*Sparrow!*'

'Yes, Miss Minter?' Sparrow struggled up onto her elbow. 'Oh!' she cried in surprise. Miss Minter was leaning over her, her red mouth and flashing eyes only inches above her face.

'Don't!' Sparrow cried.

Miss Minter held a pot of daisies poised, as if it were a weapon, ready to smash on Sparrow's head.

'Stop it!' Sparrow threw up her hands to protect herself. 'Miss!' she squeaked. 'Don't!' She scrambled up to a sitting position. Scaramouch growled protectively.

The other girls woke and sat up, alarmed.

'Did you see anything?' hissed Miss Minter through

clenched teeth. 'You saw something! What did you see? Tell me!'

'No! What do you mean? I've just woken up,' Sparrow said. To lie was automatic. It was important not to have seen the bright stuff – why? She didn't know, but it was. 'I didn't see anything at all.' Sparrow rubbed her eyes theatrically.

Miss Minter breathed out loudly. She glanced round at the other girls then looked sharply at the pot in her hand, as if wondering how it had got there. Suddenly she twirled round and smacked it down on the little table by Sparrow's bed and smiled.

'Sparrow likes daisies, don't you?' she said. 'There. Done. I didn't mean to frighten you, my angel,' she added, sitting down on the bed. 'I am always up and down, up and down and so changeable. My father used to say I was like thistledown, blowing wherever the wind took me.' Her eyes suddenly filled with tears. 'I've had a troubled life, Sparrow,' she went on. 'My father was locked up in prison, and he was innocent, innocent! My mother died when I was young. The rest of my family hated me.'

She turned and looked up through the window towards Dragon Mountain and the Academy. There was a long pause. 'Even my cousin, my cousin disowned me.' Then she sighed. She patted Sparrow's arm. 'That's why I must help you girls,' she said. 'We must fight; we must be strong together. We are family.'

'It's all right,' Sparrow said. 'I understand.'

Miss Minter clapped her hands. 'Time you were all up,'

she cried suddenly, waving an arm at the girls. 'Breakfast time! Whose turn to get the bread?'

'Mine,' Connie called, leaping out of her bed. She was dressed in an instant and out of the room and clattering down the stairs.

Sparrow calmed her breathing. Miss Minter didn't seem to suspect her of lying. Admitting to a mistake at the orphanage – like forgetting to wash the floor behind the black stove in the kitchen – meant time locked in the coalhole or the cellar or even, once, up in the cobwebby attic with the bats. So she had learned to lie and lie well.

Miss Minter nodded towards Scaramouch. 'Cats look after themselves, don't they?' she said. 'He'll be all right. I don't like animals frightfully much. Their eyes are so knowing, they seem to know something and I think they might speak and then the thought goes and they don't speak.' She jumped up and began to roll up her hair in a shining pleat. 'I'm late. Come, Sparrow. Come and have breakfast. I want you to tell me all about yourself and how you came here and all about the orphanage. All my girls are orphans, you know, unwanted and unloved. It's very sad. I love them. I can love them, can't I? Even though I'm not truly an orphan I think I can know how it feels to be one, can't I?'

'Yes, yes, I'm sure you can,' Sparrow said. She pushed Scaramouch aside gently and got out of bed.

'I want you to be my special friend, Sparrow,' Miss Minter went on, placing her slender arm around Sparrow's shoulders and brushing aside Sparrow's thick hair. 'You are like me,

Sparrow, I can see it: you are bright and clever and the world has been against you so far. But not any more, my angel. Now Miss Minter will watch over you.'

Sparrow smiled back warily. 'Creepy' was the word that sprang to mind. Miss Knip was mean and spiteful but not creepy. Miss Knip was *always* mean and always spiteful so you knew where you were with her, but Miss Minter was weird and changed mood all the time.

'Thank you,' Sparrow said quickly and escaped to the bathroom.

At the Knip and Pynch Home for Waifs and Strays the water had always been cold and the soap gritty and the towels damp. Here the bathroom was warm and steamy and the other girls laughed and joked with each other as they washed.

'Hello, face!' Sparrow said, seeing her reflection in the mirror; a rare sight. 'Hello, all that hair!' she said, brushing out her thick hair with a proper brush for the first time in ages.

'Haven't you seen your hair before?' Hettie cried. She was standing on a chair beside her, eager to plait it for her.

'Not in a mirror,' Sparrow said. 'Not properly, not for months.'

'My sister had long hair right down to her bottom,' Hettie told her. 'It was orange like a carrot. I loved it. Carroty Cari I called her. Her real name was Carina.'

Carroty Carina must have died, Sparrow thought. She didn't like to ask when or how.

'Hurry up, Sparrow,' Glori said, nudging her. 'Connie's

back. Hettie, leave her alone!'

Hettie scampered off, giggling.

'She's sweet,' Sparrow said.

'She's lonely, that's what.'

'What happened to her sister?' Sparrow asked her.

'Mmm? Oh, look at that!' Glori said, going across to the baths. 'No one ever picks up a towel, do they?' She scooped the wet towels up and hung them out to dry on the pegs. 'Are you ready? Come on, Birdie!'

Sparrow grinned. She liked being called Birdie. Glori was fun and at least here she wasn't in danger of breaking one of Pynch's new rules or disobeying an order from Miss Knip. Nor, so far, did she have a list of dull, pointless duties that she had to work through every day. Maybe, maybe she'd stay . . .

Connie had brought back bags of fresh croissants as well as bread, and three jars of plum jam. The other girls had laid the big table with plates of all shapes and sizes and patterns, glasses and mugs, spoons and knives. The dark girl called Violet, who was about twelve years old, was making coffee and hot chocolate. She wore her hair in a ponytail and had round black eyes that she made darker with black makeup. Her fingernails were bitten down to stubs, half the size they should have been, like grubby little windowpanes at the ends of her fingers.

'You ever had croissants before?' said Connie or was it Dolly? They were identical. She tossed one onto her plate.

'No,' Sparrow admitted. 'We had black bread for breakfast. Or gruel. Are they good?'

'Like eating crispy clouds of butter,' the other girl said, grinning.

Sparrow tasted the flaky pastry. 'That's amazing!' she said, rolling her eyes. 'Heavenly!' And all the girls laughed. 'I wish I could take some back to the Home. To the others.'

'I wish you could too, darling,' Miss Minter said without glancing up.

Sparrow had the impression Miss Minter had no idea what Sparrow had been talking about and was just saying anything that sounded right.

'Oh, look!' Beattie added. 'Your Scare-a-mouse has gone outside! How'd he do that?'

They all rushed to see. Sparrow pressed her nose against the cold glass of the window. Scaramouch was tiptoeing across the point of the roof like an acrobat on a high wire. He glanced back at her over his shoulder and flicked his tail. What did that mean?

'How did he get out?' she asked.

Hettie showed her a missing pane of glass in the huge window. 'Through there – there's a roof door by the kitchen too, but he doesn't need real doors, does he? Will he come back, Sparrow?'

'Oh yes, he always comes back.' He *had* to come back. He *would* come back. 'Yes,' she said again. 'He'll be back.'

'All creatures need time on their own,' Miss Minter said, addressing her newspaper.

'I wish I had a special friend like him,' Beattie said. 'Maybe he'll bring some more cats home with him?' She looked out at Scaramouch dreamily, coiling her frizzy blonde hair around her fingers. 'We could have a cat each, couldn't we, Miss Minter?'

'Quiet now, and get on with your breakfast,' Miss Minter said.

'We have a rota for washing up,' Agnes told Sparrow, showing her the slate where jobs were written down. 'And one for cleaning and for shopping and match-making. Your name's already on it, Sparrow.'

Sparrow was surprised. She didn't know whether to be pleased or annoyed or even scared. After all, she thought, I never said I was going to stay – but now it seemed she was.

'There, see,' Glori said, pointing to the list, 'you and me on match-making this morning. That's good. I can show you how to do it.'

'You make matches?'

'Yeah, we do,' Glori said. 'We're not on breakfast or tidy up so, come on, I'll show you.'

'What about Scaramouch?' Sparrow said, looking out of the window.

'Scare-a-mouse'll be fine. He can come in when he chooses. He can go out when he chooses. Come on, Birdie! Follow me!'

On the floor below there was a large room divided into two by panelled, folding doors. Three tall, thin windows, thick with grime and dust, let in a feeble light at one end. The window shutters were half-closed. A long, narrow table stood centrally in each side of the room, surrounded by chairs and covered in pots and strange, small pieces of machinery. The walls had shelves and narrow cupboards on them.

'What's that smell?' Sparrow cried, holding her nose. It was the stink she'd smelled the night before – a burning, acrid, sulphurous tang. It made her eyes smart and her nose burn.

'Phosphorus,' Glori said. 'I know. It's bad, isn't it? Makes my teeth ache something terrible. It's not so bad on the other side of the room,' she said. 'See, we need the phosphorus for the matches. Miss Minter wants it all secret,' Glori told her. 'No open windows so it can't escape and let them know – the authorities. It's not illegal, making matches, only she don't pay no taxes.'

'And she don't want no one checking on us,' Agnes said, slipping past them to take her place at the table. 'No regulations and all that stuff.'

The twins came in, along with another girl.

'Bet you don't remember their names,' Glori said and, when Sparrow shook her head, Glori told her, 'That's Dolly. See, they're not truly identical, Dolly's the dumpy one –'

'I am not!' Dolly cried, patting her tummy. 'Just padding, that is.'

'And the other one's Connie. And that's Beattie with all the frizz.'

'Blonde curls, they are,' Beattie said, smoothing her cloud of hair. 'Where d'you get a name like Sparrow, anyway?' Beattie asked her.

Sparrow shrugged. 'I don't know.'

'Thought you were an orphan,' Connie said. 'Orphanages and homes give out names like Jane and Ann. Not Sparrow.'

'Then someone called her it *before* she were an orphan, stupid,' Agnes said, tying her long brown hair back over her shoulder. 'Someone with some imagination.'

Had it been her mother? Sparrow wondered, as she had done so many times. Her father? She hoped so.

Agnes, Connie and Dolly sat down in the first section of the room.

'We've drawn the short straws,' Dolly said, making a disgusted face at the awful stench.

'As usual,' Agnes said, glancing at Sparrow. 'Why isn't it the new girl?'

'Here we go,' Connie said, ignoring Agnes's comment. 'Masks on!' Giggling, the three girls tied scarves over the lower part of their faces.

'Blimey, what a life,' Agnes said in a muffled voice. She pushed the pot of phosphorus further away. 'It's rotting my guts, that stuff is.'

'I'm glad I'm not working at that table,' Sparrow whispered to Glori.

'Miss Minter changes us around from week to week,' Glori said. 'I've been here longest, I've had more poison than the others.'

'Is it really poison?' Sparrow asked.

'Maybe not,' Glori said vaguely.

The smell was still awful but less so in the other half of the room. Here there was some simple hand machinery for making the wooden matchsticks – weird-looking tools, glue and wood. Sparrow wondered what it was all for. She wasn't sure she wanted to make matches, but then what else was she to do?

She wished Scaramouch were with her. Everything was better when he was close by.

'Come on, let me show you what's what,' Glori said. She pointed to a pile of small wood pieces. 'That's the matchwood,' she said, 'brought up from the joiners round the corner.'

'So the joiners know you make matches?' Sparrow asked.

'No – Mr Abraham thinks we burn it to keep warm!' Beattie called over her shoulder.

'This is the cutter,' Glori said. 'See?' She cranked the handle on a conical machine and the wheel rotated. Thin lengths, each three inches long, popped out at the other end. 'Ta dah! Firesticks – they'll turn into matches.'

Sparrow picked one up and rolled it round in her fingers. 'We only used tinderboxes in the Home,' she said. 'Matches were too expensive – and dangerous. Don't they ever explode?'

Connie and Agnes giggled. 'All the time!' someone shouted.

'Watch it! Hold your noses! I'm dipping!' Connie called out as she took the lid off a jar of phosphorus and a white mist swirled up into the air. Sparrow watched it linger there like a heavy cloud above the table. The air was suddenly filled with the sharp, tangy smell of phosphorus.

'What is *dipping,* exactly?' Sparrow asked and quickly learned it meant dipping the end of the sticks into the jar until a little pale-yellow blob stuck to its end.

'Lucky us. Miss Minter has put you on boxes with me,' Glori said. 'Here.'

She led Sparrow to the other table, where Kate and Billie and little Hettie were just settling down to their work.

'Sit by me!' Hettie cried to Sparrow.

'We all hate dipping,' Kate said. 'I'm back on it tomorrow.' She put a scarf over her rich, red hair and swept it out of the way.

'Me too,' Hettie said. 'But Miss Minter would be poor if we didn't help her, wouldn't she?'

'Wouldn't she just,' Billie said.

'Gives me toothache,' Kate added.

'Gives us all toothache,' Glori said. 'But it's that or –' she motioned over her shoulder with a thumb – 'out we go!'

13

A Letter

My Sweetheart, it's me, Tapper.

Hello.

Your friend, as what you know I am. So.

I'm on my way to Sto'back. Now. Just got to do this note to you.

I've got a job. It were given me by an old bat who shall remain anon-imus.

This is the job – to find something. That's not hard I think, to find something that's gone missing. I thought, I can do that. Tapper can find that all right.

My Sweetheart, you will help me. You can, so, you've got sharp eyes, I know.

The Old Blue Bear Tavern on Friday. Nine. 9 in the night time. Be there, girl!

Do you wonder what? The what is the money!

You must help.

Friday. 9.

Tapper

14

Stories

'Are you watching me?' Glori asked, pausing with a half-made box in her hands. 'Or are you away with the fairies?'

Sparrow shook herself out of her dream. She was thinking about Scaramouch. She pictured him falling off the roof or being attacked by big Stollenback cats . . . Didn't he like it here? Was he going to go off on his own? What had that look meant, that flick of his tail?

'Sorry. I just wish Scaramouch had come down here too, that's all.'

'Ah, he'll be fine. Now, watch, this is what you do.' Glori scored and folded a strip of cardboard. 'This makes the outer bit, the case. Glue here. And here.' She stuck on a strip of rough striking paper to the glued card. 'Then we make the tray like this.' She again folded and glued some soft card to make the inside box. Then she counted out twenty matches that already had their blobs of phosphorus on them and laid them neatly in the tray and slipped it into the outer case and closed it.

'Done!'

'Amazing!' Sparrow said. 'A real box of matches.'

'Now watch this!' Glori worked twenty times faster and completed a box in seconds. 'There!'

'Goodness!' Sparrow cried. 'You're so fast!'

Glori gave Sparrow a friendly punch and laughed. 'I've been doing it since I was knee high – this, and stealing pies!'

'You've always been knee high,' Billie said.

Glori groaned. 'I can't help it if I don't hardly ever grow,' she said. 'I'm sixteen, or maybe seventeen by now, and look at me,' she said to Sparrow. 'Scrawny and thin and not much bigger than a twelve year old!'

'Your feet reach the ground, though,' Sparrow teased her. 'You're perfect.'

The others giggled.

'Now you try making one, Sparrow,' Glori said. 'Go slowly – they gotta be perfect. You can decorate the cover then, 'cos we have to make them special or they're no better than the other match-girls' boxes.'

The work wasn't hard and it was the sort of fiddly thing Sparrow was good at.

'So you've only just got out of that old Home?' Kate asked her. 'What's it like being free?'

Sparrow shrugged. 'It's good,' she said. 'I think.' Was she free? She felt almost as trapped here as she had in the orphanage.

'My father left me outside a tavern,' Kate said. 'Two Drunken Dogs, it was called. Wish it hadn't been called that. I remember his face as he pressed a penny in my hand.

I remember thinking, why's he looking at me so sad? It was 'cos he knew he weren't coming back, that's why. Wish he'd just said it. I waited two days. Right worried, I was, thinking he'd got lost or hurt, and I stuck to that doorstep 'cos I thought if I left it, he'd never find me. Then I just kept seeing his eyes, that last look, and I knew he'd gone for good. He were sorry, I knew he were. He couldn't afford me after Ma died. Wish he'd said, though. I wouldn't have done that to a . . . oh no, to a *dog*!'

A couple of the girls giggled nervously.

'At least you knew him, at least you've a face to remember,' Sparrow said. 'I've only got Miss Knip's ugly mug to keep in mind and no one would want to remember that!'

They laughed. But just a moment later, Hettie's round face crumpled and she started to cry. 'Cari never said goodbye. She never gave *me* a penny,' she wailed. 'I miss her. Why won't my sister come back?'

'Oh don't cry, Hettie,' Sparrow said, hugging her. 'What happened to your sister?'

'She must've not wanted me,' Hettie sobbed, 'like your dad, Kate. Just the day before she went, she told me I was an awful nuisance and a – a pest!'

Kate glanced round at the others with an embarrassed look. 'Oh no, Het, don't think that,' she said. 'Carina loved you.'

'What happened?' Sparrow asked her again.

'Perhaps you shouldn't ask,' Billie said. 'It upsets her.'

'Cari went out selling, selling matches,' Hettie went on. 'It were wet. I remember the rain running down the window. She had a blue cape on . . . pretty. And she never came back.'

98

Hettie looked at Glori. 'You were with her, Glori! Don't you know nothing?'

Glori looked embarrassed now. She shook her head. 'Ah, Hettie, don't you fret. I bet she's got a grand place to stay. Probably working as a maid right now in a lah-di-dah house somewhere in Sto'back with a white cap and everything. Don't you worry about her.'

'But why'd she go?' Hettie cried. 'We were always together. We walked all the way from the other side of Dragon Mountain together. I miss her bad, I do.' She dabbed her eyes. 'Why didn't she tell me?'

Sparrow saw a conspiratorial look pass between the three girls; they knew something, she was sure. Something they were keeping from Hettie . . . and from her.

'Didn't she give you no message, Glori, for me, or a –'

'Now look, you've glued the wrong bit!' Glori interrupted her. She snatched the box from her little hands. 'Silly little pumpkin.'

'Sorry,' Hettie said. She inched closer to Sparrow. 'I'm so clumsy. Cari said so too.'

Sparrow patted her arm gently. 'No, no,' she said. 'Of course you aren't.'

Now she wanted to know what had happened to Cari as badly as Hettie did.

By lunchtime Sparrow had made sixteen matchboxes while the others had each completed over one hundred.

'Don't worry,' Glori told her. 'You'll soon speed up.'

If I stay, Sparrow thought. But to leave was going to be hard, she could see that, and where would she go? And the girls were so friendly . . .

The only thing she didn't like was the constant bite in the air from the horrible phosphorus that made her eyes water and her throat tight. She pitied the girls whose job it was to dip the matches – and it would be her job too, one day soon. Each time one of them lifted the lid from a jar, the phosphorus mixture exuded a white vapour that spiralled upwards like a ghostly figure.

And she didn't think she liked Miss Minter much either.

They stopped at one o'clock and went upstairs to eat. Violet had been out shopping for lunch and the table was covered in fresh fruit and cheese, long loaves of bread and plates of ham.

Sparrow was starving, but her first thought was for Scaramouch.

He had come inside out of the rain that had just started to fall and was sitting by the missing pane of glass, staring out at the rooftops. Sparrow, catching sight of him from behind, thought he looked miserable. His whiskers drooped and his fur lacked its usual sparkle and lustre. Sparrow gathered him into her arms and pushed her face against his, reassured as she breathed in his musky scent that she knew so well.

'Have you missed me?' she asked him. 'Of course you have! Are you all right? You were so tired and weary yesterday, poor thing. Are you OK?'

All morning she had been thinking about him. She relied on his sixth sense to tell her what to do, and she would leave if he wanted her to, but she hoped that he wanted to stay; at least for a while, at least until she had a plan. She just couldn't face being alone again and on the streets, scratching around for a crumb to eat.

'What do you think, Scaramouch, dear?' she whispered to him. 'Can we stay here?'

Scaramouch purred and then slipped out of her arms and out through the broken window onto the roof. He sat there, out of reach, watching her with his great big clever eyes.

'But I can't leave – not yet,' she whispered to him. 'I just need to think it out. Please, dear puss-cat, don't sit out there!'

Three grey pigeons settled on the roof near him and started strutting up and down, cooing and billing. Scaramouch might have been a chimney stack for all the interest they showed him or he them.

'Don't your cat catch birds?' Glori asked, joining her.

'*Doesn't!*' Miss Minter corrected her from her place beside the hearth. 'Correct English, Gloriana, please!'

'Sorry, miss. *Doesn't* he catch birds?'

'Never. Only things like mice,' Sparrow said.

'Maybe he don't – doesn't – like feathers? Perhaps they tickle his tonsils?'

Sparrow laughed.

'Or is it 'cos you's a bird?' Glori said. 'He don't want to eat *you*!'

Miss Minter called out, 'Will he not come inside, Sparrow, angel?' She was eating cherries from a silver bowl while the girls washed their hands and prepared themselves for lunch. 'Is he your very special friend, Sparrow?'

'He is. He will come in, he's just . . . he likes his freedom.'

'We all like our freedom,' Miss Minter said, 'but sadly we cannot all have it. Now Sparrow, leave the window and come and join us. Violet, move over, please.'

Violet glowered darkly as she vacated her seat beside Miss Minter.

'How did you get on with your chores this morning, Sparrow?'

'I got on well,' Sparrow said. She had taken Violet's chair because Miss Minter had told her to, and now she could see that Violet was cross. She didn't want to sit next to Miss Minter – Violet would be welcome to the favoured spot if only she knew.

Sparrow changed the subject. 'I keep looking at Dragon Mountain,' she said, 'hoping I'll see a spitfyre. Have they always lived up there?'

'Yes,' Glori said, sitting down at her side. 'A long, long time ago there were dragons there but now it's a spitfyre school.'

'*Academy!*' Violet corrected her.

'Years ago there was some big upset,' Glori continued, ignoring Violet. 'I don't know exactly what it was, something to do with the Director and his daughter . . . what was her name? Something odd –'

'What?' asked Hettie. 'Was it something romantic?'

Miss Minter shuddered. 'I loathe romantic, feeble, wet girls' names,' she said. She stared up at the distant castle on the mountaintop. 'Don't tell me, was it something like Esmeralda? Or Cinderella?'

The girls laughed.

'Oh yes, I think I remember . . .' Kate said.

Miss Minter leaned towards her, her eyes suddenly sharp and penetrating. 'Do you? Say it then, say it! I dare you to say it!'

'No!' Kate cried. 'I don't remember it.' She gasped, looking shocked. 'I don't remember it at all.'

'I remember the story!' Dolly cried. 'The Director did something terrible and was put in prison!'

'He'd locked up hundreds of grubbins,' Beattie said. 'That's what he did.'

'*Grubbins?*' Sparrow asked. 'Is that the same as mole-men? Those little men that dig up precious metals and –'

'That's it,' Glori said. 'And it turned out the Director was using the spitfyres to catch grubbins. He'd got hundreds of the poor things locked up in the dungeons.'

'And one of the students took over when the Director went to prison,' Billie said. 'He had a funny name . . . something to do with the weather . . .'

'*Stormy,*' Miss Minter said in a thundery voice.

'Oh yes, that's it,' Glori said, warming to her tale.

'Maybe it was really Stormy that was bad,' Dolly said. 'Maybe he hatched a plan to bring down the Director, set him up, just so he could take over. I've heard of that sort of thing happening.'

Miss Minter flashed her a cold look. 'Now you are a little closer to the truth,' she said.

'And the maid was involved somehow too,' Agnes went on. 'What did she . . .?'

'She married Stormy,' Miss Minter said lightly. There was a loud *crack* and she slipped a broken cherry stone from her lips and dropped it with a *ping* into the bowl. 'I don't know my own strength,' she said, smiling, 'do I? Yes, Stormy is a wicked man who allows a maid-of-all-work to sleep between fine linen sheets on a down-filled mattress and give people orders and –'

103

'And live like a queen!' Glori finished for her.

'Lucky beggar,' Violet said.

'Wish I could do that. I'd love a big bed with a feather mattress,' Connie said. 'I dream of one.'

'From a maid to a queen!'

Miss Minter coughed suddenly.

'Are you all right, miss?' Glori dashed to Miss Minter's side. 'You didn't swaller a pip did yous?'

'It's swall*ow*. *Swallow!*' Miss Minter snapped. 'Pronounce it properly, can't you?'

'Sorry.' Glori shrivelled beneath Miss Minter's harsh tone. She glanced worriedly at the other girls, who all looked scared. 'Sorry, I forgot. Sorry, Miss Minter.'

Billie poured Miss Minter a glass of pop-apple wine and pushed it over the table towards her.

'Thank you, Billie,' Miss Minter said. She smoothed her hair then placed a well-manicured hand on her chest to calm her breathing. 'I'm just angry. Angry that such things could take place. A maid! I ask you! None of you would ever think of doing anything like that to me – of getting rid of me, and taking my place here . . . Would you?' She stared round at them angrily; her cheeks were a hot pink. 'Speak now and let's hear what you have to say!'

'No, no, no!' the girls cried.

'Never ever, miss,' Glori said.

Miss Minter sipped her wine. 'I remember the scandal well,' she said, calmer now and looking out towards the mountain. 'I'm much older than all of you, though I know I don't look it. I lived through it. Don't believe all you hear, girls. I never thought that the Director was evil. Or his daughter. And the Director was not a grubbin!' she said forcefully. 'Impossible! I think you are more right than you know about Stormy, Dolly. Clever girl. It was Stormy who was the bad one.'

Sparrow felt a shiver ripple up her spine: no one had mentioned that the Director was a grubbin . . . where did Miss Minter get that idea? And why was she so angry?

'I wonder where they are now?' Kate said, gazing up towards the Academy.

'Oh they're still there,' Miss Minter said. 'Stormy and his maid are still up there, lording it over everyone.'

'Are they?' Violet said, biting her nails. 'Hey, is it them that try and protect the spitfyres? Is that them?'

Miss Minter smiled. 'They are the ones.' She laughed. 'And it's an impossible task,' she said. 'They will find out in the end that the spitfyres are doomed. They are nearing extinction and nothing can prevent them from disappearing off the face of the earth. Nothing. And it serves them right!'

Miss Minter's eyes were dark and cold. Sparrow thought looking into them was like looking into a frozen pond; though the pond looked like glass and should reflect, you got nothing back at all.

15

Never Forgiven

'Well done, Gloriana, Sparrow was a splendid discovery,' Miss Minter said as they sat late one night sipping pop-pear wine by the dying fire. The other girls were asleep. 'Better than you could guess.'

'Have I done good then, miss? She is sweet, in't she? She's got right tidy little fingers and can make fiddly matchboxes really good. She's learned quick too.'

'*Quickly*. Your grammar never improves,' Miss Minter said with a sigh. 'Yes, you have taught her well. You know how much I depend on you, don't you, Gloriana?'

'Yes, Miss Minter. Thank you, miss.'

'And if I don't tell you everything, all my secrets, well, that's because the less you know, the less you can tell if you're ever caught selling, you know . . . I do have secrets. Oh yes, I do, but soon they won't matter . . . I have been badly treated, and all that was mine was taken away from me . . . I have old scores to settle and by the strangest of strange coincidences, Sparrow is going to help me settle them.'

'Is she, miss? How?' Glori asked her, very surprised.

'Never mind. Never mind. But believe me, Glori, when you found her, you found me a goldmine. When I'm rich again and more beautiful than the day itself, then you and I, Gloriana, oh what a wonderful life we will lead together.'

Glori nodded and looked quickly at Miss Minter's face; yes, it was beautiful, but it was hard too, and never lit up like an ordinary face. It had no laughter lines, she thought.

'If things hadn't gone so wrong for me before, in the past,' Miss Minter said, staring into the fire, '. . . if a certain boy hadn't brought it upon himself to defy my father, I wouldn't be reduced to collecting pennies from matches.' She sighed and patted Glori's knee. 'In the past,' she said. 'In the past – but not forgotten, never forgotten. Never forgiven. They are bad, bad . . . Whose turn is it to carry it next?'

'It's Kate's,' Glori said. 'She's done it before. She'll be fine –'

'You said that about Cari!' Miss Minter snapped. '*Cari can take care of herself. Cari can run fast!* you said.' Miss Minter slopped wine from her glass. 'Looking at Hettie's miserable, lumpy face makes me sick! Sick!' she snapped. 'She'll have to go if she doesn't wipe that expression off her face. I don't blub when a girl leaves; why should *she*?'

'Cari *was* her sister. Hettie thinks she's abandoned her,' Glori said.

'Well, she has. Who wouldn't leave that snivelling little brat behind? I would. If I had a sister I'd have a brave one . . . No sisters for me. No family. Gone . . .' she trailed off.

'Get me another drink.'

'Kate knows she has to do it,' Glori said cheerily, pouring out the wine. 'She knows there's a bit of risk. We all like risk.'

'Do you? I do. I do.' Miss Minter sighed and drained her glass quickly. 'Well, it's just as well, isn't it? I must go to my room. Light me down, Gloriana.'

Glori took two big candles and led Miss Minter down a half flight of stairs to her small bedroom. It was a ritual they went through every night because Miss Minter did not like to make the journey on her own. Glori put one candle down on the bedside table and turned down the bed.

'Can I do anything else for you, Miss Minter?'

'I'm feeling brittle tonight, Glori. Like I might snap. Why?'

'I don't know, miss.'

Moonlight came suddenly streaming in through the window and for a moment they were both lit up in its silvery rays. 'Look at us!' Miss Minter cried. 'See, I shine! I'm a body of gold, all iridescent and silver! Do I look younger? Am I lovely? I feel it . . . but fragile.'

Glori held up her own pale, shimmering, thin arm. 'And I'm phosphorus white,' Glori said.

'Are you complaining?' Miss Minter's voice was suddenly spiky.

'No, no, only it *is* bad, Miss Minter, my poor teeth, the phosphorus –'

'You *are* complaining. I hate it when you complain. I won't hear it. After all I've done for you! Go to bed, Gloriana. I will draw my own curtains. And I'll have that candle, thank you,' she added, snatching it from Glori. 'Go.'

'Yes, Miss Minter.'

Glori closed the door softly and tiptoed back up to the nest in the dark, feeling her way up the stairs and so to her little bed.

16

Sewing

The days passed by pleasantly enough and Sparrow did not think about leaving again, even though Scaramouch would not spend the day inside with her – he only came in at night.

One rainy evening Connie came across the key to the old trunk by the window – it had been missing for ages – and she and Dolly opened it. It was stuffed full of old clothes.

'Where did all these come from?' Dolly cried, twirling around the room in a long black cape with a silver trim.

'It were here when we came,' Glori said. 'Everything were. We brought nothing with us.'

'So you and Miss Minter discovered this place together?' Sparrow asked her. 'You were the first?'

'Yes. We'd been sleeping in doorways and horrible little sheds and then we found the door to this place open and no one was here. First thing we did was bolt that front door so no one else could get in. Then we made our nest up here. It were like a tree,' Glori went on. 'I felt as if I was at the top of a great big elmmow tree and sometimes I thought the wind swayed the whole building. I remember. Long time ago.' She smiled. 'It was good. Anything we found here worth a penny or two we sold, straight off.'

Sparrow lowered her voice to a whisper and nodded towards Miss Minter. 'So where did *she* come from?' she asked.

Glori whispered back. 'Dunno. Same as all of us I suppose; nowhere.'

'And her father? The cousin she talks of?'

'What are you two whispering about?' Miss Minter called.

'Nothing!' Sparrow said, grinning at Glori and leaning further into the big trunk to hide her face.

The clothes smelled musty. She picked up a purple velvet jacket and shook it out. 'Glori, this would really suit you,' she said. 'Go on, try it on.'

'Oh, that's a bit grand for me,' Glori said, grinning shyly so Sparrow could tell she liked it.

'No it isn't!' Sparrow held it up against her. 'There, it's lovely. Do try it on.'

'It's too big,' Glori said, slipping her arms into it. 'Sparrow, it's huge! I'll drown in purple velvet!'

'Take it, Gloriana,' Miss Minter said. It seemed to Sparrow that Miss Minter heard and saw everything, despite never moving from her place beside the fire.

'I'll make it fit you,' Sparrow said.

'Do you think you could?' Glori looked so hopeful that Sparrow determined she'd make it the best jacket in the world.

111

'I did lots of sewing at the Home. I helped all my friends with their clothes 'cos miserable Miss Knip wouldn't buy us any stuff.'

'Honest, could you?' Glori asked. 'Would you?'

'Course I will!'

While Sparrow sat by the window sewing, Miss Minter and Glori watched her from the other side of the room.

'She can sew, that girl, it's true,' Glori said. 'You should see how neat she is. Amazing!'

'There's something peculiar about that cat,' Miss Minter said, ignoring her. She nodded towards the window. 'Why doesn't he come inside out of the cold? Look at him out there by the chimneys. Sitting on hard tiles. Perching on gable ends. Prowling about like a wild thing.'

'He comes in and sleeps on her bed at night,' Glori told her. 'I've seen him come in so quiet. He walks along the furniture, over the chest and he never touches the ground – like he's playing, or trying to be an acrobat!'

Miss Minter's eyes narrowed. 'Why would he want to be out there when he could be inside in the warmth, drinking cream from a saucer?' she said. 'Have you seen how they look at each other, the girl and the cat? As if they're talking? What's it got to say? A *cat*?'

Glori said nothing.

'Watch that cat,' Miss Minter said. 'Watch him. I'm warning you, he's odd!'

Scaramouch was curled up between two tall chimney pots but he woke suddenly, as if he sensed they were talking about him, and stared back over his shoulder at Miss Minter. His eyes glowed golden-yellow. Glori thought they looked like the eyes of a wild beast, a tiger or a lion . . . not that she'd ever seen one for real, but his eyes held such passion it was quite scary. Miss Minter was right; he was an extraordinary cat.

'Every time I look at him he looks back at me, the way a real person might,' Miss Minter complained. 'His eyes are marbles. I wonder if he's real. I *know* he's real,' she contradicted herself. 'He is a cat. Cats are very self-possessed, aren't they? Loners. There are cats in the circus doing all sorts of clever things.'

Sparrow looked up from her sewing. 'Is Scaramouch all right?' she asked.

'Scare-a-mouse is fine, Birdie!' Glori said. 'How's my lovely new jacket coming along?'

'Nearly done.'

Glori went over to her. 'You're so neat and clever at it,' she said to her. 'Is it hard to do?'

'Not really – just takes years of practice.'

'I'm glad you're here, Sparrow,' Glori said, sitting beside her. 'Not just for this jacket,' she added, 'course not. But I . . .' She faltered. It was so hard to explain but even after such a short time Glori couldn't imagine Sparrow not being here. She'd become a real friend and somehow had made Glori feel differently towards Miss Minter. That was weird; she couldn't say anything about that to anyone. And nothing, *nothing*, could ever make her leave Miss Minter, but Sparrow . . . She was really kind, kind without wanting anything back. There was something fresh and new and enthusiastic

113

about everything she did and she was funny and bright and straightforward . . . Not at all like Miss Minter. 'It's just that you . . .' she trailed off.

'Go on,' Sparrow said. 'Tell me how brilliant I am!'

They both laughed.

'Quieten down, you two,' Violet called. She had slipped into Glori's place quickly and had begun painting the nails on Miss Minter's right hand. Dolly took up another pot of polish and started on the nails on her left.

Kate began brushing out Miss Minter's long blonde hair and counting each stroke laboriously. Hettie sat and watched them wistfully.

'Gently, gently,' Miss Minter told Kate. 'I'm delicate, you know.'

'Sorry, Miss Minter.'

'Always remember, remember I'm special,' Miss Minter said. 'You must never forget that, my darlings. I'm a lady.'

Glori put on the purple jacket. It fitted her perfectly, hugging her tiny waist and flaring out over her hips. Sparrow had found seven gold buttons in the trunk – not matching exactly, but almost – and sewn them on.

'I love it!' Glori cried, twirling round. 'Thank you so much, Birdie.'

'Can't I come with you?' Sparrow asked her, as Glori got ready that evening. 'I'd love to go out for once.'

'She's meeting a friend,' Miss Minter said sharply. 'You can't. I hope you have a delightful evening, Gloriana,' she added, not taking her eyes from the newspaper she was

114

reading. 'I see here that the Academy is in the headlines again; they are thinking of starting up a breeding programme to get more flying horses. They'll have to be careful they don't lose any more spitfyres, won't they? They lost one only last month – how could that happen . . .? Did I give you permission to go out, Gloriana?'

'You did, Miss Minter, you must have forgotten,' Glori said, going suddenly pale and very still.

'I did, yes, I did.' Miss Minter pouted. 'But I'll miss you. I don't like it when you leave me.' She glanced up at the clock. 'Off you go, then.'

'Good night, everyone!' Glori called, and she flew out of the door.

Glori went down the stairs whistling. She reached the ground floor, swung round the big wooden newel at the bottom of the stairs, hopped over the black and white floor and unlocked the front door. She was the only girl, apart from Miss Minter, who was allowed a key so she could – sometimes – come and go on her own.

She slipped quietly out into the night.

The rain meant she had to cover up with a big black waterproof and no one would see her lovely, smart, purple velvet jacket. A shame. The rain pattered down noisily on her hood. She quickly rolled up the legs of her yellow and orange trousers and splashed down the lane. The dogs barked and one brutish man shouted at her but she ignored them. She licked the wet off her lips and hurried on; she mustn't be late.

At last she reached Abbey Street and there was the blue

115

lantern swinging above the tavern. The wind was rocking the wooden sign backwards and forwards, making it squeak and groan like a weary phantom. She got her breath on the doorstep, pushed the hood off her dark hair, wiped the rain from her face and opened the door just as the clock struck nine.

'What kept you?' Tapper said.

17

Turquoise Delight

Tapper was standing alone, slouching against the wall, a glass of bark-beer in his hand. As usual he had gathered space around him like other people gathered friends; even furniture seemed to inch away from him when he was in a room.

'You're late,' Tapper said.

'It's only just nine,' Glori said, glancing at the clock. 'Don't be cross with me. Be pleased to see me, Tapper, can't you? It's raining out.' She took off her waterproof carefully and flicked a drop of water from her velvet sleeve and waited.

Tapper looked her over. Up and down. He grinned at her. 'I won't be cross with you; you look a picture,' he said, smoothing his hair and grinning. 'Nice stuff.'

She smiled and stroked the velvet. 'Thanks. It's lovely in'it?'

Then he grabbed her arm roughly. 'You got money I don't know about?'

She shook him off. 'Silly. A present from Miss Minter, that's all. No worries. It were too big but it were fixed.'

'All right then.' He let her go. 'But, see, I got you something too. In't only Miss Minter as can buy things, so.'

He was put out because his present might not be so grand, Glori thought. 'Oh what is it? Do show me,' Glori begged him. Whatever it was she would pretend it was amazing.

Tapper handed her a box of sweets. She unwrapped it quickly. 'Oh my favourites,' she crooned. 'I love Turquoise Delight!' She let him take a chunk first then popped a small blue square into her own mouth. 'Delicious,' she said. 'You are thoughtful, Tapper.'

'So. Good,' Tapper said. 'What d'you want to drink? I've got money tonight.'

'I'll have a glass of pop-pear fizz please, if you're sure.'

'Nothing's too good for you!'

Tapper called out to a passing lad and soon Glori had a glass of warm, yellow, sparkling liquid in her hand.

They sat at a little round table in a corner.

'I got the letter you left for me at the wood shop,' she told him. 'Well, course I did, or how would I be here?' She smiled. 'So what's this business you're on?' she asked him. 'This mysterious "thing" you're looking for?'

Tapper picked up his drink and Glori saw how his hand shook. A pulse beat unsteadily in his temple. He was grinning like a mad thing.

'Can't you say?' Glori asked gently. 'Go on. You've got a job, a mission. Sounds like you're some sort of spy or something.' She made it sound like she was impressed;

flattery always worked on him and she liked him best when he was pleased with the world.

Tapper leaned back and grinned widely. 'A *spy*? That sounds grand! I am a sort of spy, you know. I've got a job to do for a certain Miss Knip . . . Oh Glori, you can have as many glasses of pop-pear fizz as you wish, my girl, because we're going to be rich.'

'We are?' Glori yelped. 'What a lark!'

'Shh!' he hissed, leaning closer. 'We are! So! What am I looking for? I'm after finding a girl from the Knip and Pynch Home. She didn't run away, before you ask. It was her leaving time, but just as she'd upped and gone, Miss Knip finds out something about her and wants her back. So I've to find her. That's where you come in, Glori. You can help me, because if anyone's going to find me a fresh orphan girl in the streets of Sto'back, it's you.'

It was *Sparrow* he wanted.

Glori felt as if someone had poured ice water through her veins. She turned away; fearing she could hide nothing from him. Her lip quivered.

It had to be Sparrow. Sparrow came from the Knip and Pynch Home . . . It had to be her. Oh what bad luck, what very bad luck that Miss Knip wanted *her*!

'What's up? Look at your face!' Tapper said, his voice full of suspicion. 'You know something?'

Glori smiled quickly, pushing down the fear that was bubbling up, the coldness gripping her heart.

'Nothing. Nothing. What's the name of this home?' she said vaguely. 'What did you call it?'

Tapper eyed her slyly. 'It's called Knip and Pynch,' he said slowly. 'Ever heard of it?'

Glori shook her head.

'It's the other side of the swamp. She came through the krackodyles.'

'Brave . . .' Glori said. 'Why d'you say this Miss Knip wants her? Has she done something wrong?'

'She might have,' Tapper said. He took hold of her hand with his own. 'You're all a tremble,' he said. 'Why you quaking in your boots if you got nothing to hide?' He squeezed her hand very hard so her bones scrunched against each other.

'I'm cold. It's cold,' Glori said, smiling, pretending he wasn't hurting her.

Tapper nodded towards the blazing fire nearby. 'Really?' He let go of her hand and leaned back in his seat. 'So you don't know nothing about a missing girl? Not seen no new waifs and strays wandering the streets of Sto'back? I need her, Glori, she's our ticket out of here . . . But I know you'll find her for me, so. I'm not worried. My Glori sees everything.'

The door blew open suddenly and a cold blast of wind shot through the room. They both turned towards it.

'*Miss Minter!*' Glori cried, leaping up.

Miss Minter paused, smiled round at the other drinkers and then pranced over to them on her high heels. She slipped out of her fur coat and drew up a chair at their table and sat down. 'Hello, Gloriana,' she said. 'Forgive me for interrupting you so rudely but . . . well, I was curious to see your young man.' She looked pointedly at Tapper. 'Good evening,' she said.

'This is my Miss Minter,' Glori said weakly. 'Miss Minter, this is Tapper.'

Miss Minter pulled her chair a little closer to Tapper – that's a first, Glori thought, raising her eyebrows. She'd never seen anyone else getting close to him. What was that about? she wondered.

'Let me get you a drink, Miss Minter,' Tapper said. His face was blazing red. 'Pop-pear fizz? A double?'

He sloped off to the bar.

'It's lovely to see you, Miss Minter, of course . . . but how did you know where I'd be?' Glori asked her. There was only *one* possible way, she thought: Miss Minter had read Tapper's letter to her. Why hadn't she hidden his note more carefully?

'I don't know.' Miss Minter shrugged. 'An inspired guess, perhaps? What have you been discussing? Love talk?'

Glori shook her head. 'Of course not.'

Suddenly Glori understood. Miss Minter hadn't come to see Tapper, she wasn't at all interested in his face or his prospects; she'd come because of the money mentioned in the note, that was it.

'So, Miss Minter,' Tapper said, setting the fizzing drink in front of her, 'Gloriana here was just telling me about the new girl in the nest. The one from the Home . . . What's her name?'

'Sparrow,' Miss Minter said.

Glori sagged. She was done for.

'That's the one.' He grabbed Glori's elbow in what looked like an affectionate squeeze, but was painfully hard. 'Go on, describe her again, the new one you've got. Oh what a poor memory you have, Glori, my pet.' His long lick of hair dropped between his eyes and he let it stay there, giving Glori a black, mean look through its strands.

There was something untamed about him, out of control, Glori thought, and suddenly she didn't like him at all.

'Sparrow, yes. She's got green eyes,' Glori said, staring at the tabletop. 'Light hair – lots of it. Jolly. Brave. And a cat. I was going to tell you, in a bit . . .'

Tapper's face split into a grin. 'Cat? Got her!' He slapped the table with his hand. 'Got her safe! Knips will be jumping out of her boots when she hears this! I wonder what next, now I've found our bird?'

'Excuse me,' Miss Minter said, coolly.

'What?'

'You haven't got her,' Miss Minter said with a big, radiant smile. '*I've* got her.'

Tapper's face fell.

'But why do you want her, Tapper?' Glori asked. 'You and Miss Knip? Why's there money in finding little Sparrow?'

'Oh, never you mind about that,' Tapper said, rolling his eyes. 'We shan't hurt her, not a hair on her dear little head, if that's your worry. We need her fit and well.' He paused while he thought things through. He turned back to Miss Minter. 'I see, I see what you're saying . . . Knips is out of the scheme now? You want . . . I see . . .' He offered his hand to Miss Minter. 'Partners, so?'

Miss Minter shook her head and ignored his hand. 'I'm in charge. I'm always in charge. You can work for me.'

'Oh I don't care,' Tapper said, downing his beer. 'Just so long as me and Glori get rich . . . Funny you didn't remember her name, in't it?' he added to Glori.

Glori shrugged. 'You know my memory's not so good.'

Tapper raised his empty glass and clinked it against Miss Minter's. 'Here's to us!' he said.

18

Cari

Two days later, Sparrow was perched on the wonky old trunk by the window watching Scaramouch on the roof outside. He sat with his back to her. He was cleaning the white patch on his chest, licking himself earnestly, as if it was the dirtiest bit of fur he'd ever come across in his whole life. 'Scaramouch, dear, come in and talk to me,' Sparrow begged him quietly. 'Scaramouch, please.'

The cat swivelled round to fix his golden eyes on her and meowed silently, showing the perfect inside of his pink mouth and his sharp white teeth.

'I know. I know. You want to go, and we will go,' Sparrow whispered, very aware that the other girls in the room behind her might be listening. 'We will, but not just yet. We can't. What don't you like? The food?'

He yawned and started to wash his immaculately clean whiskers with his paws.

'All right. If it's not the food, what else?'

He got up and walked to the tip of the roof point. He padded to the very edge and stopped, glancing back over his shoulder at her, and then down to the streets below.

'You want to explore? You want to go somewhere else?'

He sat down again and fixed his big eyes on her.

'That's it, isn't it? You're waiting for me? Well, I will . . . I promise, I just –'

'Who are you talking to, angel?'

'Oh! Miss Minter!' Sparrow spun round. 'Just Scaramouch.'

'Don't you have enough to do with your matchbox making? Or are you lonely? I hate it when the girls are sick,' Miss Minter said, glancing over to the beds where Beattie, Connie, Dolly and Violet all lay, brought down by a bug. 'I'm glad you're not sick,' she went on. She put her hands on her hips and stared through the rain-spattered glass at Scaramouch. 'I don't think he's a normal cat. Do you see how he's looking at me? Do you see how glassy his eyes are? What's he thinking? Cats don't think, do they? Does he want to know my secrets?'

'He's just a commonplace cat,' Sparrow said, though she didn't believe it for one moment. She stared at him longingly then got up, determined not to let Miss Minter know just how important he was to her.

'Now, angel,' Miss Minter said, putting her arm around Sparrow's shoulders and drawing her to her side. 'Glori tells me you are happy here. That's good. I want my girls to be happy. You are beginning to make some beautiful matchboxes, Sparrow, very pretty.'

'Thank you.' Sparrow did not enjoy being hugged by Miss Minter.

'I like pretty things.' Miss Minter looked wistfully around the attic at the cracked and flaking plaster, the peeling paint and cobwebs, the line of sick girls. 'This is not a beautiful place. I had fine things once; a big house and people who did what I told them to do. Immediately. I was free then.' She looked out towards the mountains. 'A long time ago.'

The sunlight suddenly cut through the heavy clouds and settled on Miss Minter's blonde hair and her whole head seemed to burst alight, shining brilliantly like the halo around the people in church windows. Miss Minter looked like a saint. Then she moved and the light went.

Sparrow suddenly found Miss Minter's glacial stare on her.

'Your hair is very beautiful,' Sparrow said sweetly. 'I wish mine was so blonde and shiny.'

Miss Minter's expression changed; she broke into a pleased smile and smoothed her hair around her neat ears. 'My hair *is* very beautiful,' she agreed. She wandered back to the fireplace and poured herself a drink from a small bottle of pop-pear juice. 'Sparrow?'

Sparrow went over to her. 'Yes, miss?'

'Sparrow, you haven't been out of this place since you came, have you? Out in the fresh air? I know you'd like to. I think you should go out selling matches tomorrow, with Gloriana.' She sat down on her pink couch. 'It's market day. We can't afford to miss it, even if the others are ill . . . Aren't we lucky to have work and be able to earn a living in these hard times, eh? How would you like to go out selling?'

'I'd love it!' Sparrow cried. She longed for the outside and here was a chance to look for Sampson's. She'd almost forgotten about her shawl. At last! She could try to find the shop.

'Good, that's settled then,' Miss Minter said. 'I think you're going to be a real asset to us, Sparrow. Stay with the other girls at all times; imitate what they do and you'll do splendidly.'

That night, when everyone was in their bed, Scaramouch crept back into the attic, leaping silently onto a bookcase, tiptoeing around the potted plants, then jumping right over three sleeping girls before landing softly on the bottom of Sparrow's bed. He crept up to her pillow, purring softly, until his head settled beneath her chin. Immediately Sparrow felt happy. It wasn't that she'd been sad, but now she felt content and complete. She rubbed Scaramouch's nose and round his ears. He lay down alongside her, the engine in his throat rolling and rattling noisily. He turned blissfully on his back, his paws floppy and relaxed, and Sparrow rubbed the soft fur of his tummy. 'I'm going out selling matches tomorrow,' Sparrow whispered. 'I won't leave you for long, I promise. Will you watch me from the rooftop? I'm going searching for our family, Scaramouch. You'll be all right without me for just one day, won't you?'

Scaramouch stopped purring. The silence was massive. He rolled over and stood up, facing the moonlit window. Each hair on his back gleamed in the silvery light.

Sparrow sighed.

127

'But how can we go? *Where* can we go?' Sparrow whispered to him.

And Scaramouch had no answer to that.

Because of the illness that had brought the other girls down, only Sparrow, Glori, Kate and Agnes were going out to sell matches the next day.

Sparrow was nervous; she'd never done anything like selling matches before. And what if she found Sampson's? What would she do then?

Each girl carried a tray in front of them, supported by a strap around their necks. As they filed out of the attic room, Scaramouch bounded lightly over and slipped through their legs to join them.

'Oh here's Scaramouch!' Sparrow bent down to stroke him. 'I think he wants to come out too. Can he? Please?'

Glori glanced back nervously to Miss Minter, who seemed absorbed in her newspaper.

'I – I suppose so,' Glori said.

Sparrow grinned. 'I'll sell ever so many matches with Scaramouch to help me.'

Sparrow hadn't been further than the matchmaking room since she'd arrived, and there were more floors and many rooms below. They passed closed doors, twisting, narrow passages and even other staircases disappearing into the shadows. Sparrow wondered what secrets the house held.

A shaft of sun through the window above the door illuminated the big hallway on the ground floor; dust motes danced in the light. The floor was littered with dry leaves.

Dust and lumps of plaster had fallen from the walls onto the floor. There were three doors and a long corridor leading off into darkness.

'All right, Sparrow?' Agnes asked her.

'Just dreaming,' she replied. If she wanted, she was thinking, she could try and run away. If she had to, she could; one of these doors must lead somewhere. Scaramouch slinked around her ankles and mewled as if he were thinking the same.

'Put the cover on the tray to protect the matches,' Glori told Sparrow as they paused by the wide street door. 'Here.' She rearranged the wide, green strap around Sparrow's neck so it was comfortable. 'You can check all your boxes are neat when we get there. Got your purse?'

Sparrow nodded. 'Yes.' She patted it where it rested at her waist. She glanced at Kate; the strap of her tray seemed to be cutting into her thin, white neck. 'Yours looks lots heavier,' she pointed out to her. 'How come? Have you got heavier matches?'

Kate looked back at her blankly then laughed loudly. 'Yeah, made of lead!' she said and lifted her tray up easily. 'Daftie! The matches are just the same as yours.'

Just then there was the clatter of footsteps on the stairs and Violet and Hettie exploded into the hall. 'Came to say good luck! Wish I was going out,' Violet cried, then doubled over in a violent fit of coughing. 'Oh, I'm so ill!' Then she scooped Scaramouch up in her arms and handed him, struggling, to Hettie. 'There you are, Hettie,' she said.

'*What –?*' Sparrow began.

Violet gave Sparrow a reassuring smile. 'Hettie *so* wanted him to herself while you go out, and Miss Minter said she could. Miss Minter said you wouldn't mind.'

'Please, Sparrow!' Hettie said.

Scaramouch began to struggle more forcefully.

'But –'

Agnes unlocked the door. 'Come on,' she called. 'All clear! Quick, Sparrow!'

Someone pulled Sparrow to the doorstep.

'Scaramouch!' she cried.

Scaramouch yowled.

'Off we go!' Glori propelled Sparrow outside, saying, 'I know, I know, but honestly, Sparrow, he would have held us up. Come on, little Birdie, he'll be fine.'

Agnes took her arm. 'Hettie will look after him. Don't worry. Miss Minter will give you some ribbon to tie round his neck if we do well.'

Sparrow shivered. The idea of Miss Minter tying ribbon round her dear cat's neck sent a shiver up her spine. 'But I wanted him to come! Couldn't we . . . I just . . .'

Sparrow was sure she could hear Scaramouch crying, even when the big door shut behind them; the sound made her go cold. 'I wanted him to come with me,' she said quietly.

'I know, I know,' Glori said, slipping her arm through Sparrow's. 'Oh Birdie . . . Mmm, smell that fresh air. Lovely!' she added, breathing in deeply and loudly. 'Great to be out.'

'I suppose . . .'

'Oh it's bliss away from that phosphorus isn't it?' Agnes said.

It was, but still, Sparrow couldn't enjoy it now.

'Scaramouch is better off inside,' Kate said. 'Truly. Let's be off!'

They went single file down the ginnel. Halfway along, Glori called for them to stand aside; a man was coming down the narrow alleyway towards them.

He was tall and rake-thin, with long, sparse hair that reached to his shoulders. There was a bag slung across his back and two more in his hands. He seemed to recognise the girls and grinned at them.

'Morning, girls,' he said with a nod. He indicated his bulging bags. 'Just off to feed the old nags.'

'Hello, Brittel,' Agnes said, and at the same time she tilted her head towards Sparrow, as if to warn him she was there, Sparrow thought.

Brittel gave Sparrow a hard, measuring look. She didn't like the way he looked at her or his face; it was sneaky and rat-like and he seemed to be sizing her up as he stared at her before squeezing past them and on down the alley.

'Who was that?' she asked Glori.

'Brittel. He does odd jobs for Miss Minter,' Glori explained. 'I think she knew him a long time ago.'

Sparrow looked behind her, wondering where the horses were that he was going to feed, but he'd already disappeared round a bend in the ginnel.

Soon the girls were spilling out into a cobbled lane where tall, gabled houses lined the road. They walked for half an hour through dark and shabby streets of boarded-up houses and falling-down warehouses. Scruffy dogs watched them from where they sat on top of doorsteps or curled on heaps of old clothes.

As they turned onto a wider street they came to a crowd of people that blocked their way. They had gathered to watch something passing by in the road and were cheering and shaking their fists at something. The match-girls stopped too.

'What is it?' Sparrow asked, bobbing up and down, trying to see over the heads of the people.

They pushed their way nearer.

A procession was going by slowly. At the front were four guards, mounted on horses pulling open wagons. The wagons held wooden cages and were followed by yet more stern-looking guards.

The cages held people, all of them chained to the wooden bars of their cage.

'What's happening?' Sparrow cried. 'Why are they in those cages? Why are they chained?'

'They're from Stollenback prison,' Kate said. 'Oh, they must be freezing in those rags.'

'The chains must hurt,' Glori said.

'They don't even have shoes. And see how dirty they are!' Agnes said. 'Poor things.'

The prisoners' eyes were downcast. Their heads drooped.

'They're crims,' Glori said. 'But still, you can't help feeling sorry for them, eh?'

'But children too, look!' Sparrow said. 'Boys, and a girl just like us. Look at her! That one. She looks so ill and thin!' She pointed.

Glori saw the girl she meant and tensed. She nudged

Kate, who sucked in air loudly and grabbed Agnes. 'It's *her*!' Kate hissed.

'Who?' Sparrow asked. 'Do you know her?' She looked again at the poor girl. Her head hung from a neck so pale and thin it didn't look strong enough to hold up her head of long, tangled, ginger-coloured hair.

'That's Cari. It's Hettie's sister,' Glori said. She took Sparrow's arm and began to pull her away.

'*What?* Hettie's Cari? Can't we do something to help?' Sparrow cried. 'Are we just going to leave her there? Does Miss Minter know?'

The match-girls dragged her back behind the crowd and they huddled by a tree.

'No, no we can't do nothing,' Glori said, keeping her voice low and turning her back on the wagons. 'She's going out. Sent off to the wastelands.'

Kate's expression was fierce as she squeezed Sparrow's arm. 'You're not to say a word. Not a word to Hettie,' she urged her.

'But –'

'No buts; Hettie's too little, she wouldn't understand.'

'But can't we do anything for her?' Sparrow said again. 'Why's she locked up? Did she do something wrong?'

Glori shrugged. 'Maybe she did, maybe she didn't. Many things are a crime in Sto'back. She's beyond our help, Sparrow. Forget her, that's all we can do.'

19

Disaster

All the fun had gone from the outing and Sparrow walked along feeling as if a dark, gloomy cloud hovered over her head, casting her in shadow. Poor Cari, and poor little Hettie, thinking Cari had abandoned her when it was Cari herself who'd been abandoned.

Perhaps Cari had been arrested for selling matches on the street? Perhaps it was against the law? Her heart thumped faster: she didn't want to be caught and put in prison. No, she reasoned, it couldn't be criminal, or the match-girls would be arrested all the time. Seeing Cari like that, and being unable to help, had upset her.

Sparrow tried to remember some of the street signs so if she got lost she could find her way back, but she had to give up. There were too many of them and she couldn't concentrate. The horror of what she'd seen lingered. What if the guards picked her up because she was an orphan or because she'd asked for that bit of pie? It was a horrible thought.

When they came to streets of shops, Sparrow perked up a little. There was so much to see, so much going on, and Sampson's might be here . . . What if Mr Sampson himself was there at the doorway, smiling, holding out his arms to her, his long-lost daughter?

'All right there, Birdie?' Glori asked.

'Miles away.' Quickly Sparrow dismissed her silly idea and tried to forget it. 'Can't stop thinking about Cari . . . But you were right about Scaramouch, Glori. Sorry. He'd have got lost or trodden on or something out here with so many people. Don't let *me* get lost, will you?' Sparrow pulled Glori closer. 'You're all I've got and I could wander around these streets for the rest of my life looking for you!'

'Don't worry,' Glori said. 'Miss Minter would be furious if I let *you* disappear. Once she's let a girl in she doesn't like to let them *out* again.'

'Doesn't she . . .? You love Miss Minter, don't you?' Sparrow asked.

'*Love?* Don't know what that word means.' Glori shrugged and stared at the ground, embarrassed. 'She's the only ma I ever knew. She might not be the ma I'd choose, like, but she's the one I got. Better than no ma at all.'

'I think she's a bit scary,' Sparrow said tentatively. 'Up and down, hard to get to grips with.'

Glori laughed. 'She might be. I'm used to her, I s'pose. We've been together years. She wouldn't ever let *me* go!'

They stopped in Middle Square. Ancient stone pillars supporting a low, sloping roof encircled it. Under its cover, stallholders had set up their tables and counters to sell their produce – eggs, massive cheeses, salamis, fresh fruit and flowers. Behind the stalls there were shops too – bookshops, tool shops, shoe and boot shops and fabric shops. Sparrow's heart began to beat faster; she could feel it thumping in her throat: all these shops, any one of them could be Sampson's; all these people and any one of them could be a Sampson.

'We'll go over there,' Kate said, pointing to the far side. 'Outside Billington's Boots and Shoes.' She gave Glori a wry smile and a wink. 'Good luck, girl.'

'You're the one needs it,' Glori said. 'Take care.'

'Isn't Kate very good at selling then?' Sparrow asked her as they walked off.

'Ah, well, you know, not as good as me,' Glori said vaguely.

Glori and Sparrow settled by a colourful flower stall in front of a bookshop.

'This is our pitch. Now take the covering off your tray,' Glori told Sparrow. 'Sort it out so it's neat. That's it. We'll stay until the tray's empty. All the pennies go in the purse. Ready?'

Sparrow nodded. 'It's not, you know, illegal, is it?' she asked quickly.

Glori shook her head. 'Would I do it if it was?'

People were streaming past them; sometimes they bumped into Sparrow, as if she wasn't even there. At first Sparrow said sorry when it happened and when it continued she started to make faces at them behind their backs. Match-girls, she soon realised, were very low in the pecking order of Stollenback society.

136

'Those matches are pretty, my dear,' said a woman, looking at Sparrow's tray. 'But I can't afford them. We use a tinderbox at home . . . Oh go on, I'll take a box as a special treat. They're so quick and easy, aren't they?'

Sparrow handed over the matches and slipped the penny into her purse. 'I've made my first sale!' she whispered to Glori.

'Well done.' Glori smiled back at her. 'Yes sir, that's right, a penny a box, very fine matches. Extra long! Every single matchstick guaranteed to light,' Glori rattled off beside her. 'Matches! Matches!'

The hours went by slowly. Selling matches was a dull job once the novelty of being out in town had worn off. Thank goodness she wasn't expected to do this every day, Sparrow thought. The cold seemed to strike up from the cobbles and through the soles of her feet. Her hands were freezing.

Every opportunity she had, Sparrow looked at the shops, trying to see their names; Read Well, a bookshop, a cobbler's called Heels & Toes, a sewing shop whose window was a rainbow of coloured bobbins, and an ironmonger's with pans and rakes and metal bathtubs stacked outside. No shop selling baby shawls. No weavers. Perhaps a weaver wouldn't be in the centre of town; perhaps they'd have some sort of mill out of town?

Sparrow's legs began to ache from standing still for so long and she leaned back against the stone pillar. She wondered how Scaramouch was without her. Hettie would be kind to him – as long as he didn't scratch her. She wasn't so sure how kind Violet would be. Poor Scaramouch. Perhaps she could find a treat to take back to him?

Sparrow shifted her tray to a more comfortable position. Glori and the other two girls had all started the day with more matches than Sparrow and now Sparrow's tray was almost empty and her purse was heavy with copper coins.

'Penny a box!' Glori called beside her. 'Beautiful matches! Burn a full minute!'

Suddenly a man wearing a tall hat stopped beside Sparrow, momentarily blocking the sun and casting a shadow over her.

'Yes, sir? Hello. How can I help you, sir?' Sparrow said. 'Matches?'

Beneath the black hat his cheeks were very pink against his white, white skin as if they'd just been scrubbed with soap. A grey moustache lay like a little upturned caterpillar along his top lip. He leaned over Sparrow's tray of matches and said very quietly, 'What else? What else could I possibly want?'

Sparrow looked back at him blankly. *What else?* 'I've no idea,' she said.

'Are you sure?' he persisted and very slowly, very meaningfully, he winked one small, grey eye at her.

Sparrow turned to Glori for help, and instantly Glori was there, stepping protectively in front of Sparrow and looking at the man with a hostile expression. 'We don't sell anything but matches, sir,' Glori said.

The man touched his hat politely and retreated, smiling a cunning smile, as if he knew differently. He vanished smoothly back into the crowd.

'What an odd man!' Sparrow said. 'What do you think he meant?'

'I don't know. You get all sorts here,' Glori said. 'Don't worry about him, Sparrow.'

Sparrow didn't worry about him. She grew more and more bored as time slowly passed. She kept looking round the square at the shoppers and stallholders, imagining what fun it would be to make cheese or spin your own wool. What sort of shops might there be on the other side of the square . . .? Impulsively she took the almost-empty tray from around her neck and rested it against the wall behind Glori's feet. She could just slip over and have a quick peep, she thought. Nothing could happen to her in the square.

She glanced over towards Kate and Agnes on the other side, where Kate's dark red hair shone in the winter sunshine like a beacon. Kate was having a very intense conversation with a fat young man and they were whispering together, heads bowed. Sparrow craned this way and that, trying to peer past the people moving in front of her. Why did the man look so strained and worried? He was only buying matches . . . There was a sudden gap in the crowd and through it Sparrow clearly saw Kate slip her hand into her tray *beneath* the matches. There was a miniscule flash of brilliant light, as if a tiny shooting star had passed between them; it was there – it was gone. The fat man was shuffling away with hunched shoulders and was quickly absorbed by the crowd.

'Glori!'

A horse and cart came through the square and blocked her view.

'*Glori!*'

Kate was selling something other than matches. She had it hidden in the tray, that's what made it heavy. Sparrow remembered how the strap had cut into Kate's neck when they'd set out. The stuff was bright – brilliantly bright. It had to be the same sparky stuff Miss Minter had taken from the safe – it had to be! But what was it? And did anyone else know she had it?

Suddenly there was a harsh shout. A burly man with a top hat was yelling horribly at Kate; his face was contorted with rage. With him was the plump young man who had just bought the bright stuff.

Kate screamed, ducked and ran.

Immediately Sparrow felt Glori grab her arm and whisper urgently, 'Got to go!'

'It's Kate,' Sparrow said, clutching her. 'That man!'

Glori's face was white. 'Yes. We must go,' she said quietly. 'Don't make a scene.'

'Guards!' the burly man was shouting. 'Guards! That match-girl is selling Brightling! Seize her!' He was pointing at Kate – or at where Kate and Agnes had been, because now they had both disappeared.

A girl shouted from the middle of the seething crowd: 'THIEF!'

It sounded like Agnes. It *was* Agnes. She'd ditched her tray, jumped up onto a barrel and was shouting at the top of her voice, 'Thief! That boy stole my purse!' She pointed into the crowd, crying, 'There he goes! He's got my purse! Please, please, help!'

People started running. Everyone was shouting. The horse

reared up, neighing, scattering empty buckets on the ground. It was chaos with everyone bumping into each other and dogs barking and running between people's legs.

Glori pulled Sparrow away. 'Come on!'

They ran, dodging this way and that, pushing against the crowd. Someone shoved against Sparrow and she felt her heavy purse fall from her waist.

'Hang on!' She bent over, quickly reaching for it.

Glori's hand slipped from her grasp.

'*Glori!*'

Sparrow struggled to reach the purse . . . gave up, turned back to Glori. If she lost Glori now, in this crowd . . . But Glori had vanished.

A woman crashed against her, apologising as she elbowed Sparrow in the neck. Sparrow cried out, swirled away.

'Help!'

She ricocheted off something soft and bouncy, yelled, spun round and flew straight into a pillar.

Her head smashed against the stone. A searing pain flooded through her, then everything went black.

20

Lost

Miss Minter stood in the empty market square, wrapped up in a big, shapeless black coat and a large hat. She had insisted that Glori took her to the place where the accident had happened that very afternoon.

'Where?' she demanded.

Glori pointed to the pillar where Sparrow had hit her head. 'They said there. I'm really sorry.'

'It's the worst thing that could happen,' Miss Minter said softly. 'Perhaps not the worst – I can think of worse – but bad. It isn't good. Should I blame you, Gloriana? Is it your fault?'

'No, really it wasn't. I –'

'Sparrow's first outing, her first time on the streets.' Miss Minter dug her gloved fingers into the pillar. 'You were in charge of her, my Gloriana. You!'

Glori winced and swallowed a lump the size of a melon. 'I'm sorry,' she said again, as she'd said a million times. 'It weren't my fault.'

'*Wasn't*,' Miss Minter corrected her in acid tones.

'*Wasn't* my fault. Anyone that ran looked like they was guilty. It was get nabbed or let Sparrow get nabbed. No choice, Miss Minter, you can see that – can't you?'

Miss Minter scanned the empty square. 'And she put her tray . . . where?'

Glori showed her exactly where she'd found Sparrow's tray, neatly propped against the wall.

'At least Kate got away with the Brightling,' Miss Minter said quietly.

'Yes.' Glori looked again at the pillar where Sparrow had been hurt. 'A gent said Sparrow were – *was* – badly hurt. Poor little Birdie!'

'Poor little *nothing*!' Miss Minter said. 'I've spent money on her, all the time she's been here, Gloriana. I've been seeing people, finding out, digging around for information. Your Tapper doesn't come cheap, either.'

Glori glanced at her nervously. 'I know, miss. Thank you.'

'Some people do have a family, it seems. Mothers and fathers. Sisters perhaps. I had a cousin once. No. Never.' She paused, took a deep breath, started again, but her thoughts seemed jumbled. 'Sparrow's family history is not as straightforward as Miss Knip imagines. Tapper's a clever lad, a smart boy. He likes you, doesn't he?' She didn't wait for an answer. 'I want Sparrow back. We must get her back. How much does Sparrow know?'

'About . . .?'

'Yes, yes – about the Brightling.'

'Nothing,' Glori said. 'She's sharp, though. This morning

143

she guessed something was wrong with the tray and when we saw Cari . . .'

'I'm not interested in Carina. Don't talk to me about Carina. It's Sparrow we must find,' Miss Minter said. She twirled round slowly, gazing at the closed and silent shops. 'Where can she be? Who has got her?'

'She can't even find her way back,' Glori said. 'I made sure, like you said, and took her a round-about way.' She was sorry she had now, as a picture of Sparrow, wandering the streets aimlessly, came to her.

Miss Minter pulled her hat down further over her face. 'We must get her back quickly. Even a few words from her – *the empty school, the narrow alleyway* – might lead people to us.'

'If she can, she'll get back,' Glori said. 'She'll come back for her cat. She won't want to leave him, will she? I haven't seen Scare-a-mouse since we left this morning . . . Where is he, Miss Minter?'

Miss Minter looked vaguely around Middle Square. 'I really can't imagine,' she said quietly, smiling slightly. 'I expect he'll turn up when he's hungry.'

21

Hilda

Sparrow's first sensation was pain. It felt as if a hammer was pounding her temples and smashing against her skull. She raised her hand to her throbbing head. *Bandages*. She opened her eyes slowly, squinting in the light.

'She's awake,' a woman said softly. 'Look! Hello dearie, how are you feeling, my lovely?'

Sparrow closed her eyes again. It seemed the safest and easiest thing to do and, really, she couldn't speak; she couldn't even think with this hammering going on.

Someone, presumably the same woman, held a glass of cool water to her lips. She sipped it then lay back on the pillow. The bed was so soft – the sheets had to be absolutely white as snow, she thought, to be as soft and smooth as this. She turned her head slightly and smelled roses and honeysuckle, and felt very safe.

'Can you hear us?' A man's voice this time.

'I don't think she's properly awake yet, Bruno,' the woman

said. 'She's all dopey. Does your head hurt a great deal, you poor, dear thing?'

Sparrow heard them quite clearly but she didn't have the strength to answer so she kept her eyes closed. She felt wonderfully safe and relieved to be able to say nothing.

She smiled to herself and slept.

The next time Sparrow woke, her head didn't hurt so much; now it wasn't a hammer she felt, but a steel band, tight around her forehead.

There was a gentle *click clack* sound somewhere near her.

She opened her eyes.

She was in a strange room with red roses growing up the walls. When she looked again she realised it was wallpaper and wondered how it smelled of roses, but then she saw a vase of real red roses on a chest of drawers.

She felt along the bed for Scaramouch. He wasn't there.

She sat up sharply and cried out, 'Scaramouch!'

A plump woman of indeterminate age had been sitting knitting by the fire – that accounted for the click-clacking noise. She had blonde plaits neatly wound round her head. Her white linen collar was spotless. Her round cheeks looked soft and very pink.

'She's awake!' The woman dropped her knitting and came to her bedside. 'Dearie, how are you?' she asked, leaning over her. 'I'm Hilda, Hilda Butterworth. Three days you've lain there.'

'Hilda Butter . . .? *Three days!* Where's Scaramouch?' Sparrow muttered, looking round.

'Oh I'm so glad you can speak, dearie. We were worried you were done for.' Hilda bit her lip. 'It was Bruno's fault. He knocked you out cold – like a slab of meat, you were.'

'Three days?' Sparrow repeated. 'I've been lying here all that time without my cat?'

'I didn't see a cat, dearie. We brought you home and looked after you because Bruno, my husband, he said it was his fault you hit your head. He got in your way. He owns a toyshop not too far from the square, and came out to see what the fuss was all about. You bounced off his big fat stomach and splat into that old pillar! Five stitches you had to have, but don't worry,' she added, as Sparrow touched her bandaged head, 'it's mostly in your hair and it won't show.' She smiled. 'No one else was picking you up, were they? They're a rum lot, our townsfolk, I sometimes think.'

Sparrow smiled weakly. 'Three days,' she said. 'I can't believe it.'

When had she last seen Scaramouch? In the hall, in Hettie's arms . . . he'd be all right. Hettie would look after him. She was a kind girl . . . an unhappy girl. She remembered Cari and a sadness shot through her.

'There, you're a dear girl, aren't you? What a nice face you've got. What's your name?'

'Sparrow,' said Sparrow.

'And where are you from, Sparrow? Where do you live? We've been so anxious – we couldn't find out who you were. We asked and asked. Your mother and father must be so worried about you.'

'I'm from nowhere,' Sparrow said quietly.

147

She felt tears come into her eyes. Her tears seemed to appal Hilda, who dabbed at them quickly with the bed sheet. 'No, no, don't cry,' she squeaked. 'What can be the matter? What is it?'

'I'm an orphan. I've never had a home,' Sparrow said.

And then it was Hilda's turn to cry. She wiped her eyes and kept trying to apologise and then started blubbing again. Finally she called downstairs to Bruno to come up.

Sparrow's head hurt but she didn't mind because this woman, Hilda, was so kind and the sheets were so smooth and the room so cosy, it was like being in heaven. *Where are you from? Where do you live?* She didn't want to remember the Knip and Pynch Home for Waifs and Strays or Miss Minter's attic or making matches. She never ever wanted to recall the awful look of hopelessness on Cari's face. She wanted to forget it all and lie here swimming in roses and white sheets for ever and ever.

'Women, women,' the man called Bruno muttered. He came stamping up the stairs with a person who Sparrow guessed immediately was Hilda's sister because she looked very similar, though not so smiley. Her name, she learned, was Gerta.

The three of them stood and stared at Sparrow.

'She says her name is Sparrow,' Hilda told them. 'And she doesn't remember anything and she's an orphan.'

'Oh is she now?' Gerta said, making a face that meant she didn't believe a word of it.

Bruno was a big man. He was almost bald and had a nose like an old potato, upon which rested a pair of wire spectacles, and ears like cabbage leaves. 'Hello, there

Sparrow,' he said, grinning widely. 'Well, well. No more talking, if it turns on the waterworks. *Sparrow?* Now, *that's* a funny name for a girl.'

'Very unlikely,' Gerta put in.

'Is it?' Sparrow asked, glancing anxiously from one to the other.

'No, of course it isn't,' Hilda said. 'Don't you look so worried. It's a lovely name.'

'I'm sorry my dear, how rude of me,' Bruno said. 'You can have any name you want,' he added, giving his sister-in-law a stern look. 'I didn't mean to be rude.'

'Let me help you sit up,' Hilda said, plumping up the pillows.

Sitting up, Sparrow could see a pale blue cover on the wooden bed, a dresser with a mirror, all polished so it shone, two chairs beside the fire, a rug on bees-waxed boards; it was homely and comforting. She reached down the bed to the empty space where her cat should have been.

A moan escaped from her.

'Does your head hurt?' Hilda asked softly.

Sparrow nodded – her head did hurt; it wasn't a complete lie. 'What happened to me?' she asked. 'Tell me again . . .'

'Oh you poor dear, don't you remember? Well,' Hilda brought her chair up close to the bed. 'There were some match-girls in the square and –'

'– And this lot weren't just selling matches, that's for sure,' Gerta said.

'What were they selling?' Sparrow knew Kate had been up to something. She fixed a blank expression on her face.

'Bri—'Bruno began, but his wife stopped him.

'Oh no dear, don't. Not now. I don't want to upset Sparrow. Something they shouldn't, that's all, dearie, something unkind.'

Bruno patted Sparrow's hand. 'See you later, my dear,' he said and headed downstairs.

Gerta folded her arms over her chest and stared at Sparrow. 'An orphan, eh? Lost your memory? Very convenient.' She winked meaningfully at Sparrow.

'You've all been so kind to me,' Sparrow said, ignoring her. 'Thank you very much.'

'It's nothing, nothing,' Hilda said. 'You are our guest. It was Bruno's fat tummy that caused the accident, so we *must* look after you. You will stay with us, dearie, until you're quite better, won't you? I mean, if you have no home and everything, where else would you go?'

Gerta shot her sister a worried look. 'Well, she can stay until her head doesn't hurt,' she put in. 'Then –'

'I think I can make decisions in my own home, thank you, sister,' Hilda said firmly without looking at her.

'I do want to stay,' Sparrow said.

'I'm sure you do,' Gerta said grimly, under her breath.

'Only,' went on Sparrow, 'only I had a cat, a big beautiful cat, like a Siamese but he isn't, he's bigger. Grander. Furrier. He has almost invisible stripes of golden honey and dark tips to his ears and . . . I've never been without him before. And now . . .'

'An orphan with a big cat? What next?' Gerta said, rolling her eyes.

'Bruno and I didn't see a cat, dearie.' Concern and worry showed in Hilda's broad face. 'We'll keep our eyes open, I promise you. They're funny creatures, cats are, and yours may well find you here. I've heard of things like that, haven't you? They have different senses from us – more ways of seeing – and they can always find their way home.'

'I hope he'll find me,' Sparrow said, glancing towards the window. 'I'm sure he *would* come and find me if he could. At the orphanage he just seemed to appear, as if he came through the mouse holes or under the door; he could always find me there.'

'I don't care for cats,' Gerta said.

'You'd like this one,' Sparrow said. 'He's wonderful. Everyone loves him.'

'I'm not everyone,' Gerta said. 'And I'm quite content to be the odd one out, thank you.'

Sparrow suddenly noticed a small painting by the window, a portrait of a young woman with green eyes. 'Who's in the picture?' she asked. The woman looked a little wild and not at all like the portly and solid figures of Hilda and Gerta. She seemed out of place, and yet there was a look of Bruno there, Sparrow thought, in the bright eyes. 'Is she family? I do like her face.'

Hilda's eyes dimmed and her smile died away. 'That's Bruno's sister. I'm afraid she was a rather foolish young woman and –'

'– Ran away from home,' Gerta said, shortly. 'She had an accident and died.'

'I'm so sorry,' Sparrow said. After a pause, she added,

151

'She looks sparky.' And she was thinking too that the young woman was very like her to look at. She felt an immediate connection, as if, even though the other eyes were painted, they were meeting and linking with her own.

Hilda smiled and patted her arm. 'She *was* sparky. It was a terrible accident; a dreadful waste. She was lovely. We all adored little Mayra; it broke our hearts when she went.'

Sparrow nodded, understanding. She could not take her eyes from the portrait. She felt bewitched.

Hilda and Gerta tiptoed down the narrow stairs to the parlour at the front of the house. Bruno looked up from the newspaper as they came in.

'Well, well,' Bruno said, grinning broadly. 'What a sweet girl! She'll stay, won't she, until she's quite better?'

Hilda nodded happily. 'Of course. I want her to, anyway.'

'I can't imagine why,' Gerta said. 'We know nothing about her. What was she doing in Middle Square in the first place? Is she really from an orphanage?'

'Oh Gerta . . .' Hilda turned to Bruno. 'Don't *you* think she's telling the truth? Please say you do, dear.'

'She wasn't even wearing orphanage clothes,' Gerta put in.

'Sparrow wouldn't lie, I'm sure,' Hilda said. 'You can see she's just not that sort.'

'I shall ask around,' Bruno said. 'It wouldn't do any harm, would it? To check if an orphanage did have a child called Sparrow – there can't be many of that name; if that really *is* her name. I feel she is honest, personally.'

'Me too,' Hilda said. 'I feel it in my bones.'

'Your bones are probably made of liquorice laces,' Gerta said. 'You're far too sweet and soft. Personally, I doubt it,' Gerta went on. 'And all that nonsense about the picture!'

They told him how Sparrow had been enthralled by his sister's portrait. Bruno looked puzzled. He rubbed his big nose and took off his glasses to rub his eyes. He smoothed his thinning hair and finally said, 'Now that is strange, because I did think Sparrow looked a little like Mayra. The hair? The green eyes? Or is it that I see Mayra's face everywhere, even in a little orphan girl from the streets?'

Hilda bit her lip. She looked troubled. 'My love, I fear that *is* the truth,' she said.

'Of course there isn't any resemblance!' Gerta said. 'How could there be? That girl is just trying it on. It's comfortable here and she wants to stay. Then you'll turn your back and she'll be gone and all the silver with her too!'

'Oh now, Gerta, for shame!' Bruno said.

'I feel confused,' Hilda said. 'I'm so ready to love something . . . I know it's a fault, I know it, but after, after the Swamp Fever took our little Emma and Matilda from us, I've been so ready and willing and then here comes this little angel out of the blue and I'm so inclined to ask her to stay . . .'

'No one could ever replace our girls, dearest.'

'Of course not. Never, but I have room in my heart for someone, Bruno. But what if Gerta's right and Sparrow's going to leave me too? I couldn't bear it.'

'There, there,' Bruno said. 'You always get upset talking about the darling girls. Dry your eyes. I think that's Sparrow

153

coming now. We mustn't show her teary faces. We must find out a little more about her, my dear,' he added quietly. 'We'll care for her and help her and find out all we can. And we'll get my brother down here too. If *he* thinks she looks like Mayra, then she does.'

'You'll be lucky if you can get Otto out of the Academy kitchens for one second!' Gerta said. 'He'll say his sponge will collapse or his pancakes flip or something.'

Bruno grinned. 'He'll come,' he said. 'For this.'

22

Tapper

Dear Nips,

It's been wot you might call a disaster up here in Sto'back as we've lost our BIRD. She didn't flap off so much as got hurt. Couldn't fly, if you see what I mean. I don't know where she is exactly at this precise moment in time but I am on the job, I am. My personal ackom-pliss is also on the lookout for her, also a certain Miss Minter who is influenshall in these parts. We are searching the streets even as I, myself, write this letter. So. We will find her soon, no worries in that department. Where can she go? Where can she hide?

She'll be back for her cat, won't she, so?

*In the meantime whiles I need more money for my
ongoing professional work.*

As much as you can afford, by return.

Ta.

Tapper

Tapper was grinning as he slipped the letter into the envelope.
A very fine bit of writing; to the point and well written, he
thought.

'You shan't get her now, Knips, no matter what you do,'
he said to the envelope. 'When I find her she's going back
to Miss Minter.' Miss Minter was better looking than old
Knip and much smarter. And Miss Minter had come up
with a new plan that meant more money.

Cedric de Whitt. Tapper rolled the name around in his head.
Cedric de Whitt. It was a fine name, a gentleman's name. The
name of the gentleman who would pay a lot more for Sparrow
than nasty old Knips, that's what Miss Minter had told him.
He'd no idea how Miss Minter had discovered this Cedric de
Whitt, but then that was none of his business. His business
was simply to find and bring back Sparrow. Meanwhile he'd
milk Knips for every penny he could.

I should have held on to Sparrow more tightly, when I had
her at Ma's, he thought. Missed a chance there, didn't you,
Tapper? he told himself. It was Ma's fault. Now Sparrow'd
slipped out of his clutches again – Glori's fault. *Women!*

Glori now had bruises on her wrists where he'd held her as tight as he could, wanting, just for a moment, to snap her stupid little arms. But he'd got over his first blind rage. Gently, gently, he told himself. Just get Sparrow back!

Tapper,

May I remind you that it is Knip with a K, as in 'know' and 'knot' and 'knave'.

I certainly shall not be sending you any money. What are you thinking of, letting the girl out of your sight? I've heard of that Miss Minter in Stollenback. She's up to no good. Don't imagine that she likes you, Tapper, there is no one she likes. No one! Don't believe what she says. It's all lies. And if you think that the pair of you can take what is mine, you are wrong. I have the locket and the locket is the proof. You won't get away with it. The reward will be mine because I am the only person with the evidence.

Find that girl. Keep her safe – away from Miss M – and then we'll talk.

My Pynch is threatening to come up to Stollenback himself to sort you out.

Miss Knip

'Oooh, I am so frightened,' Tapper said to his empty room. He laughed. 'Pynch is as fierce and scary as a custard tart.' He threw down Miss Knip's letter in disgust. 'What do I care, Knip? Me and Miss Minter're cleverer than you. So.' And who needs lockets, he thought. We'll *get* the girl and then we'll sell her to the highest bidder and it won't be you. So.

That evening he met Glori in the Old Blue Bear Tavern and passed her Miss Knip's letter to read. 'See, she wouldn't send no money,' he told Glori. 'That's why you're drinking limewater tonight. And you know what? It's all your fault, for losing that girl.'

'Isn't Miss Minter paying you?' Glori asked him, ignoring his dig at her.

'Maybe,' Tapper said. 'Knips don't know that, though. Knips is just a stingy old crow.'

Glori sipped her limewater. Limewater tasted of nothing.

'Now, how's the search going? Got any clues?' Tapper said. 'She can't have disappeared into thin air, can she, so?'

Glori was pale. She hadn't slept properly since Sparrow had gone.

'We asked around and looked everywhere . . . Phew, it was a close one though. Kate was doing really good, she'd sold some tonic to some fat gent and then another geezer come up and he said he was going to arrest her. She legged it.'

'You told me.'

'Yes, I told you. I keep going over it, I'm sorry. We'll have to be more careful now.' She lowered her voice. 'The authorities know it's the match-girls what are selling it. And Agnes said she was followed for miles yesterday, and only just lost them. Selling Brightling's getting real dodgy. I wish we didn't –'

'Miss Minter knows what she's doing. She's a proper lady, in't she?' Tapper interrupted her, leaning over the back of his chair and crossing his legs, slicking back his hair. 'How come you ain't picked up any of her airs and graces, so?'

Glori felt herself sag. She gulped down another mouthful of hateful limewater. 'I don't know.'

'No, I don't either.' He turned away from her, as if even the dirty floor was better to look at than her.

Glori glanced at Miss Knip's letter again. 'What's she on about with this locket? How's it proof, Tapper?'

Tapper shrugged. 'Dunno. Well, best get on,' he said. 'You're sure Sparrow don't know her way back to the old school, aren't you?'

Glori nodded sadly.

'What's the matter? Don't look so glum, your face in't pretty when you're glum. You know I only like you pretty.'

'Oh Tapper, can't we just leave her and forget about her?' Glori said.

'So, that's your game?' Tapper said, leaning over the table and getting close up to her. 'This is what's going on in that little head, is it? Leave her be?' His voice had sunk low and harsh.

'No. No, not really.' She shrank back from him. He frightened her. He had a sort of unsteadiness about him, so she never knew what he'd do next and now he was so angry about Sparrow. When he suddenly burst out like this, it scared her; scared her rigid. She shivered and moved away from him, rubbing at her sore wrists.

'Glori, don't you want her to be reunited with her family? Don't you want her safe in the bosom of her own flesh and blood?' Tapper sneered.

Glori nodded. 'So there is a family?'

'I never said that.' Tapper smiled. 'Miss Minter is so smart. She can worm things out of folk. You should have seen her with that man de Whitt.' He flicked his fingers as if they'd been burnt. 'She can bargain. Phew! Hot stuff!'

'What man *de Whitt*?' Glori said.

Tapper went very still. 'I didn't say it,' he said. 'Did I say . . .? Forget you heard that name, Glori!' he hissed, grabbing her fingers and bending them backwards and all the while smiling at her. 'Forget it!'

'I've forgotten it! I never heard nothing!' Glori whispered desperately. 'Please, Tapper! Ow!'

He let her go.

Oh if only Miss Minter hadn't got her claws into him . . . What a combination: both so greedy, both as explosive as the phosphorus. Both could make her so happy and so miserable.

She wished he were only hers, like he used to be; he'd been kinder then too.

'And when we've found Sparrow and got some money we're going to set up house together, aren't we, like you said?' She touched his sleeve tentatively.

'Maybe,' he said, shaking her off. 'We'll see.'

And he was gone.

23

Sampson's

Every morning when Sparrow woke she reached out for Scaramouch. Then she listened for the sounds of someone else breathing. Nothing. She was alone. Still. She missed the noise and the silly jokes and sharing things with the girls. Now it was just her and three grown-ups – two who were jolly and loving, at least, but . . . it wasn't the same. It didn't feel quite right. As the days went by she thought often of Mary and Little Jean and her other friends at the Knip and Pynch Home, wondering what they were doing. It made her feel guilty having all this luxury to herself. She missed Hettie too, and worried Glori had got in trouble for losing her. Did the match-girls miss her as well? But it was good to feel so safe; it was like being wrapped up in tissue paper, living here. And she didn't have to work; all she did was read and sew and help in the kitchen. She knew that her friends would love to be in her shoes.

'Don't get a cold sitting by that draughty window, will you?' Hilda said gently, as Sparrow sat staring out into the garden one day. 'What are you looking at, anyway? See anything interesting, dearie?'

Sparrow shook her head. 'Nothing. I was watching Bruno feeding the birds and looking out for Scaramouch,' she said. 'I thought I heard a cat.' It was terrible not having him – like someone had cut off her leg.

'It'll be that white tom from next door,' Gerta said. 'Dirty old thing, he is.'

'Probably,' Hilda said. 'But it *could* be your cat, Sparrow, dearie, so go and look if you want.'

Sparrow shook her head. She'd already seen the white cat strolling up the path, as if he lived here. He had a fat, flat face and torn ears; nothing like Scaramouch. 'That's all right, thank you, Hilda.'

She imagined she saw Scaramouch everywhere: in the garden shadows, creeping along the wall, lying on a branch in a tree. A squashed, velvet bag, lying on an armchair, looked so like him that she ran to pick it up and then almost wept when it wasn't. In the night she had to get out of bed time and time again to go to the window, thinking he was meowing outside or scratching at the windowpane to come in.

She even dreamed about him and sometimes the dreams were awful because they turned into nightmares where Scaramouch was locked up and was trying to reach her, but couldn't.

Where is he? Why hasn't he found me? she wondered for the hundredth time.

Sparrow stared hard at the privet hedge but without noticing the little glossy leaves and dark twigs; all she saw was the attic-nest and the girls gathered around the fire, mugs of hot chocolate in their hands and . . . Scaramouch. Scaramouch wearing a pink collar, sitting on Hettie's lap with the girls feeding him cheese and cream, and he was so fat and happy that he could hardly get up. He'd given up waiting for Sparrow. Hettie was his new special friend. He was sleeping on *her* bed now. He turned his big yellow eyes to look up into Sparrow's face.

'*You left me!*' he seemed to say. '*So what can you expect?*'

Sparrow let out a big, long, sad sigh. No, she couldn't blame him; he must think she'd abandoned him. He must *hate* her!

'I took Mayra's portrait out of Sparrow's room,' Gerta said, picking up her knitting and concentrating on it with a frown. 'It could do with a new frame, I thought. Mr Reynolds in the square can do it.'

Sparrow spun round and stared at Gerta in surprise. So did Hilda. Bruno made a *huff huff* sound.

'Why Gerta, that's not like you,' Hilda said. 'You don't usually concern yourself with household chores . . . but thank you, that's very kind.' She looked at Sparrow. 'But you'll miss it, dearie, won't you?'

Sparrow turned back to the window.

'Yes, I will.' Which is why Gerta's moved it, Sparrow thought miserably. She doesn't like me; doesn't want me here.

'I wondered if it was too upsetting for you,' Gerta said without looking up. 'I saw how you stared and stared at Mayra. I believe looking at her so much might make you ill.'

163

Sparrow shrugged. How could a painting of a sweet face make you ill?

When Gerta went out of the room to fetch her shawl, Hilda came and sat beside Sparrow.

'Don't think too badly of her,' she said. 'Gerta finds you being here rather difficult, not in a nasty, mean way but, you see, before you came there were just the two of us girls and she doesn't like sharing me.'

'They're very close,' Bruno added. 'Sisters.'

'I know. You don't have to apologise,' Sparrow said. 'You're all so kind to me. So generous.'

'Gerta was very sick when she was a little girl,' Hilda said, 'and spent hours in bed, poor thing, and I looked after her. Later, when I lost my darlings, Gerta looked after me. She knows how . . . how fragile I am and all she's trying to do is protect me, Sparrow. She's not sure about –'

'I know! It's my fault, I should have told you straight away that I was a match-girl,' Sparrow said. 'I didn't mean to hide it from you, not really. It was just . . .' It had taken her days to tell them the truth. 'It was just I thought you wouldn't let me stay and then . . .'

'It was probably the bang on the head that made you confused,' Bruno said, kindly. 'Don't worry about it.'

'The match-girls were kind and . . . I liked them. I didn't want to get them into trouble,' Sparrow said. 'It's hard on the streets, Hilda, when you can't even afford a scrap of pie. Honestly.'

'I can imagine,' Hilda said, patting her hand and smiling sweetly. 'Poor girl.'

'Now, Bruno, have you found out anything more about her?' Gerta asked him later, when they were alone.

Bruno shook his head. 'The shop takes up such a lot of my time. D'you know, I think I'm almost ready to retire. I'm too old for toys . . . and this sort of detective work's not easy . . .'

'Why don't you just ask Sparrow the name of this orphanage she says she's come from?' Gerta said. 'For goodness' sake, Bruno, don't be such a wet.'

'I don't want her thinking we're checking up on her,' Bruno said miserably. 'She's a dear girl and I want her to trust us.'

'Well, I'm not ashamed and embarrassed about checking up on her,' Gerta said. 'If you won't protect dear Hilda, I must. I'll ask her straight away.'

And she did. Sparrow gave her the information gladly and Gerta wrote down *Knip and Pynch* in her notebook. 'You never know,' she added, 'they might have some information about where you came from, your *real* family. That would be helpful, wouldn't it?'

'Oh no, they won't know anything,' Sparrow said. 'There was nothing to know. And Miss Knip absolutely hated me. She won't care where I am or what happens to me. Honestly, I'm the last person she wants to hear about.'

'You still don't have much colour, Sparrow. Peaky. Would you like to go for a walk into Sto'back with me?' Hilda said one day. 'We could go and see Bruno in the shop. The exercise will do us both good. You can help me post some pamphlets too.'

Hilda's face was full of cheery hopefulness and she positively lit up when Sparrow said she'd love to.

When Sparrow had recovered from her three days in bed, she had found her old clothes washed and neatly folded, and since then Hilda had given her new dresses, a red coat, soft brown boots, books and lovely soaps, everything a girl could wish for.

She could not replace the Butterworths' two little dark-haired daughters, she knew that, and she wasn't going to try. She did love Hilda and Bruno now, how could she not? But she worried that she wasn't very good at showing her love. She'd had no practice. When she had Scaramouch back and maybe had found out who she really was, *then* she would be able to be more loving, she imagined. And more lovable too. At least, she hoped so.

The weather had taken a turn for the worse and it was bitterly cold. Sparrow snuggled her chin into her coat collar as they walked down the road. They slipped the folded-up pamphlets through the letterboxes of each house as they went. They were about animal welfare, Hilda had told her. She was on a committee about stopping animal cruelty; it had become her main concern in recent years. Sparrow was too interested in being out in Stollenback to look closely at the leaflets and she dropped them through the letterboxes as quickly as she could.

She didn't recognise any of the streets. The roads were cleaner and wider and there were more window boxes and bigger gardens than in the area around Miss Minter's nest. Small trees, clipped into lollipop shapes, lined the main streets and the houses were freshly painted and well cared for. Large, bright posters advertising ZIPPO'S CIRCUS had been plastered on the walls, showing Zippo in a top hat and flourishing a whip.

'Our shop is just down here, dearie,' Hilda was saying, as they turned into a side street. 'It used to be busier round here; it's a bit run down now. Bruno is thinking of giving up, you know. It's all getting a bit much at his age and –'

Sparrow suddenly stopped dead. 'Oh, no!' she cried.

'What is it, dearie?' Hilda exclaimed, her face full of concern. 'Are you ill?'

'There, that shop!' Sparrow's heart was suddenly beating twice as fast as normal. Her mouth was dry. She pointed at an empty old shop, whose shutters hung crookedly off their hinges.

Sampson's of Stollenback.

24

Memories

Sparrow shivered from head to foot. Her dreams were dashed!

'What on earth is the matter?' Hilda cried. 'You didn't want to go there, did you? Sparrow, dearie, I can take you to a much better shop and find you something pretty if that's what you want.'

The shop looked empty and unused. The dirty windows were lined with yellowed newspaper; a pile of old leaves and scraps of paper had blown into the doorway. A CLOSED sign, festooned with cobwebs, hung in the doorway in front of a blind.

'It's not that,' Sparrow said weakly. She couldn't explain.

'There, there,' Hilda said, hugging her. 'Come to Hilda. Can you tell me, dearie?' she said. 'I hate to see you all upset.'

'It's just that, it's just . . . when I was brought to the orphanage, as a baby, I was wrapped in a shawl, a very lovely shawl, which I've left at the match factory, and the cloth came from here. It was all I ever had, Hilda, the only clue about who I really was, and I always hoped . . . I always hoped that maybe I'd find this shop and someone would be here who knew about me or . . .'

'Don't fret,' Hilda said. She looked at the shop and back at Sparrow's unhappy face. 'Come on, dearie, let's investigate,' she said brightly.

Hilda marched up and knocked loudly on the door. Nothing. Not a sound.

They pressed their noses against the dirty windows and rattled the door.

'Maybe round the back?' Sparrow suggested.

'Let's try next door first,' Hilda said, 'before we get arrested by the guards for clambering over walls and breaking into other people's property.'

There was a small, wonky cottage next door, with a window of thick glass like the bottom of a bottle. Dark red hollyhocks, frozen and browned by the sudden cold snap, grew so abundantly around the doorstep that they almost blocked the tiny green door.

Hilda knocked loudly. No one came. 'It could be empty too,' Sparrow said, 'and anyway, it was a long time ago. Eleven years.'

Hilda knocked again, even more loudly. 'I won't give up,' she said, 'and nor must you.'

At last the front door was pulled open. It squeaked and groaned as it scraped over the uneven stone floor. A little old man wearing large, tortoiseshell glasses, peered up at them.

'Good afternoon!' Hilda said cheerily. 'I'm Hilda Butterworth and this is Sparrow and we would like to ask you some questions about the shop next door.'

The man smiled, showing one single tooth in the top of his jaw. 'Oh, yes,' he said, in a quavering voice. 'Sampson's, that was. It's been empty for years.'

'Do you know anything about the people who lived there?' Hilda asked. 'Did anyone there have a baby?'

The old man chuckled hoarsely. 'I should say so,' he said. 'Loads of babies. Barrow-loads of babies. 'Bout ten years ago, that was.'

Hilda and Sparrow exchanged a meaningful look.

'Please might we come in for a moment?' Hilda asked. 'We'd like to talk to you.'

The old man led them inside to a tiny parlour and sat them down at a round table. 'I can't hardly see,' he said, striking a light on his tinderbox. 'I'm going blind and deaf, I am. A touch of that magic horse elixir, that's what I need.'

'Brightling, you mean? That doesn't work,' Hilda said sharply. She glanced at Sparrow. 'And it's illegal. And dangerous.' Hilda took out one of her pamphlets and passed it to him. 'You really should read that,' she told him. 'Read that when we've gone, and see what you think then.'

'But have you tried it? Have you?' the old man said, undaunted. 'I've heard it makes old men like me leap around like young goats!' He chuckled as he lit the lantern. 'I'd like not to creak when I bend . . . If only I could get my hands on some! If, eh? And who's going to put an ancient old crock like me into the dungeons for having it, eh? I'd like to see 'em try!'

The lantern glowed yellow and the gloomy room came slowly into view – large, dark furniture, a big oak grandfather

170

clock and dusty pictures.

'Now,' the old man went on, 'what was it you two lovely young ladies wanted to know?'

'Everything about Sampson's,' Sparrow said. 'Everything, please.'

'It is important to us,' Hilda said, 'Mister, Mister . . .?'

'Fred Fardell's the name,' the old man said. 'Well, what can I tell you?' His eyes were like owl eyes behind his thick glasses. 'Let me think. Let me think what you'd want to know . . . Mrs Sampson was a nurse. She took the babies in for the mothers and fathers that couldn't care for them – boarders, you understand – just until better times. Barrow-loads of babies, there were . . . She was a nice woman, Lydia Sampson, with a lovely smile for everyone, always a smile for me. Gave me cakes too. Soft heart. I remember her very well.'

Had nice Mrs Sampson looked after her? Sparrow wondered. Been kind to her? It would be good to think that just once in her past someone had been kind to her; it would make up for so much of the horridness later, in the orphanage.

'Her husband, Mortimer, was the weaver. Oh one of the finest in the town – such soft and silky stuff he made. But he took sick and died. It was that terrible Swamp Fever that hit the town.'

Hilda let out a little gulping noise and quickly dabbed her eyes with her hanky. 'I remember that time,' she said quietly.

'That's when it all went wrong,' Fred went on. 'Lydia couldn't manage the nursery without her husband. All but one baby went back to their mothers. All but one. Then

171

Lydia died too. That flu again or a broken heart, I don't know. The good die young, that's what they say, isn't it?' He looked reflective for a moment, then grinned. 'I must be a pretty bad chap then, eh?' he chuckled. 'I'm so old. Heh heh heh! Oh! There was another nurse, Pocket or Porridge or Picket or something. Such a plain and needy thing. Stayed there for a while after Lydia went, with this one baby, but she couldn't manage. She was no nurse and she couldn't cook, neither. I remember something, I remember . . .' He tapped his wrinkled brow while Sparrow held her breath, certain it was important to her. 'Something about this baby . . . Lydia had said the mother would come and pick the baby up. But she never came back for that baby. Yes, that was it! Nanny Porrit – now, look at that! Her name just sprang into my old head! Nanny Porrit was left with this baby and she took it to an orphanage because she didn't know what else to do with the wee mite and this orphanage was over the swamps somewhere, on the way north to Nollenback where she had family.'

Hilda and Sparrow stared at each other, wide-eyed.

'The Knip and Pynch Home is between here and Nollenback,' Sparrow said. 'You see,' she explained to Fred Fardell, 'I think I was one of those babies – which means I'm not a Sampson at all. I'm trying to find out who I am and I only have this Sampson's shawl. Do you remember the baby's name?'

Fred shook his head. 'Don't remember if it was a boy or a girl, even,' he said. 'I know the mother was young and Porrit thought she might have run away – she was a dancer

172

or something in a show. I'm sure there were some sparkles or sequins or something involved. I'm not sure. And birds.'

'*Birds?* Was the baby's name Sparrow?' Hilda asked him.

Both Hilda and Sparrow stared at him so hard Fred Fardell had to lean away. He shook his head. '*Sparrow?* It could have been, perhaps it was. I don't remember.'

'Well, thank you, Mr Fardell, you've been so helpful to us,' Hilda said. She slipped him a card with their address. 'If you do remember anything else, anything else at all, perhaps you'll come and see me?'

'Certainly I will,' he said. 'Certainly.'

'Thank you for everything,' Sparrow said, getting up. 'I think – I hope – that baby was me!'

'Can't say I recognise you,' he said, giving her a wink.

As they left, Hilda slipped some coins onto the table for him.

Hilda put her arm through Sparrow's as they set off again. 'That was interesting, dearie, wasn't it?' she said. 'Now we're getting somewhere. We must find this Nanny Porrit. It all feels right; it all fits in. Don't worry, Sparrow. We will leave no stone unturned until we find out exactly who you are! We'll tell Bruno everything and he will help us. Look!' Hilda finished. 'Here's our shop.'

Butterworth's was a double-fronted shop selling all sorts of toys. The windows were crammed with dolls and doll houses, jigsaws, birdcages, beads, bicycles and trucks. There was a train running on a track going in and out of wooden-brick arches and around big, soft bears and under a rocking horse. Hanging on invisible wires from the ceiling, hundreds

173

of spitfyres bobbed and spun against a painted blue sky. Sparrow went cold inside at the sight of them – they were exactly like the ones she'd been made to sew by Betty and Tapper Nash.

They went inside. Bruno was sitting at the wooden counter, mending a clockwork mouse. 'Hello, girls!' He jumped up. 'How grand to see you! Goodness, Sparrow, wearing that new coat, and your colouring – you look just like someone . . . someone I used to know.' He faltered, looking pointedly at his wife. He coughed. 'Well, well, now . . .' and he held out his arms to her.

Sparrow ran and hugged him. 'It's only me,' she said.

'Of course it's you. Just you, and I don't want anyone else either.' Bruno waved his arms at the surrounding toys. 'Take your pick, Sparrow. Choose something from my shop. Anything at all.'

As far as she knew, Sparrow had never had a toy in her whole life and now she felt she was too old to enjoy one, but she looked at them anyway, not wanting to hurt his feelings.

'What about a spitfyre?' he said, plucking one of the models from the ceiling. 'They're all made by hand. Look at the tiny stitches! They're very pretty.'

Sparrow shuddered. 'Mrs Nash and Tapper made them, didn't they?' she asked.

'Why, goodness me, how do you know that?' Bruno asked.

Sparrow told them about her night at the Nashes' house and how they had tricked her and locked her in her room and how she was sure others had been kidnapped and kept there before.

'Why, that's terrible,' Bruno said. 'Kidnapping! Forcing girls to make these things! I will never buy any more from that lad again. I never did like him. I've a good mind to go to the guards and tell them what you've told me but I feel sorry for his old mother. She depends on him, you see.'

'I would like a spitfyre anyway, thank you, Bruno,' Sparrow said, afraid she'd sounded ungracious. She slipped it into her coat pocket. Little Jean would love it, or Hettie, if she ever saw either of them again.

'Tapper hasn't been in these last couple of weeks . . .' Bruno went on.

'But how extraordinary,' cried Hilda. 'I saw him in town just the other day! In Middle Square!'

Sparrow felt her blood freeze in her veins.

Tapper, *here*?

Was he looking for her?

25

Brightling

So Tapper was in Stollenback. Even sitting behind the closed shutters in the warm, cosy parlour with Bruno, Hilda and Gerta, Sparrow was nervous. He was out there, looking for her; perhaps creeping up on her in the dark.

'Relax my dear, relax,' Bruno said, seeing her darting glances. 'Or did you think you heard your cat?'

Sparrow shook her head.

'I wonder if poor Sparrow isn't a little bored with us?' Gerta said. 'We are dull old things and she's young and full of energy.'

'Oh don't say that, Gerta!' Hilda said. 'It's not true, Sparrow, is it?'

'You know it's not,' Sparrow said.

Tapper was out there; that's why she was nervous.

'Well, you're all jittery tonight,' Gerta complained. 'Perhaps you've remembered where this match factory is, have you?' she went on. 'Because then we could have the

176

match-girls arrested, couldn't we?'

'I told you,' Sparrow said. 'I only saw the street once. I don't know where it was.'

'The papers insist that it is the match-girls that sell Brightling,' Bruno said.

'Do they? What *is* Brightling? Some sort of tonic?' Sparrow said. 'Why's it illegal?'

'Brightling comes from spitfyres,' Hilda said.

'It's an elixir,' Gerta said. Her eyes gleamed suddenly as she stroked her cheek. 'They say it irons out your wrinkles and makes you look twenty years younger. They say –'

'People say it does all sorts of ridiculous things,' Hilda butted in. 'But how can it cure warts and carbuncles? Be an antidote for snakebites and bee stings? Make your eyesight better and help new wives fall pregnant?'

'I know for a fact it helps your hair grow thicker and stops you going grey,' Gerta said, stubbornly. 'Cicely West used it and –'

'Poppycock!' Bruno spluttered, throwing down his newspaper. 'Utter rubbish! Don't listen to such twaddle, Gerta. Otto is closer to the spitfyres than any of us and he says it doesn't work and he should know. Spitfyres –'

'Oh! I saw spitfyres!' Sparrow said. 'I saw them breathing fire when I ran away from the Nashes' house! They were so beautiful!'

'They are, but –' He stopped and sniffed. 'A spitfyre caused Mayra's death,' he said. 'An accident. They're dangerous and wonderful at the same time.'

Hilda patted Bruno's arm lovingly. Then she disappeared

into the kitchen and came back with one of the pamphlets that she and Sparrow had been handing out earlier. She gave one to Sparrow. Sparrow read it then turned back to Hilda.

'People *hurt* the spitfyres?' she said.

'Yes,' said Hilda. 'The thieves don't care. Brightling is the spark of the spitfyre, their essence, and without it they die. It looks for all the world like bottled sunlight – sunbeams condensed into a sort of liquid dust – but it isn't sunlight. It's their life.'

Sparrow's mouth fell open and stayed open. Miss Minter had had some in her safe; she knew it instantly. And Kate was selling it at the market; it was what she'd kept hidden in her tray. *Brightling*.

'Yes,' Bruno said, misreading her expression. 'It is amazing stuff.'

Sparrow nodded dumbly.

'Is it really so bad though?' Gerta said, in a wheedling voice. 'What's wrong with taking a little of this sparking fluid from a spitfyre? Isn't it just like taking milk from a cow?'

Hilda shook her head. 'No, no,' she said. 'It's not like that at all, Gerta.'

'And it might work,' Gerta said obstinately. 'You never know for sure.'

'It doesn't, Gerta! It's a myth,' Bruno said. 'We all want long life and good health –'

' – And happiness,' Gerta said. 'You name it, Brightling does it.'

Bruno sighed. 'It does not.'

'Because the spitfyres' ancestors were dragons,' Hilda

said, 'they're fantastic, mysterious creatures. Of course, folk believe all the silly stories that get made up about them – the more weird and wonderful the better.'

'When I saw them they made me feel happy. They gave me hope,' Sparrow said.

'Well, now,' Bruno said, grinning at them all, 'talking of spitfyres . . . I had a letter from my brother, Otto, today and . . .'

'He works at the Academy,' Hilda told Sparrow.

'. . . And he told me that the spitfyres will perform at the circus on Friday night.' Bruno laughed. 'And *we're* going to see them!'

'But, my dear,' Hilda said gently, suddenly serious. 'Are you sure? Spitfyres at the circus? Won't it bring back too many sad memories? Aren't you worried there might be another accident?'

'No. I'm not worried. That was years ago. That terrible time when Mayra died, the animals were made to perform outrageous and impossible tricks. That won't happen again.' He pulled four tickets from his pocket and waved them in the air. 'Otto has got us the best seats. I can't wait!'

Hilda smiled. 'I knew all about it,' she said. 'We discussed it at our committee meetings.' She turned to Sparrow. 'Stormy – he's the Director of the spitfyre Academy – he's on our side. He's bringing the spitfyres here to try and persuade the good folk of Stollenback that Brightling is no more beneficial than a glass of water. And much more dangerous!'

26

Tapper Again

'What are we going to do now, so?' Tapper said, swirling his bark-beer around in the glass and watching it with dull, hooded eyes. 'Got no money.'

Glori licked her teeth; they ached. She'd been working on the phosphorus table and the stuff coated her teeth and seeped into her very bones; she felt as if her mouth had been hammered and her jaw was loose. 'I don't know, Tapper,' she said, rubbing at the side of her sore face.

'You don't know!' He smacked the little round table loudly. 'You don't know!'

Glori looked round nervously as people turned and stared at them. She shrank inside her jacket – her old red one; she hadn't worn the purple velvet jacket since Sparrow had disappeared. 'It's not my fault, Tapper. I've walked the streets looking for her. She's gone.'

'Haven't tried hard enough,' Tapper said. 'If you'd tried hard enough you'd have found her. 'Cos she's somewhere, in't she?'

'But I –'

'Knip's gone quiet,' Tapper said, thinking aloud. 'S'pect she's given up the search. No match for Miss Minter. What scheming, eh? Good move, that. Smart girl.'

For a second Glori thought he meant *she* was smart, but it was Miss Minter and her planning he admired.

They sat in gloomy silence.

'Any sign of that big old cat?' Tapper asked.

Glori shook her head. 'No. Violet knows something, I think, but won't say nothing.'

'Huh. Good riddance, I say. So.' He drained his glass, 'I might as well go. This in't any fun, is it, when you're so flat and gloomy.' He suddenly slapped down a pair of knitted gloves on the table. 'Oh I came across these. Got them for you. But what's the point when you're such a misery?'

'Oh Tapper, thank you!' Glori quickly put the pink gloves on. 'You are kind. I know you're kind, really. No one ever buys me presents. Ever. Do stay, Tapper,' she said, grabbing his arm. 'Don't go just yet. I'll try to perk up. It's just my jaw that hurts and –'

'Fact is, I've to see Miss Minter,' Tapper said, standing up. 'She wants my help. Friday.'

'*Friday?* Are *you* coming out with us too?' Glori said.

He winked and gave her a crafty smile. 'Yes. You're surprised Miss Minter likes me? She does. She sees what's what, and she needs me.'

Glori knew that he wanted her to be jealous, but she wasn't. She was no match for Miss Minter, nor did she want to be. 'She likes anyone who is useful to her,' she said.

'I'll tell her you said that.'

'Oh don't do that!' Glori cried. 'I didn't mean it, Tapper, honest . . .' She thought for a moment. 'If you're planning to speak to her, you'll be going back to the nest . . .?'

Tapper shrugged. 'Yeah, I suppose we can walk along together.'

Glori smiled. She was the only girl in the nest with an admirer, and that's how she liked it.

Glori climbed the stairs wearily with Tapper lumbering ahead. The nest hadn't been the same since Sparrow came and Sparrow went. She'd been almost happy with Sparrow around, Glori thought. But now everything seemed so pointless.

As soon as they opened the door, Hettie came running up. She stopped when she saw Tapper, hesitated then flung her arms around Glori. 'Glori! Glori! Did you find Sparrow today?'

Glori shook her head. 'No sign of Sparrow,' she said. She took off her coat and hung it up and went to sit beside Hettie at the table. 'Where is everyone?'

Only Miss Minter sat alone by the fire.

'Everyone else is busy,' Hettie said.

'Good evening, Miss Minter,' Tapper said, going over to her. The fire flickered forlornly and died down as he went and stood beside it.

Miss Minter nodded at him. 'I hope you've kept your mouth shut,' she said quietly, but not so quietly that Glori couldn't just hear her.

Tapper whispered something but Hettie's loud voice drowned him out before Glori could catch what he said.

'No Sparrow, no Sparrow,' Hettie sang sadly. 'Oh well, you're my big sister again today, aren't you?'

Glori smiled and patted her arm. 'Yes, course I am.'

'Sit next to me at the circus! We're going to the circus!' Hettie cried. 'Miss Minter said we were. All of us. On Friday! We're going to make special, glittery matchboxes and sell hundreds and hundreds of them!'

'Gloriana, take Hettie away,' Miss Minter said. 'Her shrieking is getting on my nerves.'

'Come on, Hettie,' Glori said and reluctantly led Hettie to her bed.

Tapper took a chair from the table, swung it round back-to-front and sat down opposite Miss Minter, leaning over the chair's back and grinning.

'Friday night at the circus, Miss Minter,' he said. 'What fun!'

While they talked, Glori sat with Hettie on her bed.

'Sometimes I think you're going to bring Cari back with you,' Hettie said, looking suddenly forlorn. 'You never do. But I won't forget her.'

'No. Good. That's right,' Glori said. *Cari*. Miss Minter had forbidden them from visiting her while she'd been in prison. Now it was too late; she'd gone to the wastelands and would never be seen again. Tough. She hadn't run fast enough. Poor Cari.

'You'll love the circus,' Glori said, turning back to Hettie with a smile. 'You'll love all the lights and things. You like horses, don't you?'

'I do!' Hettie cried. She waved a pamphlet advertising the circus at Glori. 'Look! Not only horses but littles – they're tiny people – and even cats!'

Glori laid the crumpled pamphlet on the bed and read it.

ZIPPO'S SPECTACULAR, STAR-SPANGLED
CIRCUS
SIX WHITE HORSES ridden by SIX BLONDE
BEAUTIES!
LITTLES to make you LAUGH!
DARING TRAPEZE ARTISTS to make you
SHIVER with FRIGHT!
COOL CATS to CONFOUND and CHARM you!
AND, FOR ONE NIGHT ONLY,
ACADEMY SPITFYRES!

27

Miss Knip's Letter

Dear Miss Gerta,

My compliments to you.

I was delighted to receive your letter concerning the orphan called Sparrow. I hope she is not causing you too much trouble.

She most certainly is from the Knip and Pynch Home as she has told you. She left here on her eleventh birthday.

I need to meet with you and share what I know. Please refrain from informing her of my impending visit; let it be a pleasant surprise. Also, please do not tell anyone else that she is now

*living with you because I have reason to believe
that others might be after her.*

*I will arrive in Stollenback on Saturday, early
evening, and I think you will be delighted to learn
what I know. You will find it most edifying.*

Yours most humbly and truly,

Nora Knip (Miss)

There! Gerta thought. There *was* something mysterious
about Sparrow, just as she had guessed. All right, she was
from the Knip and Pynch Home as she'd said, that wasn't
a lie – but Miss Knip was hinting at secrets too. Hopefully
she knew who her real family was and then they could be
reunited with Sparrow, and Hilda would be all hers again.

She slipped the letter into her bag. 'I'm not doing this for
me,' Gerta said quietly to her empty room. 'It's for you, dear
Hilda. Sparrow is not the right little girl for you,' she went
on, putting on her coat and adjusting her hat. 'I understand
you have an empty place in your heart, but please, sister,
dear, don't fill it with that unworthy girl!'

She checked her reflection in the mirror.

'Perfect. I do like the circus.'

28

Circus

The night was cold and starry with a clear, white-blue moon; Sparrow's favourite kind of night. She held onto Hilda's arm as they joined the crowds streaming towards Zippo's tent, which had been put up in a field on the outskirts of town. She was thrilled at the prospect of seeing spitfyres again.

The huge red and white striped tent was decorated with strings of flags, which danced in the breeze. Fairy lights were strung up in the surrounding trees and linked in a circle around the tent. Beside it were many brightly-coloured caravans, and cages where the animals were kept.

As they queued along the sawdust path to go inside, circus people, dressed in bright, glittery costumes ran around with sticks of fire, tumbling and leaping on the grass. There were hundreds of people; their breath billowing out in clouds in front of them. The air smelled of animals and hot sugar candy.

A 'little', not much taller than a seven year old, galloped up and down, bareback, on a miniature white pony. He had very blue eyes and a wrinkly face like a raisin.

'Roll up! Roll up!' the little called. 'Zippo's circus is about to begin!'

Sparrow's group was propelled along, caught up with the throng, pushing towards the lights and the open doorway of the tent. Hilda chatted and pointed things out to Sparrow and they were so absorbed that neither of them saw the match-girls with their trays of pretty matchboxes, or heard their calls.

But the match-girls saw *them*.

Glori was the first to spot her.

'Sparrow!' She lurched forward, and then stopped, biting her lip and letting her voice fade away as she stared at Sparrow's retreating figure. Glori's shoulders slumped. She blinked back a tear and turned away as if she'd seen nothing out of the ordinary at all. 'Matches! Lovely matches!' she cried, turning her back on Sparrow and edging away, out of sight. '*Matches!*'

But Violet had spotted Sparrow too. She quickly closed up her tray and sped off like the wind to find Miss Minter. Her face was alight with mischief and excitement.

'Come on, this way,' Bruno was saying to his group. 'My brother has got us front row seats. Come along, Gerta. Aren't we lucky? Good old Otto. He's so looking forward to meeting you, Sparrow. We've told him all about you.'

Sparrow hardly heard what he said. She was beyond listening, beyond speech. The lights, the people, the smells

188

of sawdust, animals and lantern oil were overwhelming. She couldn't believe that something as wonderful as this existed.

Tiers of wooden seats rose up and up around her and they were filling quickly. Everyone was talking and now and again someone laughed loudly and blew a hooter.

'It's wonderful!' Sparrow whispered to Hilda. 'It's the most marvellous thing ever. I wish I could come every day. I want to live here. I want to *be* a circus.'

Hilda laughed. 'You can't *be* a circus!' she said. 'Dear girl.' She nudged Bruno. 'Did you hear that?' she whispered. '*Now* what do you think? A coincidence, or what?'

'Shh,' Bruno said. 'Look, there's Otto.' Bruno pointed to a large man standing on the other side of the ring. 'That's my brother,' he said. 'That's dear old Otto. See him, Sparrow?' he added, waving. 'We'll meet him after the show.'

Otto was even bigger and broader than Bruno. His head was lumpy and pale, like a badly-peeled potato. His ears were huge. He grinned and waved and then stopped, mid wave, as his eyes lighted on Sparrow. He was struck rigid and his mouth fell open. He looked as if he'd seen a ghost.

Miss Minter wore a wig of black curly hair and square, dark glasses. She was draped in a full-length coat of midnight-blue velvet that reached to the floor. Her cheeks glowed unusually hot and pink with excitement and her gloved hand tap-tapped the bar in front of her. It wasn't the circus that excited her; it was her scheme for this evening.

She could barely contain herself; her eyes flashed right and left behind the dark lenses, checking and measuring.

There, just there, she thought, fixing her eyes on the tent flaps, Tapper would come in. There, and there, the lanterns must be put out. And there! She would not miss a single thing! The plan had to go perfectly. Everything must work. Oh how satisfying to hurt the Academy Director when he least expected it.

She jumped as Violet suddenly slipped in beside her. '*Miss*!' Violet hissed.

'What? What?' Miss Minter snapped.

Violet whispered quickly in her ear. Miss Minter grabbed the rail in front of her and scanned the rows of seats, around and around and up and down . . . she stopped abruptly.

'I see her.' She stared hard at the group opposite and fixed on Sparrow. 'I see her.' Her eyes had taken on a round, glazed look, like marbles. 'Go back. I'll see to this.' She slipped out of her seat, elbowing her way back through the incoming crowd to where Tapper was lurking in the dark, behind the caravans and animal cages.

'What's up?' Tapper said. He sprang away from where he'd been leaning against one of the tethered horses for warmth. 'Something up?'

Miss Minter told him.

'Well, well,' he said, grinning and raising his eyebrows. 'Ain't we the lucky ones?'

'Can you do it?' Miss Minter asked him.

'Course. I'm on it. I've enough special mix to knock out the entire circus,' he said with a chuckle. 'I'll have a word with the girls. Just so's they know.' He laughed. 'Lucky, lucky, lucky!'

Miss Minter smiled as she took her seat again. She had to have that girl! Sparrow was equally important as the spitfyres. *More important? Equally important. More?* She fixed her gaze on Sparrow, daring her to slip from her grasp again. Little Sparrow, worth a fortune. Who'd have thought it?

She breathed a sigh of relief as six littles danced around the ring and extinguished some of the lanterns; dark was good. Dark was safe.

The show was about to begin.

Everyone clapped as Zippo, the ringmaster, skipped and jumped into the ring, cracking his whip and twirling his moustache. *Slap! Slap!* The whip made the sawdust fly up around him. He wore black boots with tassels and a red and gold jacket. His eyes gleamed. Finally he came to a standstill in the centre.

The audience roared. 'Good evening, ladies and gentlemen, boys and girls!' he cried. 'Sit back and enjoy the one and only, wonderful, Zippo's Circus! The Greatest Show On Earth!' The curtains were drawn back behind him and the entire circus company trooped into the ring: clowns, ponies, littles, acrobats and . . . cats.

Sparrow nearly toppled off her seat.

Cats.

Not tigers, or lions, but big, beautiful mink-coloured cats, each the size of a small fox, just like Scaramouch. She could not take her eyes off the slinky, wonderful cats as they circled the ring, their large paws puffing up the sawdust, tails swinging gracefully from side to side. They were special cats; handsome cats with round, knowing, yellow eyes . . . Each had the same noble head and finely-chiselled nose that Scaramouch had, the same curl at the end of its long, thick tail. It wasn't her imagination; they were identical.

'Just like my Scaramouch!' Sparrow breathed. Her fingers gripped the top of the barrier in front of her. She leaned forward, totally amazed and thrilled. Just like Scaramouch!

Music blared and the acts began to trail out.

'For your first act tonight,' Zippo cried, 'please give a big hand for the amazing Felix and his Feline Friends!' A man in leopard skin had remained in the ring; his four cats sat patiently beside him, their eyes fixed on his craggy, handsome face.

Felix smiled at the crowd and bowed. The band struck up a tune. Felix flicked his hand to the waiting cats and they began to run swiftly and quietly around the ring, their tails streaming behind them, their paws padding soundlessly on the sawdust. Their mouths were open, showing sharp, white teeth; they looked as if they were laughing.

'Ladeees and gen'lemens!' Felix cried in a voice thick with a foreign accent. 'Boyz and girlies, put your 'ands togezzer please, for my four spectacular, amazing, dancing, acrobatic cats! Fandango, Pulcinella, Pierrot and Columbine!'

As each cat's name was called, it leaped high into the air, stretching out long and smooth and landing with a ripple of muscle and a shiver of fur.

'Zeeze are rare Sherbavian cats, brought back from ze furzest lands in ze world,' Felix cried. 'No-vair will you be lucky enough to see such magnificent cats as zeese!'

192

Sparrow smiled to herself. At the *nest*, she thought. You'd be lucky to see just such a one at the nest! And she felt a sharp thump in her chest, as if someone had hit her, thinking longingly of her own Scaramouch.

Pulcinella had a black nose and both Fandango and Pierrot had black tails. Columbine had white paws. They all had eyes as round as saucers and yellow as gold, circled with black. Their ears were upright, perky and tipped with dark chocolate fur. Scaramouch was, without a doubt, a Sherbavian cat.

Sparrow bounced in her seat, desperate to share her knowledge with Hilda and also keen not to miss a moment of the show.

Felix had only to click his fingers or jerk his chin and the cats leaped over high bars, walked along a tightrope and climbed ladders. They balanced on seesaws and ran up ramps, through flaming hoops and onto balls, and everything they did, they did smoothly and calmly and with obvious enjoyment.

Finally, the music grew melancholic and soft and the cats began to dance. A single beam of light picked out Pulcinella and Fandango, who stood on their hind legs and somehow, Sparrow thought, didn't look stupid or wrong or un-catlike. They danced beautifully; gracefully swaying to the music while the other two cats weaved around them, trailing their floaty tails across their bodies and under their tummies.

Sparrow was mesmerised. She perched on the edge of her seat and hardly breathed. When the act ended and Felix started to run out of the ring she felt like bursting into tears. The cats ran after Felix and leaped up onto his broad shoulders, two on each side, balancing on his outstretched arms. He turned round then and bowed and the cats one by one trickled down his back, over his bottom and floated away.

Everyone applauded loudly.

'Oh Hilda, that was *so* marvellous!' Sparrow said. 'That's what I shall do!' she went on, clapping her hands furiously. 'When I'm older, I'm going to be a cat trainer in the circus.'

All three looked at her as if she had just said something very wonderful and very odd.

'What's the matter?' she said, staring at their extraordinary expressions. 'Oh,' she went on, 'and my Scaramouch, my cat, he's just like that. Just!'

'Now, Sparrow, really that's ridiculous,' Gerta said. 'Your cat couldn't be as big as those Sherbavian monsters.'

'He is!'

'Nor as clever,' Gerta added. 'I just don't believe it.'

'He is,' Sparrow said obstinately.

'Perhaps he is, Gerta, perhaps . . .' Bruno said.

'It was quietly clever, wasn't it?' Hilda said, dabbing a tear from her eye.

'Are you all right?' Sparrow asked anxiously.

'Of course, of course, it's just memories . . .'

They had to be quiet then, as five littles came somersaulting into the ring and began to roll around and do silly things to entertain the audience before the next big act came on.

Sparrow began to dream about wearing sequins and flying on a trapeze with Scaramouch. Why not? she thought. She'd see if she could get a job with Felix; he might want an assistant and . . . but first she must find Scaramouch! She'd almost forgotten that he wouldn't be waiting for her back at the Butterworths' house. Dear, dear Scaramouch, where was he?

The acrobats and clowns came in and, although they were thrilling, she wasn't as interested. She felt hot and overexcited. She began peeling off her gloves and then stopped.

Her fingertips were glowing faintly silver in the lantern light.

She turned her hands over and over to see if she was imagining it, but it was true. She shone. She glowed just like the other girls in the nest had glowed in the dark. Quickly she pulled her gloves on again. It must be phosphorus. It had to be. It had got inside her just as it had the other match-girls. Now, as she watched the horse riders and the clowns and the man on a unicycle, she couldn't help wondering all the time what the phosphorus would do to her. She knew it made your teeth rot and jaw ache. She didn't have any symptoms of that yet and hoped she never would.

The white horses, ridden by a family of beautiful blonde girls, distracted her, as did the handsome strong man who lifted up a baby elephant. Two littles breathed fire and put themselves out with buckets of water and made them all laugh.

Sparrow laughed too and then stopped just as suddenly.

She'd right that moment made up her mind. Even if it meant leaving the Butterworths she would, because she absolutely had to. She had to find Scaramouch.

29

Spitfyres

The drum roll boomed round the tent so loudly that the lanterns wobbled and vibrations ran through the wooden seats. The audience jumped and then tittered and looked around nervously; Sparrow and Hilda glanced at each other and grinned.

The drums heralded Zippo again, who came twirling into the centre of the ring, bowing and waving. He was flanked by ten littles, wearing brightly-coloured costumes and carrying buckets of water. They began sprinkling the water over the sawdust floor.

'Ladies and gentlemen, boys and girls!' Zippo cried. 'This dampening down is just a precaution, as you'll see.' He pointed to the littles hurrying around the ring. 'We don't want to dampen *your* spirits, but there must be no chance of the arena going up in flames . . . These animals can be very sparky . . .' He rubbed his hands together gleefully. 'And now, the moment you've all been waiting for!' He had to raise his voice as a thrilled murmur of excitement rippled round the ring. 'Let me present to you Stormy and Maud, Academy Directors, and their miraculous, fantastical, super-splendiferous, extraordinary spitfyres!'

Zippo went out, leaving the arena empty. The littles had doused some of the lights so now the tent was darker.

Nothing happened.

The crowd, which had fallen silent, waiting, now began whispering and looking around, wondering what was going to happen.

Suddenly the top of the tent was drawn back and through the opening came a blast of orange and golden light; and a shower of sparkling ash fell through the air over the ring like fireworks.

'Oooh!' the crowd cried. 'Look! Look!'

Two horse shapes seemed to drop heavily through the opening and fall into the tent. Spitfyres!

Sparrow caught her breath, her hands to her mouth in amazement. Astride each flying horse sat a sky-rider, dressed in close-fitting, dark clothes.

Just when it looked as if the spitfyres would plunge to the ground, they flashed open their great wings. There was a loud swooshing sound, like an umbrella unfurling, and the spitfyres halted their fall, swooped up and began to fly.

The audience clapped and cheered.

Everyone was looking upwards as the flying horses spun round and round the tent. The spitfyres' leathery wings blew up a huge draught, making the people in the top seats cry out and clutch their hats and scarves. As the metal-tipped hooves floated above their heads they ducked and shrieked, half in horror, half in fun.

The sky-riders waved as they circled the tent. They threw down a cascade of yellow-coloured pamphlets that everyone grabbed greedily.

The spitfyres flew around and rose up and circled about the apex of the tent once more before plunging down to the arena and skidding through the sawdust to a halt.

The crowd was on its feet, applauding and shouting.

The two sky-riders slipped off their spitfyres and bowed.

'I am Stormy,' the young man said, 'and this is Maud. We are the Directors of the Academy.'

Stormy was tall, slender and about twenty years old. His eyes sparkled with fun and energy; he looked lively enough to ignite a pile of wood all on his own, thought Sparrow. He was wearing a plain, dark suit, narrow boots and a high-necked white shirt. His shoulder-length hair was brown. Maud had long, very dark hair piled up on her head and tied with white ribbons, and she couldn't stop smiling. Sparrow thought her very pretty. She began to wonder how she might join them up at the Academy . . . with Scaramouch, of course.

The spitfyres were much bigger than ordinary horses, and quite extraordinary animals. They pulsated with energy and sparkiness; they were bursting with life.

The spitfyre that Maud had ridden had a coat of dark red, black and purple that seemed to have the texture of velvet. Her hooves were speckled with violet-coloured scales. When she tossed her head, her long mane flowed like water, cascading down over her neck, sparkling with gold and silver. Her wings were huge and scaly in places; dark, dark red spread over black sinews, running through the wings in a fine network of veins.

'Hello, everyone!' Maud called. 'Let me introduce my wonderful spitfyre to you. This is Kopernicus!'

Kopernicus tossed her purple-black mane. She pranced in a circle around Maud then stopped in front of her, puffing out blue smoke from her nostrils. The smoke rose up and hung like a blue halo above them both.

The crowd roared with amazement.

'Despite being so beautiful, our wonderful spitfyres are in constant danger,' Maud said, patting the spitfyre's neck. 'People want to steal their fire-power, their Brightling!'

Stormy stepped forward. 'This is Seraphina,' he said, introducing his own spitfyre.

She shone purple or silver or sometimes turquoise or even gold, depending on how the light hit her. Her wings were the palest purple and silver. And when she moved, she shimmered like a fish under water. She huffed out and breathed a stream of small balls of fire that went bowling over the sawdust, skipping and rolling until they died out with a little hiss and wisp of smoke. At a signal from Stormy, she spun round, reared up on her hind legs and blew out a stream of spinning, multi-coloured sparks and a jet of orange flame, which shot over the ground, jumping and sparking until it fizzled out on the wet sawdust.

'Isn't she beautiful?' Hilda whispered dreamily to Sparrow. 'What a lovely, lovely thing.'

'As Maud told you, we're here today because these rare and precious animals are being stolen for their sparking fluid, for Brightling. Brightling should not be taken from them, it is part of them, it is their essence. Without it, they die.'

Sparrow sat up and listened intently.

'We must stop this terrible trade,' Maud cried. 'Look at these lovely creatures! How could anyone harm them?'

'Brightling is absolutely worthless!' Stormy said, his voice rising. 'It has no value to you. None.'

'It cured my grandma's lumbago!' someone shouted from the stalls.

A few members of the audience laughed and others cried, 'For shame!' and 'It's rubbish!' and 'No, it doesn't work!'

'I assure you it did *not* cure your grandma's lumbago,' Stormy said. 'How could it? It is –'

'My daughter waited five years for a baby,' a woman interrupted. 'Took a dose of Brightling and had one straight away.'

'No, no,' Maud said, spinning round to face the speaker. 'That wasn't Brightling! It was just luck.'

Stormy quietened the audience. Half of them seemed to believe Brightling worked, and the other half was on his side, not wishing to hurt the spitfyres.

'If you take their Brightling from them, they die,' Maud said. 'And if *you* take Brightling *you* may well die!'

'That can't be true!' someone called. 'My brother –'

Suddenly there was a shout from the back of the crowd. 'Fire! Fire!'

At first Sparrow thought the call of 'fire' was all part of the spitfyres' show. She looked round, expecting the flying horses to do something dramatic, but then, when she saw the smoke billowing into the tent from all sides in great black, thick clouds, she realised it was a *real* fire.

The cry was taken up in earnest all around.

'*Fire!*'

Smoke filled the tent so quickly no one had a chance to move before, suddenly, they were plunged into the dark as the smoke draped over them. The ring of lanterns around the arena could only glow faintly through the darkness.

'Keep calm!' Stormy called out, but he was already invisible. 'Keep ca—' His voice was cut off suddenly. A spitfyre whinnied and briefly puffed out a yellow haze of fire. Then that went out too.

The audience was already up on its feet and pushing, struggling to escape.

Sparrow turned to Hilda, who was standing up but looking dazed, and grabbed her coat for her. 'Come on,' she said. 'We must move quickly.'

'Mayra?' Hilda said in a disjointed, worried way. 'She died here, in an accident. Oh Sparrow, Bruno, what's going on?'

Bruno put his arm around her and tried to move her out ahead of him, but people blocked their path. They couldn't see where to go. Hilda's anxiety was catching – but Sparrow wasn't worried about Mayra, she was thinking about Tapper. She was sure he was here. She hadn't seen him, but why else did she have this familiar feeling of dread? What else could cause this cold, creeping sensation of impending doom?

A dot of light pierced through the smoke, darting up and down as if searching for something. It was the same brightness she'd seen at the market when Kate sold the Brightling. Before she could work it out, the lantern beside her went out and, as it died, she felt someone dash past, and the bright dot went with them.

Kate? Agnes? she wondered, nervously.

One by one, all the lanterns in the arena went out. Blackness descended, dense with smoke. All around, people shouted and pushed.

Sparrow couldn't see anything and she could hardly breathe now, as the smoke thickened and caught in her throat and eyes.

'Get those lanterns back on!' someone yelled.

'Quickly, quickly now!' That was Bruno. Where was Hilda? Sparrow tried to move towards the Butterworths. Her eyes were watering. She couldn't move at all; Gerta squeezed her from the other side; she was coughing, bent over, struggling. Desperate to get free, Sparrow was forced to clamber over the low rail and she toppled into the ring.

How could it be so dark? She coughed and coughed. 'Hilda! I'm just here!' she called.

She felt someone suddenly beside her; not someone trying to get out, not someone panicking and struggling, but someone who was bearing down on her, a black, empty, nothingness, dread and loathing . . . Again the tiny dot of light! Right up by her face. A spark. A star.

'Got ya!' a man said.

202

Glori held her tiny phial of Brightling out at arm's length; it shone like a miniscule star. When she closed her fingers round it, it vanished. *Magic*.

The blindfolded spitfyre she was leading out of the ring had come willingly; she found it dreadfully sad that it trusted her. 'Don't, don't,' she'd murmured. 'Don't let me take you like this. Fight me, can't you?'

But Miss Minter's accomplice, Brittel, that nasty, sloping-shouldered greaseball, had got to them first and fed them something to hush them up. Now the creature followed her as meekly as a lamb. She'd only to whisper its name – 'Seraphina, Seraphina' – and it came.

She led the spitfyre outside into the fresh air. All around her there were screams and shouts and bodies scrambling and shoving, but the lovely Seraphina was docile, gently puffing warm air over Glori's head and shoulders in a comforting way.

No one stopped her. No one saw them go at all.

Glori hoped Sparrow hadn't been too scared when the smoke whooshed into the ring and the lights went out. She hoped she'd got out quickly and was on her way back to her cosy home, wherever that might be. She didn't know that Miss Minter had spotted her and she hadn't seen Tapper running out with a bulky canvas bundle over his shoulder.

Moments later, Brittel and Kopernicus appeared alongside her in the cold, fresh air, and then they ran from the tent, over the field to the distant cluster of trees, leading the two spitfyres with them.

Glori felt no elation, only an enormous sadness. Seraphina

had lost her sparkle; Glori had lost Sparrow. A gloom settled over her.

'Here! Here!' Brittel shouted to the match-girls, waiting in the trees beside a wagon and two horses. Brittel and Glori led the spitfyres into the darkest shadows. 'Get those buckets!'

How Brittel loved ordering them about, Glori thought. He was in his element tonight, stealing the two spitfyres, bossing everyone. Miss Minter had told her that he'd worked with spitfyres once, at the Academy; that was how he knew so much about them.

The girls had been told what they had to do and carried the lidded buckets containing a thick brown liquid out from the back of the wagon.

Connie and Agnes began to slosh the brown stuff over Seraphina. Beattie and Kate covered Kopernicus's red hide with the dye. No one spoke. They had to work fast; the alarm would be raised any minute. Their breath billowed out around them in the icy air.

'What happened to the Director?' Kate asked, rubbing the brown colouring over Kopernicus's haunches.

'Got a knock on the head,' Brittel said.

'And that Maud?'

'Same.'

Tapper brought rolls of old fabric from the wagon and dropped them on the grass. 'Here, Glori, help me, can't you? You in a daze?'

Glori shook her head; she was. She dragged one of the rolls and laid it down alongside Seraphina, glancing back at the tent as she did so. Black smoke billowed from it. Why didn't someone come and stop them? She'd heard what Stormy had said, the spitfyres would die – surely someone must come!

Dolly and Billie rushed up from the direction of the tent. 'Did we get them? Oh that's them!' Dolly cried, staring at the spitfyres. 'They are big next to the ordinary ones, aren't they?'

'Big, and they've got wings!' Billie said.

'It's the wings we got to strap down and hide. Let's do it!' Brittel said.

'Why don't they attack us and breathe fire and all that?' someone asked.

'Fizzled out,' Brittel said with a laugh. 'My potion.' He took off the blindfolds from the two spitfyres. 'I'll give them some more in a minute.'

Quickly the girls began to bandage the spitfyres' wings to their sides with the fabric.

'No flying for you, poor thing,' Glori whispered to Seraphina as she gently tucked down her wings. 'Sorry.'

'Lucky they're the smaller ones,' Brittel told the girls. 'If it'd been Sparkit or Bluey, them from the old days, them Elite spitfyres . . . Whoa, different matter then – we'd be fighting them right now. Huge, they were, and strong! Here, we must give them some of this.' He looked round anxiously, pulling a brown paper bag from his pocket. 'Before they start . . .'

'Start what?' Kate asked.

'Sparking,' he said.

Brittel fed each spitfyre a handful of small orange benga-berries.

'They can't resist them,' Brittel said, grinning. 'The berries are doused in anti-spark potion. My invention. Stops them making fire.'

They got up on the wagon; a wagon that had arrived with a party of demure schoolchildren and a teacher with black curly hair, pulled by two brown horses. Now *four* brown horses would draw it back home again.

Brittel took up the reins and flicked them. 'Off we go!' he called and he guided the wagon out of the field.

In the lane beyond, three glow-worm dots of light danced. It was Miss Minter, Violet and Hettie, waving phials of Brightling.

Brittel stopped for them and they climbed up onto the front seat.

'We missed it!' Hettie said, forlornly. 'The smoke came in and we missed the show.'

Glori sat her down beside her and put her arm around her. She exchanged a knowing look with Violet. 'Never mind. I'm sure we'll get to see them again.' Hettie didn't know what the match-girls had really been doing; Miss Minter said she was too young to keep their secrets.

'Tremendous!' Miss Minter said. 'Well done! Perfect. Perfect.' She laughed. 'And well done, Violet, for spotting Sparrow!'

Violet glanced over her shoulder at Glori and smiled smugly. Glori tensed. The others had seen Sparrow too!

'There's something on the floor back here,' Agnes said, nudging the canvas bag at her feet. 'What is it? Looks like legs . . .'

'That's our little friend,' Miss Minter said. 'That's Sparrow.'

'*Sparrow!*' Glori cried. Her heart sank like a lead weight. 'How? It *can't* be!'

'It is! Two spitfyres richer and Sparrow returned!' Miss Minter said. 'We had a very profitable night! And,' she added under her breath, 'those hateful Directors got what they deserve.'

30

A Visitor

Miss Knip stood on the pavement beside the orphanage cart and straightened her new black bonnet (made by the orphans to her specific design) and adjusted her shawl (knitted by the orphans in the finest lacy cashmere). She squeezed her shiny new krackodyle handbag against her chest. The handbag had been bought that day in Stollenback in anticipation of the reward she was going to get from the Butterworths.

'You will wait for me here, Barton,' she said to her driver. 'I may be some time.'

'Yes, ma'am.' Barton nodded to the horse. 'Me and Horace won't budge.'

Miss Knip stood at the gate for a moment regarding the neat little house in front of her and checking that the name and number matched the ones on her letter from Gerta. Very nice house, she thought, eyeing it up and down and trying to calculate its worth. Then she stepped lightly up the path and knocked on the door.

It was not Gerta Butterworth who opened it, but a large man with a knobbly head. He glared at her.

'Yes? What is it?' he said roughly.

Miss Knip took a few steps back. 'Mr Butterworth?' she ventured.

'I'm Otto Butterworth,' he said, smoothing long strands of hair over his bald patch. 'I expect you want my brother Bruno. Who are you?'

'I've come to see –'

But before she could get any further, Gerta squeezed past Otto. 'Excuse me, Otto. Sorry. I asked Miss Knip to come. You *are* Miss Knip?' she said. 'Do come in. I'm Gerta. This is Otto.'

Gerta took Miss Knip through to where her sister and brother-in-law were sitting in the parlour. Gerta seemed unsure, worried. There was an odd, tense atmosphere in the room. What was wrong? Miss Knip fretted.

Bruno stood up and shook her hand. 'Bruno,' he said.

'And this is my sister Hilda,' Gerta told her. 'Please have a seat.'

Miss Knip chose a hard, straight-backed chair and sat down, glancing at Hilda as she did so.

Miss Knip knew the signs of grief well, having caused them many times herself in the orphanage, and she could see that Hilda had been weeping.

'Miss Knip is from the Knip and Pynch Home, where Sparrow was. I asked her to come,' Gerta said, 'before . . . you know . . .'

Again Miss Knip felt a small doubt creep in. She watched Hilda dab at her nose with a damp, lace hanky and warned herself to tread carefully.

'That's right,' Miss Knip said, removing her bonnet gently. 'I know about the girl.'

'Do you know where she is?' Hilda shouted, leaping out of her seat.

Hilda gave Miss Knip such a fright that her bonnet flew up in the air and she only just managed to catch the precious thing. She laid it like an eggshell on a nearby stool, not taking her eyes off it while her brain laboured furiously, trying to work out what was going on.

Hilda was helped back to her seat, wobbling unsteadily and sobbing. 'Now, now, dear,' Bruno said. 'Hush.'

'Isn't Sparrow here?' Miss Knip said, composing herself and turning to Gerta. 'You said . . .' She paused. Surely, surely her plan wasn't going to backfire now? She stared at Gerta through narrowed eyes. 'You said she was here.'

'So *you* don't know where she is either!' Hilda cried with a little moan. 'Oh, my dear girl! Where can she be?'

Miss Knip looked to Gerta for help. 'Sparrow isn't here with you?'

'No, she . . .' Gerta stood up. 'We're all rather upset. She's gone missing; we think she was kidnapped. And we are trying to get her back, but please, in the meantime, I want my sister to know what you know about Sparrow.'

'Yes, do tell me – tell me everything,' Hilda said.

Miss Knip sniffed and fished about pointlessly in her new handbag, buying time. Her reward was looking doubtful now.

'Sparrow came to the Knip and Pynch Home ten and a half years ago,' she told them. 'I have the paperwork to prove it. She was brought to us by a woman called Nanny Porrit –'

Hilda's shrill screech stopped her in her tracks.

'*Nanny Porrit? Nanny Porrit?*' cried Hilda. 'Then we were right! She *is* the baby from Sampson's. Oh my dear girl, and she's slipped from our hands!'

'Correct,' Miss Knip said calmly. 'Sparrow came from the Sampson's nursery here in Stollenback. She'd been there since she was born . . .'

'Who was her mother?' Bruno said.

Otto suddenly took a heavy step towards Knip. 'Come on, woman! Her mother's name?'

Miss Knip recoiled. What a dangerous person, she thought – slightly insane, possibly violent. She squeezed herself back in her chair and tried to look calm. 'I had a visit from this nanny, this Miss Porrit,' she went on, not replying to Otto, 'and –'

'When? When?' Hilda cried.

Miss Knip hesitated. It wouldn't look too good if she told them it was weeks ago and she hadn't acted on the information received immediately. 'Just a few days back,' she said quickly. 'As soon as Nanny Porrit told me about Sparrow, well, of course, I planned to contact you – Butterworth being such a well-known name in Stollenback. Then when a letter came from you, Miss Gerta . . .'

'Do you have proof? Are you saying you have proof of her identity?' Bruno asked her. 'Because we have our suspicions . . .'

'That she is a liar?' Miss Knip jumped in eagerly. 'That she is a bad, wayward girl who needs to be treated firmly and whipped to keep her in order?' She added a little smile. 'It works, you know.'

'Absolutely not!' Otto and Bruno roared together.

'*Never!*' Hilda said.

'I thought she was bad too,' Gerta admitted, looking embarrassed. 'But she's a nice girl, really she is.'

Miss Knip looked at them in silent amazement. They were mad, all of them, she thought.

'We think she is our sister's child,' Bruno said, nodding to his brother.

'When I looked across the circus ring at Sparrow it was like looking at a young Mayra,' Otto said. 'The girl has her green eyes and perky little way of looking at things, and that hair . . . It was Mayra sitting there.'

'Which makes her our niece,' Hilda said.

'I am so glad,' Miss Knip said through gritted teeth. 'That's wonderful . . . So, you recognised her!' She patted her krackodyle handbag. 'I have the proof. Nanny Porrit gave it to me.'

Otto banged his ham fist down on a table, sending a silver pot leaping into the air.

'Show it to me now!' he roared. 'Now!'

'Really, there is no need to shout, Mr Butterworth,' Miss Knip said, trembling slightly. She pulled out the locket and dangled it on its chain, smiling slyly at them. 'Obviously I am expecting some remuneration before I . . .'

Otto grabbed it from her.

'Thank you!' Otto blasted her with such a glare she felt her skin was being roasted. He passed the locket to Hilda and they gathered behind her to look at what was inside it.

Hilda shook her head. 'Poor Mayra,' she said quietly, staring at the tiny portrait inside.

'That's definitely my sister,' Otto said. 'Even says so, right there – Mayra Butterworth.'

'Nanny Porrit told me the baby's mother had disappeared,' Miss Knip said. 'There was no money to feed it so Nanny Porrit brought it to us . . . I must say, I was expecting a warmer and more polite reception and . . .'

No one was listening to her. They were handing round the locket and examining the portrait again, studying it from every angle.

'Dear Mayra,' Bruno said. 'If only you'd come sooner, Miss Knip!'

Miss Knip sniffed. It was all Sparrow's fault, she thought, her fault for leaving, for ever coming, for having that cat – why, its meowing had put her off that evening and delayed her speaking to Porrit. She sat tensely and squinted at them, pursing her lips up tight and hating them greatly.

When they went on ignoring her, Miss Knip coughed loudly.

'What's the matter?' Otto asked her, giving her such a look that she was silenced again.

'Cosmo,' Bruno said suddenly. 'He must have been the father.'

Otto nodded. 'Cosmo was the circus owner,' Otto reminded Hilda, 'and she adored him.' He paused. 'I wish I'd known that my little sister had a baby. She never told us . . . She must have felt ashamed. She wouldn't leave that circus. I tried so hard to bring her back.'

'Did Cosmo abandon her?' Hilda asked.

Bruno shrugged. 'Who knows what went on between them?'

'After the accident, Cosmo went wild,' Otto reminded them. 'Crazy. He packed up the circus and vanished abroad. Did he know about Sparrow? We must find him and tell him!'

There was silence for a few moments and Miss Knip, who didn't care anything for their conversation, stared greedily at a silver pillbox on the sideboard. She was just about to reach for it and slip it into her pocket when Gerta whisked it away and handed it to her sister.

'There you are, dear,' she said to Hilda, at the same time throwing Miss Knip a dark look. 'Time for your pill.'

'I'm sorry to interrupt, but time is of the essence and I must be leaving soon,' Miss Knip said. 'Could you tell me – where is the wayward child now?'

'She disappeared at the circus last night,' Bruno said.

'Hah! She was always a sly little thing –' Miss Knip began.

'I won't hear a word said against her!' Hilda cried. 'She'd never do anything sly! She must have been kidnapped, that's the only possible explanation.'

'It's probably best if you leave now, Miss Knip,' Gerta said. 'It was very good of you to come and to bring the locket but as it turns out, we didn't need any proof. I have made a terrible mistake in not believing in her –'

'But if you hadn't, dear, and hadn't asked Miss Knip to come, we wouldn't have the hard evidence,' Hilda said kindly. 'So don't worry about it.'

'Yes, thank you for coming,' Bruno said, going towards the door eagerly.

'Perhaps *you* will show me out, Miss Gerta, if I can't be of any further help,' Miss Knip said, hugging her handbag to her bony chest, a handbag that was much lighter and emptier than she'd intended. 'I've taken a whole day getting here,' she said bitterly as she was shown into the hall. 'I've come right across the swamp. I'm not young you know; it was a vile and uncomfortable journey.'

'I made a mistake about Sparrow,' Gerta said. 'And I will pay for it if she never comes back . . . How much do I owe you?' She opened the front door.

'Well, I was thinking about a hundred –'

Gerta didn't appear to hear her. 'How will my dear sister ever forgive me?' She looked distracted. 'I'm sorry you had such a long journey. Here is five pounds.' She was already closing the door. 'Goodbye.'

31

Returned

Sparrow slowly became conscious. She remembered the circus, the beautiful spitfyres and the smoke. She remembered the strong smell of something coldly chemical and the feel of the heavy canvas bag over her head and the awful helpless feeling of having her legs knocked out from under her. She remembered feeling full of rage . . . Screaming and kicking.

Very slowly she opened her eyes. A headache was beginning to pound in her temples.

'*Scaramouch?*' Her fingers patted the top of the bed, searching, searching.

'Hello, Sparrow.' It was Glori, looking down at her as if from the other end of a long, long funnel.

Sparrow shut her eyes again. 'Where's Scaramouch? I was dreaming about him . . . Is that really you, Glori?' she asked, keeping her eyes shut. 'Are you . . .? Am I back in the nest?'

'Yeah, you're back. Are you OK, Birdie? It's just you and me here. You've been out cold. It's Sunday night and they've all gone to see some dancing. What d'you need? Can I help you? You're white as a blooming sheet.'

'What happened?' Sparrow opened her eyes again. She squinted at the light. 'What about Hilda?'

'Who's Hilda? Miss Minter gave you knock-out drops,' Glori said. 'I swear I didn't know they was going to do it. Told you Miss Minter didn't want you to leave!'

'But how did they know I'd be there?'

'Didn't,' Glori said. 'Luck or bad luck or something.' She grinned lopsidedly. 'Nice to have you back, Birdie. There's some hot pie here if –'

'*Scaramouch?*' Sparrow gasped, struggling up. 'Where *is* he?'

She turned back to Glori quickly, wincing as a wave of sickness rolled through her.

Glori shrugged. 'I don't know – Oh Sparrow, don't!' she cried as Sparrow tried to get out of bed. 'D'you have to?'

Sparrow collapsed back on her bed.

'Where's Scaramouch?' Sparrow cried, looking towards the big window. 'The missing pane's blocked up! How could he get back in?'

'It were really cold,' Glori said. 'That were it. Miss Minter said it were too cold. It's only a bit of card over the gap. And he could push it; I swear he could. I checked. One push and he'd be in. But no one's seen him, Birdie, no one at all. That's the truth.'

Sparrow looked out at rooftops that were white from a recent snow shower. The sky was a deep, steely grey behind them. She began to shiver.

217

Glori draped Sparrow's new coat over her. 'There, in't that nice?'

Sparrow stroked the coat. 'Hilda will be so worried.'

'Aren't you pleased to be back with us?' Glori asked her. 'I hope you're pleased to come back. I did miss you, Sparrow.'

'I was happy,' Sparrow said. 'The Butterworths were kind to me. They were like – they were like a proper family, Glori, and I was starting to feel –'

'Ah, but they weren't family, were they? Not *real* family,' Glori said brightly. 'We's your proper family, Sparrow. Think how we get on. We look out for each other, don't we?' She leaned over and patted Sparrow. 'There, there . . . oh, what's that?' Her fingers had touched against a soft lump in the coat pocket.

'Have a look,' Sparrow said.

Glori took out the spitfyre that Bruno had given her. 'Oh, that's lovely, that is. Such tiny stitches and pretty wings and everything; like a real one.'

Sparrow shook her head. 'It should be lovely,' she said, 'but this nasty bloke Tapper made it; him and his awful mother – well, no, they didn't make it – they get girls to make them for them. They're the ones who tried to lock me up and force me to sew – I told you about them. I bet lots of Knip and Pynch girls have got trapped in there. So there's no love in that toy, Glori.'

Glori pushed the spitfyre back into the coat pocket so she couldn't see it.

'Got proof?' she asked, avoiding Sparrow's eyes. 'I've heard Tapper's a good fellow, nice young man . . . Wouldn't

218

people have looked for those girls when they disappeared?'

'Once you leave the Home you're on your own,' Sparrow said. 'No help from anyone, *ever*.'

She leaned over and pulled her bag out from under her bed and took out her *Sampson's of Stollenback* shawl. She showed Glori the maker's name on it. 'That's why I came here in the first place,' she told Glori. 'That was all I had to link me to my past. I found out I wasn't a Sampson but I think I was in a nursery there. I want to know where I come from, where home is —'

'The nest is your home,' Glori interrupted. 'You're back home now.'

Sparrow sighed and turned to the window forlornly. 'Nowhere is home without Scaramouch,' she said.

32

Exit Miss Knip

Miss Knip prodded Barton's slumped form with the tip of her finger. 'Wake up, wake up!'

Barton shot upright with a grunt, quickly slipping his bottle of bark-beer into his pocket. 'Back already, Miss Knip?' he said cheerily. 'Have a good time?'

The horse, which hadn't drunk bark-beer and was cold and grumpy, tried to kick her.

'Oh control that old nag, can't you? No, I did not have a good time! Help me up, man! Give me a hand, can't you?'

Barton clambered down from the cart and helped Miss Knip onto the padded seat behind him. He arranged a blanket around her knees. 'Where now, miss?' he said, yawning broadly.

'The Home,' Miss Knip said, looking pointedly down the road in what she imagined was the direction of the orphanage. 'Knip and Pynch.'

'What? All the way back across that blooming swamp

tonight?' Barton said, glancing at the sky. 'It's freezing, Miss Knip, and if it snows –'

'Do as I say.'

Barton shrugged and got up into his seat. He took up the reins in his cold hands and headed out of town. They made slow progress. Night was falling. The road was already icy and the horse lost his footing a couple of times and his hooves slithered noisily over the cobbles.

Leaving the town behind, the darkness of the countryside slipped around them like a black velvet cloak. Barton lit the two lanterns on the front of the cart.

'We could try and find somewhere to sleep,' he called out. 'There's a tavern off on the –'

'No,' Miss Knip called back. '*Home!*'

She was so bitterly disappointed that all she wanted to do was get back to her orphanage and be mean to someone. She'd pick on scrawny Fiona Feathers with the unblinking eyes. She was hard to break, hard to make cry, but she could do it. Oh yes, indeed she could, and would. Miss Knip's own father had done it to her, little Nora Knip, night after night; locking her in the darkness and cold of the cellar, where the rats nibbled her ankles and tugged her hair until she begged to be let out. So she would do it to Fiona Feathers. There's no point in resisting, Fiona, she thought; no point in trying to fight back because there's always someone stronger and harder who will push you under. If only it were Sparrow she could lock in the cellar, and Sparrow's desperate cries she'd listen to – but that had always been the problem: Sparrow never did utter so much as a squeak and never begged to come out.

Miss Knip was so deep in thought she did not notice the cold of the black night. She did not see the glory of the stars as they sprinkled the sky with sharp pinpricks of silver. She missed the moon's wonderful white light, bathing everything about them, and the sound of the horse's hooves clip-clopping along the road. She didn't hear how, as they crossed the lowlands, all sounds grew softer, cushioned by the marshy path through the swamps. Nor did she see how Barton's head sagged onto his chest, or how his eyes closed and he slept.

Horace the horse walked on, dreaming of his warm stable at home.

Gerta was to blame for this bad day, Miss Knip told herself. In her imagination she began to skewer long pins into a small figure of Gerta. In the background she could hear Fiona Feathers begging for mercy. They'd pay; they'd all pay. She clutched her handbag with her measly five pounds in it and wished that everyone she knew were stone dead.

She did not see or hear the krackodyles slithering around the cart in the reeds. They were listening, watching and sniffing the air. Something on the cart bothered the krackodyles; it was something to do with the narrow-bonneted person at the back of the cart. *Sniff. Sniff.* There was something there and it shouldn't have been there and they didn't like it. It was wrong and it upset them . . .

A large krackodyle began to follow alongside the rolling cart; his red eyes gleamed, his jaw opened and closed in anticipation. Two more krackodyles followed, then three and four, leaping and sliding and running through the muddy swamp to keep up, as Horace, seeing them all around, stepped up and went faster.

Suddenly one krackodyle jumped, snapping its jaws like a nutcracker. Miss Knip was jolted from her dreams by the sound. '*Barton?*' she called.

The horse shied, neighed shrilly and lurched forward at a sudden gallop.

Miss Knip's handbag, made of finest krackodyle skin, flew up in an arc and sailed out of the wagon.

Miss Knip screamed and lunged for her bag.

Just at that moment, a krackodyle snapped near Horace's ankles and the horse twisted violently. Miss Knip was thrown the other way and tossed over the side of the cart like a rag doll.

She hit the swampy mud with a wet splat and lay there dazed, staring up at the stars.

She didn't see her handbag slowly slip under the black water, back where it belonged, amongst its brothers and sisters.

The krackodyles inched around Miss Knip. They were sniffing and snorting, creeping closer and closer, red eyes gleaming and white teeth bared: *snap, snap!*

Barton woke with a start.

'Whoa, whoa!' he called. He gathered up the reins and brought the horse back to a gentle trot. 'There, there,' he murmured. 'Don't take on so, Horace. Calm down, them krackodyles won't hurt you. All right back there, ma'am?'

he called to Miss Knip.

Not hearing anything, he assumed she was asleep and, pulling up his collar against the cold, settled Horace into a steady walk. His head soon drooped and he was dreaming again. He didn't wake until he reached the Knip and Pynch gatehouse, very much later that night.

33

Lying

'Darling little Sparrow!' Miss Minter cried, coming across the attic with her arms outstretched. 'You angel. You're awake! Are you feeling better?' She took Glori's place on the narrow bed. 'How lovely to have you back!'

Violet had come in behind her. They were close now, those two, Glori thought with a smile. She'd have minded a month ago, now she didn't.

'We have been so worried about you, haven't we, Glori?' Miss Minter said.

Glori rubbed her aching jaw thoughtfully. 'Yes,' she said quietly. 'I have been.'

Miss Minter was lying. She didn't care about Sparrow at all. She always lied about everything, pretending to like Sparrow when all she was doing was hoping to make money out of her . . . it made Glori weak to think about it. *You make money from our hard work. You squeeze it out of us, so stop pretending!* was what she wanted to say.

'We have all missed you, angel,' Miss Minter said to Sparrow. 'Dear little Hettie will be so pleased to see you. So thrilled. Oh angel, you're looking sad. What's the matter?' She looked around the attic room as if trying to guess what the problem was. 'It's that cat, isn't it?' she said. 'It's because that old pussycat has gone.'

'How? When?' Sparrow asked her. 'Did he go straight away or was he around for a few days after I left?'

Miss Minter smoothed her hair. 'I can't remember, angel,' she said.

Glori noticed a little muscle twitching beside Miss Minter's beautiful, pink mouth; she was lying. Again. Then she glanced at Sparrow's face and it was the saddest face she'd ever seen. Please be happy, Glori urged her silently. A happy Sparrow would want to stay with them.

Miss Minter brightened suddenly. 'But, darling Sparrow,' she said, 'now you've returned safely, your lovely big cat will come back too, won't he? Why don't we put some milk out for him on the roof where he liked to sit? Then he'll come home, won't he?'

'I suppose we could try some milk,' Sparrow said, doubtfully.

'And some nosh,' Glori said. 'Something Scare-a-mouse really likes, hey? What d'you think? Sardines?'

'Well, of course we could try that – or rather, *you* could.' Miss Minter stood up and smoothed her skirt. 'Were we a little rough with you when we brought you home, Sparrow? But it was the only thing to do! We could have left you – no, we couldn't leave you! Silly girl. We *had* to kidnap you. We were in a hurry. It was essential that nothing hampered our plans . . . Speed up! Faster, faster!' she stopped suddenly, as if realising her thoughts were running away with her, and managed, with an effort, to readjust her expression. 'It was a surprise to see you there at the circus, angel. Like magic. Fate. Agnes spotted you, I think. I'm not sure . . .' Miss Minter began to walk away. 'I'm not sure if . . . Were they nice, those people, the old, odd-looking people you were with?' She kept her back to Sparrow.

'Yes,' Sparrow said. 'They were very nice. I think they liked me – I reminded them of someone . . .'

'You mean they only liked you because you were like some other girl?' Glori said.

'No . . .'

'But they weren't like us,' Glori said, 'were they?'

'Not *family*,' Miss Minter said. 'We are your family. Aren't we, Glori?'

'Yes, miss. I told her that too,' said Glori.

'They were kind and –'

'Dull,' Miss Minter finished for her. 'Kind and dull.' She yawned. 'You'll have much more fun here. We have fun, don't we, Glori? It's an adventure, living in the nest. Hiding from the guards. Selling under their very noses . . . Set the table, will you Sparrow? The others will be up for supper soon. The dancing was such fun! Make a pot of tea, Glori. Violet, go down and get a bucket of coal. Hurry, hurry!'

'I don't mind going,' Glori said. 'Violet always gets it.'

'No.' Miss Minter's voice was sharp. 'Violet will get the coal.'

'Yes, Miss Minter,' Glori said. She winked at Sparrow

as Miss Minter went back to her place on the pink chaise longue by the fire. '*She's* never dull, is she?'

'She's a bit mad if you ask me,' Sparrow whispered. 'What am I going to do now?' she added.

Glori took her hand. 'What d'you mean?' she said softly. 'You're going to stay with us, aren't you? You're our mate. You're our little Birdie and we want you to stay here in this cosy, warm nest what we've made.'

Sparrow tried to smile. 'I know,' she said. 'But . . . the Butterworths will be so worried. Somehow I should let them know I'm safe. And Scaramouch . . . You see, Glori, I pictured him here, warm and cosy and well-fed . . . Now I'm here and he's not . . . I never imagined that, not ever. Now I know something's really wrong! I have to find him. You don't think Miss Minter knows anything, do you?'

'Course she don't know nothing,' Glori said cheerily. 'Nah. You stay and give that old window a stare. Look hard enough and your cat might just feel you willing him home.' She could not look Sparrow in the eyes. 'I'll do the table. Oh my, Hettie will be so chuffed to see you!'

'It's Sparrow! It's Sparrow!' Hettie cried, rushing into the room. 'She's come back. I knew you'd come back, Birdie, I knew it.'

'I never meant to leave,' Sparrow said, laughing and hugging her. 'It was an accident.'

The other match-girls followed Hettie in and most of them were pleased to see her, Sparrow thought. That made her feel better.

'We thought you'd gone for good,' Violet said, sitting down and taking a slice of bread from a plate on the table. She glanced at Miss Minter then back to Sparrow. 'Now we shall have less to eat again,' she added.

'That day, at the market – you just vanished,' Agnes said.

'Glori looked and looked for you,' Billie said.

'What *did* happen?' Kate asked her.

'Hey, it's nice to be missed!' Sparrow tried to sound light-hearted but inside she felt heavy and sad. Poor Hilda, poor Hilda, she kept thinking. She glanced at Miss Minter, who was reading her newspaper but listening too, Sparrow could tell. She went on brightly, 'What happened was, some great big fat belly got in my way and I banged into it. *Kerplong!*' She bounced up in the air. 'And I came off it like it was a trampoline and went *whack* into a pillar.'

'Ow!' Hettie said, rubbing her own head.

'Exactly. Then the big fat belly, which belonged to a really nice man called Bruno Butterworth, took me home. Oh what a place, girls! It was so grand! And Bruno and his wife Hilda were so kind to me! Fed me chocolates and cakes and as much pop-apple juice as I wanted. Their own children had died,' she added more quietly. 'Two girls.'

'Weren't they glad?' Violet asked. 'Glad to be rid of them little girls and have everything to themselves?'

'Oh no,' Sparrow said. 'They were sad as anything. They'd loved them.'

'I got the pneumonia once,' Violet said. 'Nearly finished me off. My ma said she wished it had. Just one less mouth to feed, and she'd've got by. So she said. Nine of us, there was.'

'She were just joking you,' Connie said.

'She weren't, you know,' Violet said.

'The Butterworths weren't poor,' Sparrow said.

'What luck! Is that why you've such a lovely new coat and fancy boots and stuff?' squealed Agnes. 'Oh, you should have stayed with them, Sparrow!'

The room fell silent.

'Whoops,' Beattie said, looking round nervously.

All the girls stared at Miss Minter; her profile gave nothing away. She went on reading.

'But Sparrow couldn't do that,' Hettie's small voice rang out clearly. ''Cos Miss Minter stole her back.'

'Pass me some jam,' Miss Minter said sharply. 'And Hettie, go and wash your hands, they're filthy. Agnes, you need to tie back your hair. Beattie, *your* hair needs combing – what a frizz! Billie, go and make your bed, it's a disgrace.'

The girls sped off to do her bidding.

'Now, let's eat quietly. Like the nice young ladies we are,' Miss Minter said, as one by one the girls came back and took their places for supper. 'Are we young ladies with good manners?'

'Yes, Miss Minter!' the match-girls chimed.

34

Exploring

The following day Tapper arrived. He threw himself into the attic noisily; slamming the door so hard plaster dropped from the ceiling, mice scattered and spiders shivered in their webs.

'Any food left?' he called out to no one in particular as he tossed his hat onto a peg. He cheered when after a wobble it stayed put. 'Hello, girls! It's blooming cold out. I'm famished. What d'ya say, Glori?'

Glori felt her skin shrink.

'Hello, Tapper,' she said quietly. She glanced at Sparrow and back to Tapper; feeling caught between them. She saw Sparrow shiver and go pale.

Miss Minter was sitting at the big table with some of the match-girls, reading them an account of the theft of the spitfyres from the circus.

'. . . *A daring and outrageous gang of thieves have made off with the two finest spitfyres from the Academy in a spectacular robbery that has the whole of Stollenback up in arms,'* she read. *'The Brightling Robbers have struck again!'*

'Listen to that,' Tapper said. 'Those naughty robbers, eh?' He grinned. 'Outrageous, in't it?'

Miss Minter beckoned him over to the table. 'Come and sit down. We've got some talking to do.'

One by one the girls peeled away from the table, taking their plates and cups to the sink. 'Just finished.' 'Got to go.' 'Must get back to work,' they muttered until only Sparrow and Glori were left. Miss Minter had placed a hand on Sparrow to hold her back.

'You're looking a picture, Glori,' Tapper said. 'Get us a hot drink, will you? Chocolate would be good.'

'Then you can go, Gloriana,' Miss Minter said.

After handing Tapper his drink Glori went out of the room. What were they going to talk about? What were they going to do with Sparrow?

She didn't join the other girls in the match room; she waited by the door, trying to hear what they were saying. Something was going on and she needed to know what it was. There was a place on the stairs – an empty cupboard – she'd hide there and then, if they went out, she'd follow.

'Stay,' Miss Minter had said and Sparrow sank down again on her chair and looked at her plate. 'You know each other, I understand,' Miss Minter added.

'Ah yes, little Sparrow!' Tapper said, flopping his legs up on a chair and reaching for the slab of cheese. 'Remember me, eh, do you?' He poured coffee from the pot on the table

232

into his hot chocolate and stirred in two spoons of sugar. He felt at ease in the nest and didn't mind letting Miss Minter know it.

'Yes,' Sparrow said without looking at him. 'I remember you.' She sat on her trembling hands.

'Not scared of me, are you?' he asked with a laugh. 'You should be, mind! You and your cat made a right mess of my roof,' Tapper went on, leaning back in his seat and chewing loudly. 'What d'you mean by running off like that? You won't get out of here so quick, I can tell you.'

'Be quiet, Tapper,' Miss Minter said without taking her eyes from Sparrow.

Tapper sat up sharply. 'What's that, Miss Minter? *Quiet?* Certainly. Just teasing dear little Sparrow, that's all. Perhaps it's them knock-out drops making her so quiet, is it?' he went on. 'I did give you a lot, so. Had to. Knew you'd kick and, sure enough, you was rougher than a bear with a bee-sting. Glad to be back, are you? Back with the girls?'

Sparrow looked from Tapper to Miss Minter and back again. She shuddered.

'Of course she's happy to be here, Tapper. But she's missing the cat,' Miss Minter said. 'We don't know where it is . . .' There was a pause. Then Miss Minter sighed. 'Well, Sparrow, perhaps you'd better go and join the others downstairs, if you have no conversation,' she said at last. 'Box making for you today.'

'Yes, Miss Minter.' Sparrow got up quickly and ran from the room.

Tapper shifted closer to Miss Minter. 'So?' he said. 'We've got her back safe and sound. Glad, aren't you?'

'Yes, Tapper, I am very pleased with the turn of events,' Miss Minter said without looking at him. 'Now we have our product, we can go back to de Whitt.'

'And my Glori'll never let her go missing a second time,' Tapper said. 'She's learned her lesson.'

'And I have my trump card,' Miss Minter said slyly. 'If Sparrow tries anything, says she wants to leave, I'll tell her about Scaramouch . . . Threaten to kill him.'

'Oh I see, so! That cat! Well done, Miss Minter!' Tapper said. 'Always one step ahead, in't you? Sparrow's none the wiser, eh? Hasn't twigged anything?'

'Sparrow is stupid. She loves her cat. The cat will be her downfall. Mine was my father. But I've risen from the ashes, Tapper, I rose up like the phoenix and, like the phoenix, I shine with fire!'

'You do, it's true,' Tapper said, looking at her admiringly. 'You're all golden today. Don't you go taking too much of that Brightling stuff, will ya? It's no good for you, it ain't.'

Miss Minter laughed. 'You don't know anything. It's marvellous stuff, Tapper. You should try it. Give some to that cranky old mother of yours. Make her dance.' She stopped suddenly. '*Everyone* should take it. Brightling makes the world a better place.'

Tapper eyed her doubtfully. 'How's them new beasts doing?' he asked, changing the subject.

'They're settling in,' Miss Minter said. Her face lit up with a smile and she hugged herself, closed her eyes and laughed. 'Seraphina!' she said with a little giggle. '*Seraphina!* The Director's very own special spitfyre! I have got her!'

234

'You have,' Tapper agreed, watching Miss Minter with vague unease. 'What's so special about her then? I expect he'll be a bit upset, will that Stormy bloke,' he went on. 'I would, losing a pet like that, if I had one, like. So.'

'He will be broken-hearted!' Miss Minter cried. 'Devastated! Cast down into the depths of despair . . . I hope!' She laughed. 'I do so hope! I have waited years to pay him back, Tapper; you have no idea how I've longed to hurt him.' She dug her fingernails into her own palm. 'Now at last he is suffering as I have suffered. He is in pain just as I was in pain.'

'What the blazing dragon did he ever do to you?' Tapper asked.

Miss Minter's eyes flashed. 'He ruined my life,' she said. 'He totally RUINED MY LIFE!'

Sparrow got as far as the match room and stopped, with her fingers on the handle. She could hear the girls' voices on the other side of the door. The bitter smell of phosphorus stung her nose. She glanced back up the stairs; it was as if she could feel the cold weight of Tapper's presence on the floor above, pressing down on her. The acrid phosphorus smell made her eyes water. She wanted to get out. She just wanted to get out and to find Scaramouch. To see Hilda and Bruno . . . What if the front door had been left unlocked? Perhaps there was an open window? Suddenly she spun round and bounded all the way down to the ground floor.

She pulled at the front door, twisting the big brass handle furiously.

It was locked.

Sparrow looked round the hall. There was no sunshine streaming in through the windows today, as there had been that day she'd set out to sell matches, and the hall was gloomy and dark and forbidding. She turned slowly and went back upstairs. How difficult would it be to find Butterworth's toyshop? she wondered. If she could just get there and explain to Hilda and Bruno . . . they'd be so worried about her . . . Oh where was Scaramouch?

A sudden sharp noise below made her stop in her tracks.

Someone was unlocking the front door.

There was the rattle of keys, the door opened, closed, and was carefully locked again. Footsteps crossed the black and white marble floor; a man's footsteps, she could tell. Who? Not Tapper.

She peered over the banisters. A very thin man with sparse, long dark hair and a bald patch was crossing the hall. He had a brown bag slung across his sloping, bottle-shaped shoulder and he carried a couple of large, glass containers. Without hesitating, he set off down one of the corridors.

It was Brittel; the man they'd passed in the ginnel. What was he doing?

Sparrow ran quickly and lightly down the stairs, her heart thundering. There was no sign of Brittel when she reached the corridor, so she made her way cautiously along the dark, narrow passageway, fearing he might return any moment.

Another door opening and shutting told her he was coming back.

There was a room beside her so she slipped inside. It was an empty classroom with dusty, wooden desks and a map of the mountains on the wall. She was there only a few moments before Brittel passed by, whistling. Seconds later the front door shut with a deep, loud clang. The key turned noisily.

Quickly Sparrow darted out of her hiding place and ran down the corridor. The door at the end wasn't locked and she pushed it open.

Here was a vast, secret, inner courtyard, surrounded by very tall, narrow trees. For a second she stood there, poised as if on the edge of two totally different worlds. She looked around, dazed and surprised, breathing in the cold, fresh air greedily. Was this a way out?

The trees were so dense that she could only just make out the tall buildings behind them; they were almost completely hidden, rising up high into the sky on all sides. She took a few steps further in, determined to investigate. The snow had barely reached this hidden place and only a thin layer lay over the centre of the yard.

Something moved.

She stopped.

On the far side, partly hidden from view, were stables – stables with *horses* in them. She remembered Brittel had mentioned nags . . .

Sparrow went quickly towards them, weaving her way through the old wheelbarrows, boxes, crates, straw and broken furniture that littered the yard. Four horses' heads showed over the stable doors.

The hairs on the back of her neck began to prickle. Her mouth went dry.

'Oh dear,' she whispered as she drew near. 'Oh dear.'

The first horse was a huge, dirty-brown thing with strange, scaly skin around its nose and eyes. It had a short, chopped-about mane. Its head drooped so it was resting on the stable door as if the horse were too weary to hold it up. It was so impassive it didn't even seem to notice her. The next was the same; tired and listless, dirty and unresponsive, but she rubbed its forehead and at last it raised its head and looked at her. What strange eyes it had . . . The third and the fourth horses were more alert. They tossed their heads and greeted her with puffs of smoke . . .

Smoke!

'You aren't horses!' Sparrow said, and jumped at the sound of her own voice. 'Oh my, you're spitfyres!' she whispered. She stroked the smallest spitfyre and her hand came away brown. 'Disguised!'

The spitfyre stared back dolefully. Sparrow rubbed its velvety nose and stroked the scaly, furry forehead. 'Poor thing,' she said. 'Poor thing.'

A bright fluid began to gather around the spitfyre's eyeball and collect in the corner like a drop of liquid gold.

'Are you crying? Please don't cry! Don't be sad,' Sparrow said, nearly crying herself. 'What's happening? Where are your wings?' She peered over the stable door. 'Where are your lovely wings?'

The spitfyre rubbed against Sparrow's shoulder in a hopeful way, leaving a fleck of gold on her coat.

Spitfyres.

The circus.

Miss Minter.

Brightling robbers.

'Now I see!' Sparrow glanced around nervously; there was no sign of that nasty thin man. She pushed open the stable door and squeezed in beside the fourth spitfyre, the smallest and most chirpy. She wasn't afraid; the animal was not much bigger than an ordinary horse and, anyway, it was tied up. Besides, it never occurred to her to be scared.

It was gloomy and hard to see inside the stable. Sparrow felt along the animal's flanks and at last her nervous fingers found the bindings that held down its wings.

'Oh you dear, poor thing,' she whispered. 'You can't even open them out!' And all for a golden liquid that didn't work, she thought, caressing its lovely neck and trying to untangle its mane. Stupid. Greedy. Horrible.

Whistling!

Brittel was coming back!

Sparrow dived into the back of the stable and crouched there, in a mess of hay and animal feed and buckets. If the spitfyre kicked out she'd be dead. If Brittel found her she'd be dead. And if neither of those things happened, she thought, holding her nose, the smell of spitfyre pee would almost certainly kill her.

The spitfyres had begun to shuffle and shift nervously and to utter soft whinnies and guttural sounds in their throats like growls. Heat poured off the spitfyre's flanks and Sparrow expected at any moment that flames would burst out; but there were no flames, not even sparks.

Something metal clanked against the cobbles. Glass chinked against glass. The man came near then stopped by the stable; Sparrow could just see his silhouette in the doorframe.

'By the dragon!' he swore, bolting shut the stable door with a clang. 'Brittel, you fool! You left it open! Thank the stars I tied you up, Seraphina, or you'd have been off . . .'

Seraphina? Seraphina! She *had* been so beautiful. Rainbow-coloured, glimmering and full of life . . .

'Now, my beauties,' Brittel was saying as he busied himself just outside the doorway. 'It's time.'

Seraphina began to jerk her head against the rope and kick.

'Gently, Seraphina,' he said. 'Brittel won't hurt you. I'm not a clumsy oaf like that Tapper. I do things soft and gentle.'

Brittel fixed another rope to her head so that the spitfyre could barely move. Glass clinked again and the stable door opened. Brittel came inside and took hold of the spitfyre tightly. 'There we go. Just a few drops.'

Seraphina let out an awful whinny and Sparrow had to clamp a hand over her mouth quickly to stop a cry from escaping.

'Hush there. I know about spitfyres. What? You don't believe me?' Brittel said, stroking Seraphina's neck. 'And why not, when I worked years in the Academy kitchens, making your food, eh?' He unravelled a very fine tube from a roll of cloth and fitted it to a small bottle. 'I know about spitfyres. I know *all* about spitfyres, even if the bosses never let me near them at the Academy. Not once did I get invited up to the Academy proper. Not even for a cup of tea. There. Now, keep still. It won't take a minute, you know, and it doesn't hurt.'

Sparrow's heart began to thump and thump, the hammering seemed to fill her head and pound around her temples. She felt sick and useless. She leaned out from her hiding place and saw how Brittel held the tube up to the spitfyre's glistening eye. He placed the end in the tiny pool of liquid and captured the golden tears; tears of liquid sunshine.

Brightling.

35

Cedric de Whitt

Through a crack in the half-open cupboard door, Glori had seen Sparrow leaping down the stairs. It was hard to let her go by like that, but Glori knew if she followed her she'd miss her chance to track the others. Not long after Sparrow, Tapper and Miss Minter set out together.

Glori slipped out of her hiding place and followed them out of the front door. To her surprise, Tapper and Miss Minter turned away from the centre of Stollenback and headed for the river and the poorer part of town.

It was icy cold and Tapper hunched himself up inside his thick coat and dug his hands into his coat pockets. Miss Minter wore a big fur coat and hat, and pink, sequined gloves. The cold was keeping most people off the streets, though they did pass several groups of uniformed guards.

Miss Minter and Tapper were too confident, Glori thought. They never once looked back. If they had, they'd have seen her little figure wrapped in a long cloak, darting along in their wake, nipping in and out of gardens and crouching behind walls.

Tapper tried taking Miss Minter's arm but she shook him off.

'I don't like going out in the daylight,' Miss Minter said as they passed some guards. 'I like staying inside. I like my nest.' She looked around nervously. 'I used to enjoy going out. Before. But not now. Perhaps I will not go?' She stopped suddenly.

'Come on, Miss Minter,' Tapper urged her. 'De Whitt would rather we meet in the night too,' he said. 'I understand, Miss Minter, I do.' He kicked aside a mound of snow in his path. 'This de Whitt's a busy man. He sails soon, off to some sunny clime, lucky dog. This was the only time he could see us. That's what he said. Oh to go to the sunshine, eh? Tropical beaches, sand and turquoise seas and –'

'People look at me in the light,' Miss Minter said, pulling her hat lower over her forehead. 'And I do not like being hurried.' She put on sunglasses. 'I do not like being told what to do. I hate being . . .' She stopped suddenly. 'Look at that!'

GENEROUS **REWARD** FOR MISSING GIRL
KIDNAPPED FROM ZIPPO'S CIRCUS.
A SMALL, DEAR GIRL WITH GREEN EYES
AND DARK BLONDE HAIR
NAMED '*SPARROW*'
IF ANYONE HAS ANY KNOWLEDGE OF
HER WHEREABOUTS WILL THEY PLEASE
GET IN TOUCH WITH HER UNCLE, BRUNO
BUTTERWORTH

Then the poster gave the Butterworths' address. Tapper chuckled. 'They want her back bad, don't they?' he said. 'And look, *"uncle"*. Well, if de Whitt won't pay for her, we can go back to our first plan and give her to them, them *Butterfingers*!' he laughed. 'See, Miss Minter, *Butterfingers* – 'cos they had her first and lost her. How big's a "generous" reward d'you reckon?'

Miss Minter was not smiling. 'But how do they *know* she's their niece, Tapper?' she said in a strangled voice. 'How, when it was our secret?'

Tapper rubbed his head. 'I never said to no one . . . there were only Miss Knip could've known.'

'Then *she* told them,' Miss Minter said, fisting up her hands. 'She went to them for money. I'm sure of it.' She laughed suddenly. 'But by then Sparrow had flown. Sparrow is ours! Still, I wish they didn't know.'

'What difference if they do?' Tapper asked.

'Because now they *care*,' Miss Minter said. 'And because they care, they're looking for her. Before, no one was looking. Safer, that's all.'

Tapper nodded. 'I see. I understand,' he said, wondering if he did.

The Hotel Belvedere, where they were meeting de Whitt, was a bad choice, Tapper thought. It was dilapidated and ancient; a big wooden building, creaky and slipping slowly into the river behind it. Inside, every room was damp and the wallpaper was mouldy and peeling off the walls. It smelled of mud. He didn't like it.

They sat down by the fire in the panelled hotel parlour, rubbing their hands in front of the flames.

The two men who had been sitting near them in the cosy warmth of the fire, got up and moved to another seat in the corner, glancing at Tapper nervously.

Tapper was not usually bothered by his negative magnet effect; but this time he looked round nervously. Things felt wrong here. It was this old hotel, he thought. Spooky. Haunted. He felt as if someone were shadowing him. He looked all around the parlour, checking the faces of the men in case he recognised any, but he didn't. There was a picture on the wall with a gent in it who stared at him, but that didn't account for this bad feeling he had. He glanced over his shoulder, the coats hanging on the wall moved, as if filled with invisible bodies. Then the door blew shut with a bang and he jumped. Perhaps it had been the wind in the clothes? He shivered again and hunched miserably into his heavy coat.

'Funny old place,' he said.

'My fingers are so cold,' Miss Minter complained, taking her gloves and hat off. 'I'm hot and cold. I'm up and down. You should have made him come to *me*, Tapper. I do not like being ordered to do things. Go and get me a hot pop-apple wine, a very large one. Why couldn't he come to me?'

He scowled at the bargirl and she backed away. This feeling of being watched vexed him. He didn't like it, not when he was doing secret business. Or was it just because he was up to secret business that he felt this way? He sat down again as soon as he had their drinks, hunching his shoulders.

'Cheers!' He took a long swig of his bark-beer but even

245

that didn't help. He shivered. 'What did we have to pick this dump for?' he said.

A large, smartly dressed man with a fine, white moustache walked over to their table and, bending down, addressed them quietly.

'Minter. There you are,' he said.

'*Miss* Minter,' Miss Minter said sharply. 'I will not do business with rude and ignorant people; let me say that immediately. Not even if they are likely to make me a fortune. Manners. Manners, please.'

'Hush, hush,' the man said, glancing round anxiously. 'There are ears everywhere. Good to see you again.' His skin was dark and had the texture of leather, as if it had been beaten and sundried. His hands were large and the nails perfectly manicured. He shook hands with Miss Minter and then Tapper, after which he wiped his palm down his trouser seat and sat down. 'I'll have a small bark-beer, young man.'

Tapper glowered but went to buy him the drink, his eyes darting left and right as he went.

'So, we meet again,' de Whitt said to Miss Minter. Then, glancing at Tapper's retreating back, he went on, 'I don't like that young fellow, I told you. There's something quite wrong about him. Did you have to bring him?'

Miss Minter smiled. 'He's all right,' she said. 'He does what I tell him to do.'

De Whitt shrugged. 'As you will.'

Tapper returned and handed de Whitt his drink.

'So, you have found the girl again?' de Whitt said.

'We've got her, all right,' Tapper said with a chuckle.

246

'And she's safe.'

'*Safe?* That is imperative. She must be held under lock and key, with no chance of escape,' de Whitt said.

'She is watched over by my girls,' Miss Minter said. 'There is no way she can get out.'

De Whitt breathed out deeply. 'Good –'

'Yes, well,' Tapper interrupted, wanting to get on and get home, away from this being-spied-on feeling. 'What's the plan then?'

De Whitt looked serious. He leaned over the table and lowered his voice again. 'You must keep the girl until I leave Stollenback,' de Whitt said.

'And when will that be?' Tapper jumped in.

De Whitt gritted his teeth and addressed Miss Minter. 'It will depend on the captain of the ship and the tides. I believe Thursday night. I suggest you tell her that she is going to be reunited with the Butterworth family, since they seem to be so keen to have her back, then she won't be suspicious.'

'Cracking!' Tapper said. 'You could keep her here a while. Get to know each other first.'

De Whitt ignored him. 'The moment the captain says we sail, I will send a lad to you with the message. Then you must bring her. There will not be much time.'

'Oh yes, and then what?' Tapper said. 'Is the deck slippery?' he asked with a chuckle, leaning back in his chair. 'If it was *slippery*, and the sea was rough, she might fall overboard, so?'

De Whitt smiled and fingered the tips of his moustache,

rolling them into points. 'There is always the possibility of an accident at sea. Such a dangerous place, a sailing ship . . . You do not have to concern yourself with that. I will see that she never returns. Once she is out of the way . . .' He paused and smiled. 'Cosmo's will leaves everything to this girl, Sparrow, his natural daughter. With no Sparrow, the fortune comes to me, his cousin and only remaining kin . . .'

'*And* to the person who has facilitated the operation,' Miss Minter said softly. 'That, de Whitt, is me.'

'And me!' Tapper added.

'Tapper, leave this part of the business to me,' Miss Minter said sharply. 'Mr de Whitt, we have gone to great lengths to get this girl for you and we have kept her safe. The cost has been extortionate. Without us you would have nothing, and now you will be very rich . . .'

De Whitt looked down at the table and spoke in a low voice. The bargaining began.

Tapper sat and shivered and wondered what sort of dreadful, mournful ghosts lived in the Belvedere and what he'd done to make them haunt him so.

36

Seraphina

The trickling sound of liquid draining into the glass jar went on for several seconds while a glow, like dawn breaking, spread out around Seraphina's head.

'You won't last long, Seraphina,' Brittel said. 'You're too highly strung. Stormy's pet, eh? You'll pine away quite quick, you will. Those two old boys back there; they're nearly finished – drained dry of their tears, they are. They lasted well. Kopernicus will carry on a bit longer, she's strong, but Miss Minter'll have to be thinking about another source of Brightling soon, that's the truth.'

He finished what he was doing and Sparrow heard him pottering around, perhaps taking tears from the other spitfyres and tidying things. Then he was calling out, 'See you all tomorrow!' as he crossed the yard. As soon as she heard the house door close, Sparrow jumped up and squeezed round to the front of the stable.

'What did he do to you, Seraphina? Are you all right?'

She ran her hand gently over the spitfyre's beautiful neck and peered into her large eyes. They were dry; all their golden lustre had vanished. 'They're taking your magic tears,' Sparrow whispered. 'They're stealing Brightling from you. You poor, dear thing.'

The spitfyre rubbed her nose against Sparrow's shoulder. Sparrow stroked her dirty coat and stared into her dark, sad eyes. 'I will stop this. I promise I will . . . somehow!' She laid her forehead against the spitfyre's neck. 'Can't you burn him or kick down the door or something?' she whispered. 'Isn't there anything you can do to fight back?'

Desperate to do something helpful, Sparrow found a bucket full of water and a cloth and, standing on another, upturned bucket, began to wash some of the brown colour away from around Seraphina's nose and mouth. She tried to comb out her mane. She did not know that Stormy had done these same kindnesses for this same spitfyre, years ago when he'd found her, filthy and neglected in a cave. But the spitfyre remembered, and she trembled at the gentle touch. Something inside her, a yearning for home and her master, grew stronger and stronger.

The spitfyre's fine purple, pink and blue coat gleamed out from under the brown. 'I daren't do more,' Sparrow told her. 'Brittel will notice. He'll know someone's been. But is that a little better?'

She thought suddenly, painfully, of Scaramouch. If Miss Minter could do this to the spitfyres – then what might she do to a cat? 'I'll save you somehow. All of you,' Sparrow said to the spitfyres. 'And I'll find Scaramouch too. Somehow,

somehow! Try not to weep, try not to make any tears for Brittel. Be brave!'

She slipped out of the stable and bolted the door carefully behind her. She checked to see that she hadn't left any signs of being there and went out through the same door she'd come through, back up the stairs and all the way up the dark staircase to the match room.

Her mind was racing, but by the time she got there she had composed herself and opened the door, smiling.

'Here she is!' Dolly cried.

'You've been ages!' Hettie said. 'Is Glori with you?'

'No, I don't know where Glori is. Miss Minter kept me.' She went round the first table and stopped by Connie. 'How's it going in the match-making department?' she asked, forcing herself to sound bright and pushing the images of the tortured spitfyres to the back of her mind. 'You're on cutting today, are you?'

Connie nodded and pointed at the pile of neat matchsticks she'd made. The smell of newly-cut wood fought against the smell of phosphorus, but lost.

'Come and sit by me,' Hettie called. 'Help me make my boxes.'

'I'm coming.'

'It's nice to have you back,' Connie said. 'You're always so cheery, Sparrow.'

'Tell us more about the family you were with,' Agnes said, as Sparrow took her place at the table. 'I want to know everything. Did the man, that Bruno, did he shout a lot?'

Sparrow laughed as she sat down. 'Of course he didn't. He was very kind and sweet. They had a toyshop.'

'Toyshop!' Hettie cried. 'Oh I wish I could go there,' she said. 'I'd do anything to have a toy. A real, pretend spitfyre made of velvet, that's what I want.'

'Funnily enough, that's just what I have,' Sparrow said. 'Bruno insisted I took one. I'll show you. It's upstairs in my coat pocket.'

'Goody!' said Hettie.

'You smell funny,' Violet said, sniffing Sparrow's jacket. 'Where've you been?'

Sparrow shrugged, cross with herself for not remembering she might have picked up the scent of the spitfyres. 'It must be that old bag that Tapper tipped up over me,' she said. 'It was disgusting.'

'Did you have your own bedroom then?' Billie asked her, leaving the dipping to come and join them. 'I'd love my own bedroom – no offence, girls!'

'Yes, I did. It had rose wallpaper and the mattress was so soft it was like sleeping on a cloud!'

'Oh you lucky thing!' Beattie shrieked. 'Tell us more! Tell us everything you ate and everything you drank!'

Sparrow did her best, describing the food, the rooms and what they had done each day.

'Sounds boring to me,' Violet said, turning back to her work. 'I'd've hated it.'

Sparrow was hardly concentrating on what she said; her thoughts were on the spitfyres she'd just found because – she realised suddenly – these girls must know about them. If Seraphina and Kopernicus had been kidnapped at the circus the same time as *she* had been kidnapped, they had probably helped. She hoped they didn't realise what a terrible thing it was that they helped Miss Minter to do.

'Oh do go on,' Hettie urged her. 'Tell me more.'

'Sorry, what?' Sparrow said. Without noticing, she had come to a complete halt and they were staring at her. She went on quickly, 'Hilda, the lady, she wanted to keep me,' she said, pushing all the bleak and upsetting thoughts of the spitfyres away. 'She was lonely, you see, and she liked me.'

'She could have *me*,' Hettie said, looking up at Sparrow with her big round eyes. 'I'd be really good and help and do the cleaning and everything.'

'Do you know, I think they'd love you,' Sparrow said truthfully. 'You're just perfect for them, but . . .'

'You're Miss Minter's,' Violet put in.

'For ever and ever,' Connie added.

'Like Glori.'

'That Tapper,' Sparrow said cautiously, 'what does he have to do with Miss Minter?'

The girls shrugged and looked vague. No one was clear about it. 'Don't know,' Billie said.

'He's foul, worse than a black pit of despair,' Connie said, giggling. 'That's what we call him, the *pit of despair*!'

'Don't say that in front of Glori,' Agnes put in quickly. 'Glori really, really likes him.'

'He's her *boyfriend*,' Hettie said clearly.

'Oh.' Sparrow stared round at the others. 'Is he? Really?'

'What can she see in the *pit of despair*?' Violet said wearily.

'A way out,' Dolly said.

'Freedom from phosphorus!' Beattie added, banging the

lid down on the jar.

'She thinks she can change him,' Connie added. 'She thinks she can turn him into a good person; like my ma used to think she could change my pa and stop him drinking . . . Uh uh. No way!'

37

Discoveries

Glori slithered out from under the heavy, damp coats and mackintoshes hanging on the back wall of the Belvedere parlour and ran . . .

She had heard everything. She knew everything.

She came to a stop and stood outside in the freezing cold, staring around wildly. They were going to hurt Sparrow! This man, Mr de Whitt, was planning to, to . . . kill Sparrow, push her off the ship – and they were helping him! Never in her darkest moments had she thought that they would sink so low.

Glori set off again in haste, getting away from the Belvedere as fast as she could, but with no clear plan.

The snow that had fallen in the night had almost gone. Water dripped from the eaves of the houses. The pavements were glassy and when she lost her footing and slipped, it sent a jolt of pain searing through her jaw. No one ever said, but she knew what the pain was: phozzy jaw, caused by the phosphorus. That's what made the girls glow in the dark too, turning them all into little ghosts, one way or another.

Miss Minter knows what the stuff does, Glori thought. She knows but still she does nothing about it. If the girls really were Miss Minter's family, why didn't Miss Minter look after them better?

Breathless, confused, Glori finally stopped her crazy rush and began walking. Finding herself not far from the street where the Butterworths' toyshop was, she went to it. The large window was completely plastered over with posters.

MISSING MISSING MISSING

Glori had half-noticed the posters before, thinking they were for the stolen spitfyres; now she saw they were for Sparrow. The Butterworths wanted her back. She remembered Miss Minter had said something about it but her thoughts had been in such turmoil . . . She read the poster carefully. Twice. Bruno was Sparrow's *uncle*? That made the Butterworths Sparrow's true family . . . And she had helped kidnap her back. Wanted her to stay!

No! Sparrow must be given back to them!

Glori made to open the shop door, but catching sight of the twirling spitfyres hanging from the ceiling, she stopped.

Toy spitfyres.

She turned and walked away. No love in those spitfyres, Sparrow had said. Glori walked ten paces off then she spun round and walked back, went ten paces past the shop in the other direction, doubled back and finally went in.

'Hello, may I help you?' The big man smiled kindly at her. *Bruno*. Oh he was a nice, cheery sort, with that big tubby belly and a proper, chuckling smile that lit up his brown eyes and made her want to smile too, only nothing could make her smile now.

'I'm just looking at the spitfyres,' Glori said in a small voice.

The smile faded from Bruno's face as he looked up at the hanging toys. 'Oh yes, those spitfyres . . . pretty things, aren't they, my dear.' Then he muttered to himself, 'I meant to take them down and stop selling them . . .' He shook his head. 'I'm forgetting things!' he said to Glori. 'Don't you mind me. You go ahead, my dear. Please take as long as you want.'

The spitfyres were lovely, if you didn't know how or where they were made, Glori thought. Beautiful. The real spitfyres were gorgeous too; she'd always thought so. It wasn't right what they did to them, but . . .

'Oh! No!' she gasped. 'It's . . .' She reached for one of the spitfyres with a shaking hand.

'All right, dear?' Bruno asked her. 'Can you manage?'

She nodded dumbly.

The fabric of the spitfyre was a tiny flower pattern, orange and pink and purple. Of course lots of people *might* have that fabric, she thought, lots and lots . . . it was just an old scrap of silk, a scarf she'd had from an ancient, kind lady, long ago. But it was unusual. Different. She turned the spitfyre over and over, hardly seeing it now, only remembering that scarf, and remembering giving it to Tapper as a keepsake. 'I'll keep it by my heart,' he'd said, patting his jacket pocket. 'For ever.'

What a sad life she had, she thought, with a sniff. What a hopeless life. Everything she'd believed in and wanted to love, was a lie. Maybe she could never be properly happy, she thought. She had inside her a sadness that came up unexpected – often from the very things that should bring happiness – and here it was now, overwhelming her because she knew Tapper was untrue.

'Who makes them?' Glori said in a tiny voice; not really wanting an answer. Bruno looked very uncomfortable now. 'Ah, well a young man called Tapper Nash brings them to me and, and . . . I'm not entirely sure who makes them.' He coughed. 'I'm changing supplier,' he added. 'Mr Nash isn't the man I thought he was.'

No, Glori thought, that is so true.

'How about something else, my dear – one of these lovely dolls?' Bruno asked her, waving his hand to show her a shelf of beautiful, porcelain dolls.

'Oh no, no thank you. I've got to go.'

She was outside the shop again so quickly that her head was spinning. She set off back to the nest, taking long, purposeful strides, thoughts reeling. She needed to be in the nest, she needed Miss Minter to tell her she was wrong to doubt Tapper. She wanted to hear how Miss Minter needed her and she wanted to sit by the fire with her and sip hot chocolate and feel all was right in the world.

The posters were everywhere. How had she not read them properly before? MISSING MISSING MISSING. There were hundreds of them. They haunted her journey and followed her path so she could think of nothing else except that

Sparrow had a real family – a family who wanted her.

All of a sudden a hand slammed down heavily on her shoulder.

'Glori!'

'*Tapper!*' she spun round, feeling her cheeks burn and blaze guiltily. 'You gave me a fright,' she managed to squeak. Oh what if he knew? What if he knew what she'd done, where she'd been? Her heart did one heavy thud then began to race and thrash about like something caught in a trap.

'You shouldn't have such a guilty conscience, girl. Seen the posters?' Tapper asked her, nodding towards one. 'Rum, eh? Now they're saying she's like family and everything, but we all know she's an orphan.'

'I don't know, is she? I don't know . . . I've got toothache, Tapper. I can't think. I'm feeling bad.' She looked along the street; the nest was close, she longed for the nest. 'I need to –'

'Come on, my girl, let's go have some food,' Tapper said, linking his arm through hers. 'Things are looking up again and we're in clover.'

'I'd rather not, Tapper, really . . .'

Tapper froze. '*Rather not?* I don't think so. I want lunch with you, my girl, and lunch with you is what I'll have.'

'Yes, Tapper.'

They soon had a table in the busy tavern.

'See how they move out for me, eh?' Tapper said as they sat down on seats still warm from the first occupants. Tapper smiled into his bark-beer and Glori miserably watched the bubbles disappear.

A steaming rabbit pie was placed on the table for them.

'I'm not hungry,' Glori said, pushing her pastry round her plate. 'Sorry, Tapper.'

'Eat.'

Glori tried, but the pastry tasted like cardboard and the meat was like chewing leather.

'Here. I'll eat it.' He scooped up the rest of the pie. 'I'm always hungry. I'm hungry for life, I am. Oh Glori, are we going to have a good time, you and me?'

'Are we?' Her voice came out cracked and feeble.

'What's up?' he asked, tossing his hair aside and fixing his cold eyes on her. 'Come on, tell me. You know you will in the end.'

'Nothing,' she said, rubbing her jaw.

'Glori, you can't keep nothing from me and you know it.' He suddenly grabbed her arm, squeezing it tightly. 'Glori, speak up. Don't make me be mean. I don't want to be mean, but you make me.'

'I'm not very well,' she said. 'It's my teeth.'

He picked up a fork and stabbed it inches from where her hand lay on the tabletop, digging the prongs in deep then rocking the fork backwards and forwards. '*Glori?* I'm warning you . . . Glori, don't . . .'

She had to tell him something . . . she pretended to crumble.

'Sparrow told me . . . She said she'd been in a house by the swamp and it was *your* house and you'd *made* her sew the spitfyres and locked .er up. I saw the spitfyre, Tapper. I saw it and it's true.'

Tapper laughed.

'She's a one, that Sparrow,' Tapper said, smiling at his pie, which immediately stopped steaming. 'I must have a little word with her when I get back to the nest. She was a guest in our house, Glori, and my ma fed her and looked after her like she were her own dear daughter. What a little minx to lie about it.'

Glori tried to look relieved but didn't feel anything except certainty, certainty that he was lying.

'But you *do* make spitfyres for them Butterworths?'

'How was I to know she were connected to them? How? That's just bad luck . . . or good luck. Oh I know, I know what this is leading up to,' Tapper said. 'You've seen the posters and you want us to send her back to them, don't you?'

'Why not, Tapper?' Glori cried, grabbing his arm. 'She could have a real, loving family then and belong somewhere. A *real* family and they're so kind and –'

'How d'you know they're so kind?' he interrupted her.

'I mean . . . I mean she told me they were kind. Nice. It's what she said.' Glori cast her eyes down and quickly sipped her drink.

Tapper leaned back in his chair. 'It ain't going to happen, Glori, no way.' He shook her off when she reached out for him. 'No. And don't paw me!'

'But why not?' Glori took hold of his hand again, pleading. 'Please, Tapper. We could just do this one good thing and make her happy. Then you and me, we'd still be all right. We could –'

'You've forgot about the money,' Tapper said coldly.

'But we'd get the money. The Butterworths' reward.'

'No.' Tapper snatched his hand away. 'No.'

'But why not?'

Tapper turned away and stared at the wall. A black spider scuttled off down a deep crack. 'I can get more for her, that's why not.'

'Who'd pay more for her than her uncle?' Glori asked, although she knew. She waited, wanting him to commit himself, to fall into her trap. If he was prepared to let Sparrow go to de Whitt and certain death then she was all set to do anything – anything – to save her friend.

'Never you mind. All I'll say is we'll get more. I promise. We'll get more.'

'But she's got a *real* family! What we all want!'

'Speak for yourself,' Tapper snapped. 'I don't want my old ma!' Then he grinned. 'Yeah, she's got more family than you can shake a hat at, has Sparrow. Now leave off. I've done with talking about Sparrow. Talk about *us*. Talk about that little house we're going to get and what fine clothes we'll have, eh? I've found the place, right near the nest it is, and you'll love it. End of discussion.'

38

Free

The other match-girls were asleep; the fire had burned down low.

Sparrow looked over at Glori's sleeping shape. Glori had been upset when she came in, too ill to talk, she'd said. Sparrow had wanted to ask her about the spitfyres outside in the yard. She hoped Glori didn't know about them, that she wasn't part of *that* business. Glori was too kind, too caring to be so cruel.

She was going to help those creatures tonight. She had to.

It was quiet and still. She turned back her covers gently and crept out of bed. She pulled on two jumpers and two pairs of socks; took her coat from the peg and picked up her boots. Her breath clouded in front of her; her teeth rattled in her head.

She tiptoed silently out of the attic.

At the top of the long flight of stairs she stopped, lit a candle using stolen matches and put on her boots. Then she made her way down.

Her heart seemed to have ballooned and was filling her throat, thumping massively in her chest, booming in her ears. If only Scaramouch were here, she thought. Dear Scaramouch, please find me Scaramouch, if you're here somewhere. That's what she'd do next, she thought; after helping the spitfyres, she'd go into every single room in this place, every single room and look for him.

She crept down the stairs, feeling for the rail in the dark, and on through the draughty, echoing hall. What if the door at the end of the corridor was locked? What if Brittel kept watch at night? She reached out for the door nervously, turned the handle. It moved. It opened.

Freezing air rushed in at her.

The wind rustled in the tall trees and made a horrible, sad moaning sound as if the entire courtyard was alive with phantoms and trapped spirits.

Her candle went out.

She stood and waited, letting her eyes adjust, trying not to let her fears take over. No lighted windows showed in the tall buildings behind the trees. There was no sign of life anywhere; she felt very alone.

The four stalls in the stables glowed with a dull, orangey light. The heat from the spitfyres had melted the ice on the roof and water dripped from it. She made her way across the cluttered yard towards the animals. In the first stable the grey, dirty spitfyre lay on the floor, weak and still. It hardly moved when she went in.

'Dear spitfyre,' she whispered, kneeling beside it. 'I've come to save you.'

The spitfyre opened its eyes and blinked at her blankly. 'Come on,' Sparrow said. 'Come on.' She undid the rope from around its neck. 'You're free. Look, you're free.' She pointed to the open door. 'This is your chance.'

The spitfyre hauled itself up onto its knees and then slowly stood, panting, its sides heaving with the effort. 'There, you did it! You did it!' she said. 'Well done.' Next she ripped off the cloth that was wound around its body. The moment its wings were free, it lifted its head and its ears pricked up and life came flooding back into its eyes as if some internal energy source had been turned on. It shook out its mane and flicked its tail from side to side. Gobs of thick dirt and old paint fell from its coat. 'Lovely thing!' she said, patting its neck. 'You feel better already, don't you? Go outside, move around and flap those wings about.'

The spitfyre staggered out into the yard. Its hooves made such a clatter on the stones she was immediately frightened someone might hear. She pulled armfuls of straw from the stable and threw it down, trying to cover as much of the stone as she could.

Then quickly she went into the other stalls and did the same for the rest of the spitfyres.

Kopernicus and Seraphina, the circus spitfyres, hadn't been kept prisoner there for so long and were not so weakened. Their eyes gleamed with unshed, golden tears. They puffed out miniscule sparks and thin smoke rings. Whinnying softly, they walked round and round the yard, stretching their legs and opening and closing their wings. They seemed to glow with an inner light and soon the whole yard was warm and lit by them.

As the spitfyres beat their leathery wings up and down, the wings plumped up and refilled with blood. They changed colour from paper-white to pink and purple and orange and yellow as the tiny blood vessels filled and nourished them. 'You are so lovely, so marvellous!' Sparrow said. 'How could Miss Minter, or anyone, ever hurt you?'

Round and round the spitfyres went, jumping carefully over the rubbish, snorting out orange and yellow sparks, stopping now and again to beat their wings, blowing and puffing to each other, tossing their heads, flexing their limbs.

Suddenly, Seraphina reared up on her back legs with a high-pitched whinny.

Sparrow quickly backed away as the spitfyre pawed the air and then crashed down with a hollow clatter to the ground, throwing her head from side to side as if she were shaking something off.

'Hush! Oh be quiet!' Sparrow cried, looking round at the blank windows, dreading a light appearing. 'Gently, Seraphina, gently!'

But the spitfyre was unstoppable. She arched her neck and spat and roared like a dragon. Again and again the spitfyre gazed round at the confines of the yard, and then stared up to the night sky.

Sparrow looked up too, at freedom.

'Go, go if you can!' she urged the spitfyre. 'Go.'

Seraphina tossed her head and whinnied as if to say she would. She spun round on a tight circle, like something clockwork winding itself up, then she suddenly leaped over a heap of barrels, up onto the shed by the stable, up onto the stable roof and up onto the very top of the roof. Her hooves slipped and slates came loose and slithered, crashing to the ground. Right on the top of the pointed roof she somehow balanced, wings held out like a tightrope walker might hold a pole. She looked again into the sky above and began to thrash her wings, preparing to jump. The other spitfyres watched her, pawing the ground expectantly.

Seraphina tensed, bent her legs as if they were springs, clamped her wings tight to her sides, and jumped. Straight up, she went, like a giant rocket. Skimming the tops of the trees, she unfurled her wings and began flying; up, up into the dark night sky. Orange flames streamed from her mouth; she looked like a shooting star.

Sparrow clapped her hands. Wonderful! Glorious! Oh what a pity there is no one else to see this, she thought, as Seraphina flew off over the rooftops and disappeared. Well done, Seraphina! Farewell!

The other spitfyres were electrified; it was as if Seraphina's escape had empowered them; the yard was hot and sparky and tingling with energy. Kopernicus was up onto the stable roof in two giant strides. She pirouetted, leaped, and then spiralled up into the darkness. Soon he had flown away over the houses and trees. Gone.

Sparrow ran back to the first spitfyre, who looked dazed and confused still. 'Come on, come on,' she urged it, patting its flanks. It was very weak. 'This is your only chance – come on! You must go! You must!'

'Stop right there!'

Sparrow spun round.

Brittel.

She screamed and ran but he was too quick; in an instant he'd leaped over the clutter and caught her, immediately clamping his hand across her mouth before she could utter another sound. He forced her arm up her back, twisted her about and marched her back towards the house.

'Idiot. Stupid little brat! Fool!' he spat, close beside her ear.

Sparrow kicked and struggled. She tried to bite his hand but each time she did he just yanked her arm harder and more painfully. 'Stop! Keep still!' he hissed.

There was a sudden roar, the air swirling and whooshing around them, making Brittel swing round just as the third spitfyre soared into the air.

It flew up off the stable roof and then suddenly swooped down low, its hooves brushing Brittel's head. A shower of hot ash sprayed over him. Brittel nearly let her go; he was torn between avoiding the pain, catching the animal and stopping Sparrow. She felt him waver and she almost yanked herself free, but then he had her again, his grip tighter than ever.

'You stupid little fool!'

He pushed her up to the wall and held her there, her face pressed into the stone while he kicked open a low metal door beside them with a loud clatter.

Behind them they heard the fourth spitfyre trying to clamber onto the stable roof. Brittel swirled round as tiles clattered to the ground and smashed on the cobbles. The spitfyre wheezed. It was weak. It had no strength. Sparrow urged it on. *Go, go,* she willed it.

The spitfyre whinnied, blew out a gust of black smoke and made it onto the roof.

Go, go!

Its hooves slipped, its wings thrashed and suddenly, with a startling cry, it soared into the air, throwing out a shower of silvery sparks and clouds of dusty ash.

Sparrow's own heart flew up into the stars with it.

'By the dragon, she'll kill you for this,' Brittel said, watching the orangey-golden glow fade into the sky, 'if you don't rot down there first.'

He doubled her over and pushed her roughly through the low opening in the wall, and bolted the door behind her.

39

Coal Cellar

Sparrow was falling. Not free falling, but sliding down a steep, metal chute. Instinctively she made herself into a tight ball as she shot down the narrow shaft, bumping and banging against the edges, rolling and sliding faster and faster until she somersaulted onto a pile of coal at the bottom.

So, she was in the coal cellar.

She couldn't see a thing; it was pitch black. Her shoulder hurt. Her left hand stung from where it had scraped against the metal slide. She lay for a few seconds, trying to decide if she was badly hurt or not and listening to the awful sound of her breath – short and hard and rough. It was freezing and damp. The air was thick with the smell of coal dust and something sharp and drainy.

She began to shiver and sat up and hugged herself.

The darkness was incredible. Not a chink of light anywhere. Wherever she turned her head it was the same; the same dense, impenetrable blackness.

She had a sudden vision of the spitfyres launching off the roof, and grinned. At least I did that, she thought. At least I set them free.

She rolled off the pile of coal cautiously. The lumps rattled around her to the floor. Someone will come and get coal, she thought. We have a coal fire nearly every day . . . Who goes for the coal? *Violet*. It was always Violet, her least favourite person. But even Violet wouldn't leave her here . . . would she?

And I'm not scared, she told herself. It's only blackness and I'm used to that. The coal cellar below the kitchen at the Knip and Pynch Home was the same, and how often had she been left down there? This was home from home. Someone will come. If the spitfyres can escape, so can I. I can and I will.

She stood up warily and stuck her arms out and waved them around. She couldn't see them. Nothing. She took a step forward and another and cracked her head on a low archway. Lights danced in front of her eyes.

When the pain and lights had subsided she moved forward again, this time ducking down and bending almost double. With one hand above her head, feeling for the low ceiling with her fingertips, she inched forward and, when the ceiling disappeared, she stood up again. Her fingers were covered in crumbly plaster and cobwebs and so was her hair. Not nice, but it could be worse, she told herself. She must have come through a sort of doorway into an adjoining room. There must be a door out into the main house, but where? Perhaps there had been one back in the coal room. Should she go back

271

and work her way around the entire room, searching for it? She stood for a moment, thinking, wondering what to do.

It was dark and totally silent.

And then she heard the trickle of rubble, soft and crumbly and very alarming.

Her heart went *bang*. She stood stock-still.

The blackness was deep, totally impossible to see through. She spun round, trying to locate the sound.

There was something there.

'Hello?'

She turned in a complete circle, straining her ears. She heard it again. More tiny, shifting sounds, something moving over loose bits and pieces, broken slates or tiles or . . .

A cry cut through the air.

The hairs on the back of her neck rose up and she shivered violently.

'Oh! Oh!' she cried. '*Scaramouch!* Is it you?'

'Meow! Meow!'

It *was* Scaramouch. She would have recognised his call even if a thousand cats had been down in the cellar and all crying at the same time.

'I'm coming, I'm coming!' she cried. 'Oh Scaramouch, I can't see, keep calling! Don't stop!'

She inched forward, keeping her fingertips in contact with the wall, and crept towards his voice.

'Meow!'

'I know, it's not nice. Oh dear Scaramouch, where are you? How long have you been here? Are you all right, my dear Scaramouch? I'm coming!'

She banged her knee on something and nearly fell. Tears of frustration pricked her eyes. 'I can't find you, I can't get to you!' It seemed she was going round and round and all the walls felt the same and his voice was no closer.

'Meow!'

That was nearer! She wiped her tears away quickly.

'Yes, yes, I'm here!'

She could sense him very close by.

Beneath her fingers now she could feel some sort of wooden partition built across the end of the room like a prison cell. His call came from very near by, from beyond it. She could sense him pacing from side to side, his paws making the smallest sounds on the crumbling rubble. He was close, so close . . .

She heard him scratching and tearing at the wood.

'Scaramouch! I can't see you! Dear Scaramouch!' She could only reach through the wooden bars with three fingers, but that was enough. He found her fingers and rubbed against her and pushed his head against her again and again. His purrs were deep and loud.

'There must be a catch or a door or something!' she said, running her fumbling fingers up and down and across the wood. *There!* Right at the top, a metal latch, and it wasn't even locked – no need, she thought, Scaramouch couldn't reach it. She lifted the latch and flung open the door.

He leaped into her arms and she gathered him up and kissed him again and again. *Scaramouch!* Her dear Scaramouch was back where he belonged. He purred like an engine as he snuggled up to her chin and pushed his forehead into her face while his big paws kneaded her shoulder. 'My lovely!' she crooned, sinking down with her back against the wood and stroking his smooth, fine fur until her hand ached. 'That mean Miss Minter! Only *she* would do this to you. Who brought you food? Was it Violet? Someone must have. Oh poor, poor puss. I missed you so much. It's so wonderful to see you again – well, to *feel* you again.'

'Meow!'

'Exactly. Just that much.'

They sat for a while, with Scaramouch draped around her like a thick scarf, then he began to struggle gently away from her. She could feel him standing just by her, even though she couldn't see him.

'It's all right for you,' she said. 'You can see – but I'm blind as a bat, probably blinder. You want to take me somewhere? OK. Where?'

Scaramouch set off, but it was impossible to follow him in the dark. She tripped over something and fell hard onto her knees, grazing the palm of her hand and knocking her chin. She tried not to cry but she felt like sitting down and weeping buckets.

'Meow?'

'No, no, I'm fine, it's just my lovely coat,' she said as brightly as she could. 'That's all it is, Scaramouch. That's why I'm sad. Hilda will go mad when she sees it. Oh puss, how can I follow you when I can't see?'

Scaramouch began to walk up and down past her face. His tail flicked her nose softly, back and forth again and again.

'I get it. Excellent.' She lightly took hold of the tip of his long tail and slowly got back on her feet.

'Meow!'

Scaramouch stepped forward and Sparrow, crouching like an old woman, holding his tail, hobbled blindly after him.

They walked only for a minute. He led her to a corner of the cellar where she felt a heap of dry, dusty earth and rags and they sat down on it. It was much warmer here than the stone floor and when Scaramouch snuggled onto her lap, she grew cosily warm.

She was sleepy now – it was still the middle of the night. 'Do we just sit here, then?' she asked him, yawning.

'Meow.'

'Well, if you say so. Dear Scaramouch, we should never have come here, should we?'

She wasn't afraid of anything now she was reunited with her cat. Stroking Scaramouch was soothing, and his constant purr was relaxing. Whatever happened, she felt, as long as they were together, they would be all right. Soon, no doubt, Miss Minter would be down to sort her out, but right now, she had to close her eyes.

They both slept.

40

Betrayal

'Sparrow's gone,' Hettie said.

It was the following morning and Hettie was shaking Glori awake and speaking loudly into her ear. 'She's not in her bed.'

Glori sat up quickly.

'Her bed's cold,' Hettie said. 'I felt it. She's not in the bathroom. Where is she, Glori?'

Glori felt icy all over. Had they taken her to de Whitt already? Oh please no. If they had she would never forgive herself. Never. She should have warned her last night. She should have been less selfish and not thought about her own worries.

'She's probably gone on an errand for Miss Minter,' Glori said. Her voice sounded flat and unreal to her. 'Don't worry.'

She got up slowly and dressed but her fingers couldn't find the buttons on her shirt and her knees kept buckling. Something was wrong. Something was wrong.

At last Miss Minter appeared, her nose uncharacteristically red and her normally immaculate blonde hair had flyaway strands. No lipstick either. Glori had never seen her without her lips painted.

'What is it?' Glori said. 'What's the matter?'

Miss Minter scowled at her and her eyes flashed dangerously.

'Sorry, sorry,' Glori said quickly. You never asked Miss Minter questions.

'Sparrow's gone!' Hettie said. 'Oh Miss Minter, you've got snow on your lovely hair!'

Miss Minter threw her coat at Hettie, ordering her to hang it up, and then she sat down by the fire. 'Build this fire up,' she said. 'Nothing is the matter. Get the table laid. Make some hot chocolate. Girls, girls!' She called out to the others, who were still in bed. 'Time to get up.'

The match-girls began to stir. Hettie stacked more logs on the fire and a shovelful of coal.

'Glori,' Miss Minter said, 'don't go out. Don't leave the room until I tell you.' She turned and stared into the leaping flames. 'This is going to be an interesting day.'

The girls stayed in the nest.

Glori and Connie were sitting playing cards. Glori kept dropping her cards as she rubbed her jaw.

'Keep still, Glori,' Connie said, nudging her.

'Sorry. Ow, ow,' she muttered. 'My teeth ache something dreadful.'

'Join the club,' Agnes said, making a funny face.

'What's the matter?' Miss Minter said, glancing up from her newspaper. 'Yes, yes, your jaw hurts. There's nothing you can do about it. Don't bother me.'

Glori caught Agnes's eye and they exchanged a worried look.

'I need . . .' Miss Minter began, then stopped. 'Is that someone at the door? Go see!'

'It's Tapper,' Beattie called and threw down the keys to him.

Tapper came in and tossed his snow-spattered coat onto the chair by the fire. 'Cold out,' he said, shaking snow from his hair. 'Freezing.'

Glori watched the snowflakes on his coat refusing to melt. She moved over to the window and sat on the trunk looking out at the snow. Where was Sparrow? Was she out in the cold somewhere? If they'd taken her to de Whitt, why weren't the pair of them looking pleased?

The girls gave up their seats by the fireplace to Tapper, leaving their hot chocolate to grow cold, and huddled on their beds, whispering amongst themselves.

'What's wrong? Where's Sparrow?' Agnes asked, coming and sitting beside Glori. 'Miss Minter's in a right state.'

'I don't know,' Glori said. 'Do you know anything, Violet?' she called softly. 'You're very close these days.'

Violet looked offended. 'Not as close as you! Anyway, you should ask your Tapper.'

Tapper and Miss Minter sat with their heads close together, whispering. Both looked tense. Something was amiss; their plan must have gone wrong, which meant Sparrow was . . . where?

278

'Don't sit around doing nothing, girls!' Miss Minter called out. 'Get on! Get to work. Leave us alone!'

The match-girls crept about, collecting their things.

Glori sidled up to Miss Minter on the pink chaise longue. 'My jaw hurts real bad, Miss Minter,' she said, pressing her hand against her face. 'Please could you spare a penny for me to see the doctor?'

Tapper glanced at her suspiciously. 'What d'you want with a quack?' he said.

'I don't know what this awful pain is,' Glori said. 'But it's bad. My teeth are loose and my bones hurt.' She looked at Miss Minter, giving her one last chance to admit that the phosphorus did it, but Miss Minter was busy adding up figures in a little notebook.

'Oh go then, Glori, if you must,' Miss Minter said without looking up. 'But you can pay for the luxury yourself. And don't be long! I want you back here within the hour, d'you hear? I need you.'

'Yes, Miss Minter!'

Tapper glanced at her distrustfully, his eyes narrow and calculating.

Glori was so relieved she hardly noticed; she just dragged on her coat and went.

The toyshop wasn't open, but Glori had the Butterworths' address from the poster.

She ran until she was breathless and her sides were aching and she had to sit on a bench and get her breath. Passers-by stared at her as she sat there unravelling.

'Get a good look?' she asked them, pushing up her trailing ribbons and strands of dark hair. She probably looked wild. She felt wild; like some hunted thing. I know too much, she thought grimly. I can put them both in prison. They'd do away with me too, if they knew, and not get a penny for it and not care.

What if she were too late to save Sparrow? She hugged herself against the cold. She had to be in time.

Memories flooded in. She remembered the things Miss Minter had done for her. She remembered the first nights in the nest, just the two of them. Miss Minter had dark hair in those days and was more posh and proud than a queen. She'd wept at night. Every night. Talked of how she'd been a grand and fine lady. She never did that any more. Miss Minter had given her food and showed her how to cook and steal . . . How could she give up her dear Miss Minter? And Tapper? He was her man, the only one she'd ever have, and the only one who'd ever wanted her.

Slowly Glori stood up and turned back the way she had come. No. She couldn't do it.

As soon as she began walking again, her thoughts started up. Round and round. Miss Minter and Tapper meant to give Sparrow to de Whitt. For money. They were selling her. So, that wasn't so bad; even Glori had been happy to sell her to the Butterworths . . . but Tapper and Miss Minter meant to *kill her*.

She spun round again and started running towards the Butterworths' house. Birdie deserved something more than the nest, more than Miss Minter, more than being pushed off a ship in the fog as it sailed out to sea. She deserved the best, and that meant her own family.

She hammered on the door. By the time Gerta opened the door, Glori had gone back down the path and had her hand on the gate, ready to flee.

'Yes?' Gerta looked Glori up and down, taking in her dishevelled hair, her dirty orange trousers and wild eyes. 'Yes?'

Glori turned back slowly and went up to the door.

'Is this where Bruno Butterworth lives and the nice Hilda?' she said.

Gerta stiffened. 'Yes.'

'I've got to see them, please. My name's . . . oh my name don't matter but I must see the lady called Hilda. It's about Sparrow! It is urgent!' she added, as Gerta did not move or change her expression. 'It is a matter of life or death.'

'*Sparrow?*'

Glori nodded furiously. 'Life or death!'

'Come in, come in quickly. Mind you wipe your dirty boots there,' Gerta said. 'And don't touch a thing with those mucky fingers. Hilda – Mrs Butterworth – is just finishing her breakfast.'

She opened a door and led Glori into a small, bright room with vases of winter greenery and pale orchids. There was a small fire and several candles burning, so the room was bright and jolly; it had an odd effect on Glori; it made her want to cry.

'Hilda, this young – thing – has something to tell you. She says it's about Sparrow.' Gerta stood, watching Glori with her hands folded over her front.

Hilda started up so suddenly that she upset her teacup. 'Oh my dear!' she cried, leaping up. 'Do you know where she is?'

Glori nodded. 'Can we just speak together, you and me, in private?' Glori asked her, glancing round at Gerta. 'She's stern. She makes me nervous.'

'Of course. Gerta, do you mind?'

Gerta frowned and went out, but as Glori could very well tell, she stayed on the other side of the door, listening.

'I ran,' she explained. 'I would have come before, I nearly did – got to the shop, but I wasn't sure they'd go so far – but, now she's gone . . .'

'Start at the beginning,' Hilda said gently. 'If you know something about Sparrow then I must hear it. I will help all I can.'

'Oh you are kind,' Glori said, sinking down on a stool by the fire. 'Sparrow said you were. Is it true she's your real niece?'

'Yes.' Hilda pointed to Mayra's portrait. 'That is her mother – *was* her mother. When she died Sparrow was taken to the Knip and Pynch Home for Waifs and Strays. We didn't know she existed, or we'd have had her here. Gladly. She was alone in that dreadful place for more than ten years, poor dear.'

'Then she came to Sto'back,' Glori said. 'Miss Minter got her. My fault, that.' She paused. If she'd never picked Sparrow up, never offered her that pie and a place to sleep . . .

'Go on, dear,' Hilda said.

'Miss Minter heard Sparrow was worth something to the

282

right people – that was you, miss. Miss Knip found that out first . . . Miss Minter's got this friend of mine . . .' Glori hesitated, not wanting to give up Tapper's name. 'Anyway,' she went on, 'forget about him. What happened was, Miss Minter meant to sell Sparrow to you, only she found out that there was someone else who'd pay even more.'

'*What?* Who? We are her only family. Who else would offer a reward for her, dear thing that she is.'

Glori smiled grimly. 'No, you wouldn't think it, would you? But see, there's this gent, a cousin I think, called de Whitt – Oh!' she cried suddenly, as another awful thought crossed her mind. 'Oh Miss Hilda, I *didn't* help grab her at the circus. I swear I didn't. I saw her but I told no one. But the others, they told. I saw you and saw she was happy and I wanted to leave her – I swear!'

As quickly as she could, Glori explained all she knew about Mr de Whitt, Cosmo's cousin and only other relative, who wanted Sparrow dead so he could claim her inheritance.

'You see,' Glori finished, 'when I heard them talking I knew what they was up to and I couldn't let them.'

'I see,' Hilda said, standing up and pacing round the room. 'You are very brave to come here. I appreciate it enormously. You are a true friend to Sparrow.'

'I am!' Glori cried. 'I am!'

The door was flung open suddenly, crashing back against the wall. 'But where is Sparrow now?' Gerta cried. 'We must save her!'

Glori stood up shakily. 'That's it,' she said. 'That's why I came now. She's in danger. They – Miss Minter and this – *my friend* – they've got her, I think. She disappeared last night. I 'spect she must be hidden somewhere. I'm praying she's still all right. But something has gone wrong with their plans because they're all jumpy and Miss Minter went out this morning and she never ever goes out without her lips done pink. You got to act now, but, but . . .'

'What is it? Is it this friend you mentioned?'

'Yes,' Glori said. 'He's not a good one, I know he in't; he's got like *heart rot* or something, but he's all I've got. Please, please can we give him a chance to get away? If I tell you where they are, the match-girls, and who they are and what they do, will you let me warn him?'

'But Glori,' Hilda said gently, 'surely you don't want to go back to this man? A man who steals children? Ransoms them? You say he's not a "good one". I don't understand . . . how could you care for someone so heartless?'

Glori shrugged. 'I don't know, Miss Hilda,' she said. 'He's not good at all and he is wicked, but there you are. I've never had much and to have him is better than not to have him, if you see what I mean. I've betrayed him, but he'll never find out if I can get him away now.'

'Very well, Glori, whatever you want,' Hilda said. 'Now, sit down here at the table and take some tea and some toast, I insist, and in the meanwhile I will explain everything to my husband.'

'I suppose you expect the reward my brother has offered,' Gerta asked when Hilda went out.

'I don't want no reward,' Glori said quickly. She rubbed at her jaw and aching teeth. 'I've no use for any reward now and anyways I don't deserve it.'

284

41

Rage

Glori came away from the Butterworths' house with a heavy heart and her head spinning so she couldn't walk straight. It was the right thing to have done. It was the wrong thing. Tapper would kill her. Miss Minter would throw her out. She was lost. She was crazy. But little Birdie would be all right. Birdie would have her family and be so happy.

It was going to be all right for Sparrow.

As she turned the corner into a side street, someone grabbed her hair and yanked her backwards, slamming her into the wall.

'Glori!' he snarled. 'Been out visiting your dear old doctor, have you?' He pushed his face up close to hers.

'Oh Tapper!' Glori cried. 'What are you doing here? You're hurting me. Let me go!'

Tapper shook his head. 'Never. I'll *never* let go of you.' He looked all around; the streets were empty. He took her arm roughly and frogmarched her down the lanes, past boarded-up warehouses and the old greenhouses and into the deserted park. Glori remembered how in the summer they'd walked there and gone boating on the busy river; now the trees were leafless skeletons and the grass was muddy and bare and there wasn't a soul to be seen.

'Spitfyres have gone!' Tapper snarled at her. 'Anything to do with you?'

'*Gone?* No. I've never . . . Tapper, I've never been near them. I haven't!' She almost felt relief. She wasn't guilty of this. She breathed more easily. 'I don't know anything about the spitfyres,' she said. 'Promise.'

'Sparrow did it.'

'She freed the spitfyres? How? Is she all right?'

'What's it to you? Why'd you care about another blooming orphan?' he snapped at her, pushing her across the muddy lawns towards the brown river.

'I like her. She's a real friend. Not like . . .' It was on the tip of her tongue to say Miss Minter, but she couldn't. 'She's never let me down.'

'And I s'ppose I have?' he said bitterly.

'No, you haven't. You never! Oh Tapper, where are we going? Let's go back. I'm really cold. I promised Miss Minter I'd be back straight away. I went to the doctor and –'

'Doctor's called Butterworth is he?'

Glori felt her strength drain away; her knees went weak. He knew. He knew! Of course he knew. 'I didn't tell them anything, not really, I promise,' she said. 'Just that Sparrow was safe, so they wouldn't worry. I knew they were worrying, Tapper! Ow!' she cried as he yanked her arm. 'I never told about you.'

They were on the wooden jetty now. Far away down the river, a small fishing barge was chugging softly towards them. The water lapped against the posts and knocked the cluster of rowing boats so they clunked dully against each other. The air was very cold.

'What are you doing? Where're we going?' she asked. But she thought she knew: he meant to throw her in. He was going to kill her.

Tapper ignored her. He pushed her into one of the small boats and got in beside her so roughly that it rocked and the cold water splashed her.

'Tapper!' she cried. She hardly dared look at him; his face was immobile and white. His hair hung lankly over his eyes, eyes that were horribly glassy and empty.

'Thought we was friends, Glori. Thought you and I was going to be happy together, and now what am I to think?' he said, untying the boat and pushing off from the jetty into the swirling water. 'You run off telling stories about me. You betray me. Me, your man!'

'I swear I didn't. I only told them about de Whitt – not about you. Believe me, I swear I didn't say a word about you. Not a word.' She clung to the sides of the little boat. Her fingers were quite blue with cold. Tapper was always menacing but now, now he was really terrifying. Oh how could she save herself?

He grabbed the oars and set out, rowing past an island of scrub in the middle of the river, away from everything. Some ducks quacked a warning at them.

Glori crouched as far from him as she could at the other end of the boat.

'What are you going to do to me?' she cried, staring out at the surging, dirty water. 'You wouldn't hurt me, would you? Would you?' She paused as the boat cut on through the water, further and further from safety. 'Ah, it don't matter anyway, Tapper, I'm doomed. Don't you know I'm doomed?' Glori laughed suddenly. 'Never seen how I glow at night, Tapper?' she asked. 'That's the phosphorus, that's what does it. Poison in my blood. Never wondered about my jaw and my bad teeth and the pain in my joints? *Phosphorus*. I'm full of it. I'm exploding with it, I'm . . .' She stood up. 'See, I'm a gonner, Tapper, I'm done!'

'Shut up!'

In the distance the fishing barge hooted softly and suddenly.

Glori lost her balance, her foot slipped and, before she could right herself, she'd toppled out of the boat and into the freezing water.

'Tapper! Help!'

The brown water surged over her head so, for a second, she was under. She held her breath and forced herself back up again, bobbing to the surface, sucking in air. She couldn't see; her hair was in her eyes. She groped blindly for the boat.

Oh the water was ice cold, so cold that her legs and arms went numb instantly. Her wet, heavy clothes were dragging her down; she could feel them pulling on her shoulders and hips as if strong hands were tugging her down to the riverbed. She went under again. Rising up the second time was harder; she was like a lead weight now. She pushed herself round in a circle, half-blind, searching for the boat. There it was; one wooden oar so close . . .

'Help me, Tapper. Help me!' she gasped, reaching for the oar. The oar seemed to retreat from her fingers . . . She groped for it again, staring up at Tapper.

'Please, Tapper, please!'

Tapper stared at her. Her beautiful hair, that he'd so admired, was wet and dark, ugly as slimy seaweed. He watched her fingers clutching at the end of the oar, watched them slip off, reach, slip off, and try again. She was getting weaker. The next time she reached for it, he snatched the oar from her so that it wasn't there. She looked up at him, grasped at thin air, her fingers grabbed at nothing and with a sigh the water closed over her head.

Tapper leaned over the side of the boat. Her face was hanging there, white and blue and ghastly. Her open eyes were staring and accusing. Her mouth was open; she was still saying his name. He could hear it, he could hear her calling him from far, far away.

'*Tapper* . . .'

The fishing barge was nearer; he heard its chugging motor and it hooted twice. They mustn't see him.

He turned away quickly. *Dragon's teeth!* Why had he looked into her eyes just now?

He rowed to the bank as quickly as his shaky arms could do it.

'*Tapper, Tapper, Tapper, help me!*'

He hit himself on the side of his head with the flat of his hand, trying to stop the voice. But it followed behind him all the way to the road and beyond. *Tapper. Tapper. Tapper.*

Ditching the boat, he set off back to the nest. Halfway there, he turned off and headed for the Old Blue Bear Tavern. The place was almost deserted. 'Bark-beer,' he told the barman. 'Make it a big one.' He took his drink to the darkest corner and sat down, expecting the bearded old man there to move.

The man didn't.

The brown terrier who'd been dozing on the floor woke with a start, sniffed the air and whimpered. His white-haired owner shoved him with his foot. 'Quiet!' he snapped.

Tapper was shivering uncontrollably. He stared at his trembling fingers and wrapped them around the glass to still them, but the beer jumped and jittered as if it wanted to escape his hands. He peered into the bark-beer and there was Glori's face, bobbing beneath the foam. He slammed the glass on the table and turned his back on it.

The man with the white beard and rheumy, red-rimmed eyes still hadn't got up from his place. 'Morning, mister,' he said, grinning a toothless grin at Tapper. 'Cold in't it?'

'What do you mean by sitting by me?' Tapper said. 'Don't you see? No one sits by me! No one!'

The old man laughed and rubbed at his beard thoughtfully. 'I sit where I will.'

'Why are you staring at me?' Tapper demanded.

'I'm looking at the fire.'

'You're staring at me!'

The old man chuckled. 'Why would I do that?'

Tapper stared at him. 'What can you see? What can you see?' He got up and kicked the table so his glass fell with a crash to the floor. 'There! There!' he shouted. 'She's gone!'

He raced out into the street again.

What to do? Where to go? He began walking blindly but soon heard someone creeping along behind him. Someone was following him. He glanced over his shoulder but the road was empty. He walked on, only to stop again minutes later as the footsteps pattered along behind him. *Glori's* footsteps, he recognised them.

He spun round – no one.

Tapper.

Now a dense fog was gathering and the road was misty and sinister. He turned round and headed back the way he'd come but now and again something loomed up unexpectedly at him out of the fog and gave him a fright: a man with a black beard, a tree shaped like a skull, a cart rumbling along almost silently. And still she was behind him; whichever way he went, Glori was there, trailing him, following behind him, watching his every move and sporadically calling out his name . . . *Tapper!*

Tapper burst into the attic and flung himself down at the table.

'Well?' Miss Minter said. 'Did you follow Gloriana?'

'Yes. Yes, I did. We're lost!' Tapper cried.

Miss Minter grabbed his arm and pulled him closer. 'What? What do you mean? What happened? Where is she? She wasn't going to the doctor's, was she?' she cried. 'She lied. Tell me everything.'

The match-girls, normally so anxious to leave the room when Tapper was in it, now gathered around, perching quietly on the furniture like a flock of starlings, their heads on one side, listening.

'She went . . .' Tapper began. He glanced over at Glori's empty bed nervously, knowing she'd never sleep there again. He dragged his eyes back. 'I followed her, she went to the Butt—'

'*Butterworths!*'

'She must've told them everything!' he said with a groan. He looked again at her bed; just for a second he'd seen a movement there, a small rearranging of the sheets . . .

'Why? Why did she do that?' Agnes interrupted.

'Be quiet!' Miss Minter snapped. 'Gloriana betrayed ME!' Her face was pale and her hand shook.

'What about Sparrow?' Hettie's little voice piped up. 'Where's she gone?'

Miss Minter became very calm and cold. She sat up taller and clasped her hands together. 'Sparrow has betrayed us all,' she said. 'She has released the spitfyres . . .'

'What?' Connie cried.

'How?' Beattie asked.

Miss Minter shushed them. 'It doesn't matter. It *does*. No. It's done and the wicked girl has been dealt with.'

'I don't know how, but Glori knew about de Whitt,' Tapper said, turning his back to the row of beds. 'She told the Butterworths everything.' He didn't care now whether Glori had or hadn't. He didn't care that she'd sworn she'd not given up his name – she'd gone against him, sneaked behind his back. He couldn't allow that.

'How?' Miss Minter said. 'How could she know about de Whitt?' She paused and peered intently at Tapper. 'Where is Gloriana now?'

Tapper stared into space and shook his head.

Miss Minter didn't ask more. She looked round at the frightened faces of the match-girls. 'Right, girls,' she said. 'This is it. We've discussed it before, and you knew it might happen. Time to go. Pack a bag quickly. Our dear friend, our trusted Gloriana, has betrayed us. There may be guards knocking on the door any second now.'

The girls let out a collective moan.

'Where shall we go?' Connie wailed.

'Anywhere.' Miss Minter said calmly. 'Just get out. All of you! Get out and don't come back for a long time.'

'But we *can* come back?' Agnes asked her, already stuffing clothes into her knapsack. 'Later? Can't we?'

'Yes, yes,' Miss Minter said. 'This will all blow over, I'm sure. It must. When it has, I will leave a mark, a cross on the door. Orange. No, yellow. My favourite colour. It will be safe again. Meanwhile, GO!'

'Can't I stay, Miss Minter?' Violet whispered. 'I don't want to be on my own again.'

'No one can stay. I can't look out for any of you now.'

The match-girls had been hurriedly gathering their things and now they made a dash for the door, stumbling, shouting and dropping shoes and clothes behind them as they fled.

Only Hettie remained. The nest was her home and the only place that she knew, the only place her sister might come and look for her, so she had to stay. She slipped into a corner behind the old leather trunk at the window and crouched there, unseen.

The room was suddenly quiet and bare and desolate.

Tapper seemed to breathe more easily without the girls there. 'Sparrow safe?' he asked.

Miss Minter nodded. 'Yes. Brittel caught her in the yard last night and locked her in the coal cellar. He was glad to pay her back.'

'What'd she ever done to him?'

Miss Minter laughed. 'Long ago, Otto threw him out of the Academy. Otto is her uncle. What a laugh, eh? They're even now, he says.' She laughed, then the laugh died as she remembered. 'We do not have any spitfyres. She let them go. Little idiot. But we do have *her*.' She glanced at the window. 'Look at the lovely thick fog! What could be better? I can't think of a more perfect time to take her to de Whitt!'

42

Escape

Sparrow was woken the next morning by Scaramouch's sandpaper tongue, rasping her cheek. But was it morning? She didn't know; everything was still black as ink around her.

'What? What is it?' she muttered, yawning. She rubbed and rubbed her eyes but still couldn't see a thing. Then she remembered: she was in the cellar.

She stretched her aching legs and arms. She was cold and hungry.

'Meow!' Scaramouch moved away, leaving her chilled.

'Where are we going?' she cried. 'Not too fast!' She got up slowly, shivering. 'Ow! Scaramouch, hold on! I'm stiff and cold.'

She found and took hold of the tip of his tail again and let him lead her through the horrible darkness. At last, tripping, stumbling, they came to an opening in the wall. Scaramouch stopped. Sparrow could smell fresh air and sensed an open space in front of her. Her spirits lifted.

Feeling around quickly, she discovered a hearth and an iron grate – a fireplace.

'Now what?' she asked the blackness.

She felt Scaramouch leap up past her, onto the grate. Even as her fingers touched him, she felt his fur slip away from her and he was gone.

'Meow!' His cry sounded hollow, softened by the thick wall between them. He'd gone up the chimney.

'Oh no, Scaramouch. You can't be serious?'

'Meow.'

He was.

So she would have to do it.

She reached for the grate and sat on it with her head inside the chimney. Sitting like that was not nice. The soot made her choke and cough and if it hadn't been for the fresh air swooping down coldly from high above, she couldn't have done it. She looked up – nothing. Not even a dot of light at the top.

'It's going to be a long climb, she said.

'Meow!' He was already further away, she could tell, and moving off. A shower of dust and soot and twigs fell on her.

'Hang on, I'm coming!'

She stood up very slowly. If only she could see, she thought. She was scared of smashing her head against something, frightened of touching something unpleasant like a dead bird or . . . Oh stop being such a sissy, she told herself. Get on with it.

The inside of the chimney was rough and uneven, lined with bricks that had been laid so that they were not flush with each other but jutted out and formed make-shift footholds. I suppose we're not the first, she thought, imagining the poor little chimney sweeps who once, long ago, had cleaned these chimneys.

Scaramouch called for her to hurry. 'Meow!'

'Coming!'

Her toes sought out the tiny ledges, she braced her back against the wall, her fingers gripped the protruding bricks and she began to shuffle and drag herself up the chimney. It was hard, especially doing it blind. Her legs were soon tired and aching and her hands were sore and scratched.

'Wait – wait, Scaramouch,' she called. 'I can't keep up. I need a rest.'

She stopped and wedged herself with her knees bent and her back jammed against the bricks.

She couldn't see up or down. 'My legs are burning!' she told Scaramouch. 'My head hurts. I'm thirsty. I can't see.'

He only answered with a soft, trilling '*Meeee-ow.*'

'Yeah, I see. Encouraging up to a point!' she said with a smile.

She stayed put, getting her breath back. She couldn't go back down now, but how much further was there to go up? 'I've heard about people finding the skeletons of chimney sweeps in their chimneys,' she told the invisible Scaramouch. 'They'll know it's me by my lovely red coat. Ruined,' she went on, wiping her dirty, sweating hands down it. 'Hilda will be so disappointed. And my boots will be scuffed! Heaven knows what my hair looks like.'

'Meow.'

'Yes, well it's all right for you, you've only got fur and whiskers.'

She gathered her strength and even though her thighs felt as if they were on fire and her fingers throbbed and every single nail was broken and torn, she went on and on and on.

'Meow! Meow!' Scaramouch's cry was suddenly quite different. Not an alarm, more a call to say, '*Look!*'

So Sparrow looked up and, for the first time, she saw light. It was still far away, but there it was, a small patch of sky.

'There's light at the end of the tunnel!' she yelled, and her shout brought soot and dust toppling over her face, making her splutter and cough and laugh. 'We'll do it, Scaramouch, we will!' Looking up she could even see Scaramouch now; he was on a wide ledge with his front paws resting on the stone above and his tail only inches from her face.

Sparrow felt lighter. Her legs had some spring in them again. Out, she was going to get out! Every few feet that she climbed now, she stopped and glanced quickly up to the square of daylight, thrilled to see that it was growing bigger. And every time she looked up, there was Scaramouch, looking down at her with his lovely yellow eyes, urging her on. The air grew colder and clearer, as if it were coming down to meet her, and she breathed it in greedily. As she got nearer and nearer the top, desperation took hold of her, desperation to get out of the chimney and into the open. It overwhelmed her so that even when Scaramouch was standing on the very rim of the chimney, she forged ahead.

She nudged Scaramouch out of the way. As he jumped over the side, Sparrow hooked her elbows over the edge of the chimney and hoisted herself up into the cold air.

'We're free!' she cried.

Around her lay a sea of fog, from which terracotta-tiled roofs, turrets, chimney stacks and pointed gables emerged like the masts of ghostly ships. Rooftops were spread out for miles around. Sparrow looked about, suddenly fearful.

Just exactly where were they?

43

Chase

Hettie, who had been hiding by the trunk, jumped up with a shout and pointed through the window.

'Sparrow!' she cried, her face breaking into a grin. 'Sparrow's come back for me!'

Tapper and Miss Minter spun round in amazement.

'What's *Hettie* doing here?' Miss Minter said.

Tapper leaped up, already on the move. He saw the cat and Sparrow on the roof and had the roof door open immediately and was rushing towards them. Hettie dashed out too, but Miss Minter was right behind her and swiftly scooped her up and held her arms tightly behind her back.

'Not you!'

Sparrow tried to run. Scaramouch bounded up onto a high wall.

'Go away!' Sparrow yelled as Tapper advanced, his arms reaching out for her. 'Leave me alone!' She darted this way and that; but there was nowhere to go. She ran to the roof's parapet, looked over at the nearest building, saw the terrible drop and veered away.

'The gap's huge,' Tapper said behind her. 'You'd never make it.'

She glanced again at the lower roof. Could she? Dare she?

'I wouldn't. You'd be strawberry jam on the pavement,' Tapper said, grinning. 'You can't get away,' he added. 'Might as well give in.'

Miss Minter shouted, 'Stay right there, Sparrow! Don't try anything. If you do, Hettie's dead!'

She was dragging Hettie to the edge of the roof and Hettie was struggling for all she was worth, kicking and crying. Miss Minter tripped and tottered and wobbled on her high heels. Her hair was falling down and her eyes were wild.

'Watch out, Miss Minter! Take care,' Tapper called.

'You wouldn't!' Sparrow cried. 'Please. That's little Hettie! You *couldn't!*'

'I would!' Miss Minter screeched. 'You know I would. I would. I could. I might. I will . . .' She shook Hettie as if she were a doll. 'Watch me!'

Hettie burst into tears. 'Miss Minter! Don't!' she sobbed. 'It's me, Hettie. Don't be scary. *Sparrow!* Help me!'

Miss Minter took a shaky, high-heeled step right to the rim of the roof, flinging Hettie down so she lay half over the parapet, her legs dangling over the edge.

Hettie clutched wildly at her. '*Miss Minter!*' she screamed.

Suddenly Scaramouch let out a blood-curdling cry. He flew across the roof like a rocket and leaped on Tapper. Tapper screamed as the cat launched at him, claws out. He was thrown onto the roof tiles, yelling in pain as Scaramouch raked his face with his claws.

Tapper fought and lashed out at him, trying to push him off, but Scaramouch was like a crazy, wild beast, scratching and biting.

Miss Minter abandoned Hettie and ran to Tapper. She grabbed Scaramouch by his tail and hauled him off.

'Got you, you horrible monster!' she cried.

The cat's claws ripped through Tapper's jacket as he was pulled off. Miss Minter stood, holding the cat by his tail, laughing. Scaramouch twisted and turned, yowling and spitting.

Sparrow ran to them.

'Stay back!' Miss Minter warned. Then, laughing, she began to whirl Scaramouch round and round, leaning back as she gathered momentum, so the cat became nothing more than a blur of fur whizzing through the air.

She let him go.

She flung him away. The cat sailed past Tapper and right off the roof into nothingness.

'Scaramouch!' Sparrow ran. 'No! No!'

Tapper got up and wiped the blood from his cheek. He was laughing hysterically. 'Flying cats!' he said. 'Well done, Miss Minter. Flying horses, flying cats . . .'

Sparrow knelt at the edge of the roof, hardly daring to look down.

Scaramouch had landed on a tiny window ledge. He was shaking his head, dizzy and confused. He wobbled uncertainly on his legs.

'Are you all right? I'll get you, don't worry, I'll get you!' Sparrow called to him. 'Don't worry, Scaramouch! I'll –'

'Shut up!' snapped Tapper, yanking her upright. 'That cat's dead meat!'

Sparrow pulled away from him and ran to Hettie, who was sobbing. She put her arm round her. 'You'll be fine,' she said. 'Don't worry. We'll all be fine – you, me and Scaramouch.'

'I never have been much to look at,' Tapper said, mopping his bloody, scratched cheek. 'Now . . .'

'Never mind that,' Miss Minter said. 'We must take her and go. De Whitt . . .'

But even as she spoke they both became aware of a strange noise overhead. They stared up into the misty sky where grey fog swirled above them – thick, and then thin.

WHOOSH, WHOOSH!

Now the grey fog was lit by orangey yellow, as if on fire. Showers of sparks cut through the murkiness and lit up the sky in a rainbow of amazing colours.

'Dragon's teeth! It's *spitfyres*!' Tapper cried.

Miss Minter was frozen to the spot. She stared up at the two advancing spitfyres. She seemed unable to move as she watched them circling above.

They were preparing to land.

They were coming . . .

Tapper turned and ran.

He raced over the roof, leaped onto the parapet and, with a mighty roar, jumped across the gap onto the next roof. He landed flat on the slanting, icy tiles and straight away began to glide down towards the narrow gutter, his feet slipping and slithering as he tried to get a hold.

At last he found a foothold and began to haul himself up, dragging himself to the ridge of the rooftop. He stood there for a moment, wiping the streaming blood from his face, smoothing back his hair. He glanced back at the circling spitfyres with a smile. They wouldn't get him!

Then he was up and off again.

But it was slow going and hard work.

He crawled along the rooftop and made his way around a large chimney stack, clinging to it with both hands, then climbed over a garret window and onto a flat square of roof. The fog was patchy and now and then a ray of pale sunshine broke through, bouncing off the windowpanes and sparkling on the frosted tiles.

Suddenly he heard something. He stopped. Someone was creeping along behind him. His heart missed a beat. There it was again. He glanced back, peering into the mist.

'Who's there?' he called.

Dragon's teeth, he cursed. Someone was *always* following him.

Now his heart was pounding and his hands slick with sweat. The lock of hair dangled over his eyes and each time he swept it back it fell forward again, blinding him.

He struggled on. Across a skylight, over a low railing and then jumping down to a lower roof, flanked by walls. He must reach somewhere soon . . .

Another noise.

He stopped and looked round, teetering on the edge of a parapet. A beam of light cut through the fog and he saw

. . . Glori!

Glori was coming after him.

He felt his whole body go rigid. He nearly lost his footing. Glori!

Sweat broke out all over his body. *Glori!* He set off again, faster, twisting now and then to look back over his shoulder. The fog lifted, and then fell, swirling around his face, so he was surprised when a spiked turret or a garret window suddenly appeared. He could hear Glori's little footsteps and her breathing now too, getting closer and closer.

He turned back. He wanted to tell her to leave him be. *Leave me alone!*

The fog swirled and settled, then parted, as if someone was drawing back curtains, and in the clearing he saw Glori advancing with her arms outstretched, reaching for him. Her face was white and her lips were blue. Her long, lovely hair was plastered wetly around her face and she was smiling at him. Smiling and smiling, and coming nearer and still smiling.

He turned and scrambled over a sea of tiles, clung to a length of railing, swung from that onto another low wall. Every scrap of roof seemed identical. Each corner brought another wall, another roof, and another blank, shuttered window.

He inched along a gully until he could clasp the black drainpipe at the end. He stopped: he'd come to a dead end. He looked up and there were more steep walls and, above, more pointed, impossibly high roofs. He'd have to jump, but it was too foggy to see where to jump. He'd have to wait, wait for a puff of wind to clear the fog. He was shivering and yet his hands were wet with sweat, they couldn't grip the drainpipe, and his feet were slipping on the tiles. He turned back briefly and saw Glori, still coming towards him, crawling on all fours along the gutter, balancing like an acrobat as she inched nearer and nearer.

Her saucer eyes glowed yellow in the mist.

'Go away!' he shrieked. 'I'm sorry! I'm sorry!'

The fog was swirling thicker and denser than ever but he had to move. He stared through the fog, thought he saw the edge of a flat roof below.

'Keep back, Glori!'

He looked again and she was still coming; using her tail to balance as she tiptoed towards him. 'Meow!'

He let go of the drainpipe and launched himself into the void, hands outstretched. He flew through the air, arms windmilling and legs running . . .

There was no flat roof below.

Scaramouch turned and padded back, silently, along the rooftops.

44

The End

'Where has he gone?' Miss Minter said, staring at where Tapper had been. 'Everybody leaves me. He was a nuisance. *You* are a nuisance,' she said, glaring at Sparrow. 'You are just money. You are a walking gold mine. And an interfering nuisance.'

Sparrow ignored her rambling. She was staring up into the sky. She patted little Hettie, whose arms were so tightly wrapped around her that she couldn't move. 'Don't listen to her, Hettie. Look at the lovely spitfyres,' Sparrow said, as the flying horses came swooping closer and closer. The riders on their backs waved and Sparrow waved back. 'Look, Hettie, they're coming to save us. Aren't they wonderful?'

The two spitfyres landed gently on the roof with a mild clatter of hooves and a rush of warm air and sparks. 'That's Kopernicus and Seraphina,' she told Hettie. Her heart lifted and swelled with happiness. 'They've come back! They'll save us!'

The sky-riders immediately dismounted, threw off their goggles and ran towards them. It was Maud and Stormy from the Academy. They were both dressed in soft, dark, tight-fitting costumes with long boots.

Maud shook out her hair. She ran to Sparrow and anxiously gathered her and Hettie into her arms.

'Are you all right?' she asked Sparrow, then turned to Hettie. 'And the little one?'

Sparrow nodded. 'We're fine. Fine.' She had never been so glad to see someone, ever. 'It's her, you need to get her!' She pointed to Miss Minter.

Miss Minter had made no effort to escape. She was tottering backwards and forwards as if she were drunk.

'My name is Miss Minter,' she said. Her eyes flashed dangerously. 'Where is de Whitt? We had a meeting. All arranged. Out to sea we go! My name is Miss Minter. I am a lady!'

Stormy advanced on Miss Minter.

'De Whitt has sailed,' Stormy told her. He winked at Sparrow. 'He's gone. Bruno saw him off. Your plan to sell Sparrow to him is done with,' he went on. 'De Whitt is lucky he didn't end up in prison.'

Sparrow was confused. Who would want to *buy* her? But then, she thought, if Bruno had seen this de Whitt character off, then Bruno knew what was going on. The Butterworths had helped and there was every chance she'd see them again. That was good. Very good. She squeezed Hettie gently. 'It's going to be OK,' she said.

'Meow!'

They turned as Scaramouch appeared and bounded over the roof to them.

'There he is!' Hettie cried. 'He's all right!'

Sparrow scooped him up in her arms and hugged him.

'What a clever cat!' she crooned to him. 'You made it back all on your own!'

Meanwhile, the spitfyres were walking in tight, menacing circles around Miss Minter, puffing and blowing out hot, ashy blue smoke.

Miss Minter swayed on her high heels and watched the flying horses warily.

'They don't like you, Miss Minter,' Stormy said. He was very close to her, ready to grab her if she tried to run. 'I wonder why?'

'She locked them up, that's why,' Sparrow said. 'She stole their Brightling.'

Miss Minter laughed. She turned to the Director. 'You're so stupid, Stormy, you don't even realise what riches you're sitting on up there at the Academy. You have all that Brightling, and you don't take any yourself. You could. It's worth a fortune.'

Stormy was looking puzzled. 'Who are you?' he asked her. 'I think I know you. Do I know you?'

Miss Minter cackled. 'Make these animals leave me alone. I hate animals. I hate spitfyres and cats. Loathsome. Why are they looking at me like that? I don't like it.'

'They know what you did to them,' Maud said. 'They don't trust you.'

'You don't know who I am either, do you? You pasty-faced

little maid-of-all-work, *Cousin* Maud!'

Cousin Maud?

Sparrow saw recognition dawning in Stormy and Mauds' faces; they couldn't believe what they thought they saw. She'd never seen such expressions of amazement and . . . horror!

'Oh my . . . it's *you!*' Maud said quietly, looking intently at Miss Minter. 'You've dyed your hair. It has to be ten years since we last saw you . . .'

'*Araminta!*' Stormy said. 'It's Araminta! The Director's daughter,' he added, for Sparrow's sake. 'When he went to prison she disappeared – along with a couple of the Academy spitfyres.'

Miss Minter shrieked with laughter. 'That's right. Took all their Brightling too! Lovely stuff. Stormy was a stupid, interfering boy. And you, *Maud!*' she added, pointing a finger at Maud. 'How dare you even look at me! You are my maid! My underling. I wipe my feet on the likes of you!' She laughed again and her laugh turned into a shiver so violent that it rocked her from side to side so she nearly fell over. 'I never had a cousin called Maud. Never!'

'You've taken Brightling, haven't you?' Stormy said. 'How much? It's dangerous, it –'

'Ha!' Miss Minter interrupted. 'You would say that. Lies. Lies. Lies.'

'It destroys,' Maud said. 'That's why we came to the circus, to try and warn people. It affects the brain. The tears of one sad creature can only cause tears in another . . .'

Miss Minter quickly took a bottle of Brightling from her pocket. She held it up to the spitfyres defiantly. 'I love it!'

she said and before Stormy could reach her, she had drained the bottle dry.

'Don't look!' Maud cried and swung Hettie round so she couldn't see the horrible effects of such a large dose of Brightling. Sparrow knew she should turn away too, but could not.

Miss Minter's hand remained poised with the small bottle at her lips. Now, slowly, her arm dropped and hung loosely at her side. Nothing happened for a whole minute, and then the top of her head began to smoke. Her blonde hair snapped off her head as if it were made of glass. It splintered at her feet.

Miss Minter yelped and put her hands to her throat as orange fire burst out of her mouth. She roared and spat out more flames and clouds of smoke. She began to twist and turn, faster and faster until, like a Catherine wheel, she was just a blaze of sparkling lights and brilliant flashes of colour.

When she stopped she had gone. There was nothing left but a heap of grey ash.

That night, Sparrow lay again in her rose-patterned bedroom at the Butterworths' house, feeling secure and happy. Her left hand lay gently on Scaramouch's warm back.

Now she knew who it was in the portrait that she loved so much: it was Mayra, her mother. She could stare and stare at her to her heart's content. She knew too that Cosmo, the circus owner, had been her father. Otto had given her an old circus pamphlet with a picture of the Great Cosmo in it that she would always treasure.

Sleep didn't come easily that night.

Miss Minter had died a terrible death . . . How would she ever get rid of that awful image? She would try very hard to wipe it out of her mind but it would be hard.

No one knew exactly what had happened to Tapper but a body had been found on the street – a man who'd fallen a great height, and Bruno said it sounded as if it were him.

Where was Glori? Had she run away, like the other match-girls? She had heard how Glori had gone to Hilda and done all she could to rescue Sparrow, and she wanted to thank her. Sweet Glori. She hoped she was happy, wherever she was.

It turned out that as soon as Bruno heard the details of Miss Minter's plan he'd gone with the guards and challenged de Whitt. De Whitt was a coward, and had escaped onboard a ship and sailed away.

Scaramouch was snoring – so was Hettie, who was sleeping peacefully in the spare bedroom. Everything was settled. Well, almost . . . because she still felt unfinished. Even knowing about her family, that she was Sparrow Butterworth, hadn't brought the total happiness she'd hoped for. Actually, she supposed she was Sparrow de Whitt – Cosmo's name. But since he'd never married her mother, she would happily stick to Butterworth.

Stormy had told her that he was an orphan too. 'I used to think that when I found my parents,' he'd said, 'if I ever found out who my parents were, I'd be happy because then I'd know exactly who I was and what I was.'

'Yes, yes. Me too,' Sparrow had replied.

'But, d'you know,' Stormy had said, grinning, 'it wasn't

312

like that at all. I never did find them. I haven't a clue who my real family is, but I've found Maud and the spitfyres and I love the Academy. All those things make me who I am. I am Stormy, without knowing all that other stuff.'

'That's enough?' Sparrow had asked him, amazed.

'Yes, it really is. Listen, Sparrow, you are a strong and brave person. You saved my spitfyres – they would certainly have died if you hadn't set them free. You survived the Knip and Pynch Home. You don't *need* a family to make you into a whole person. You never needed to know who your parents were to be you. You are whole. A whole Sparrow!'

Sparrow smiled as she remembered his words. Stormy was right.

And she was so happy to be here with the Butterworths again. She was going to wallow in their kindness. Being loved properly, like this, was a new and wonderful experience and she was going to get as much of it as she possibly could – as much as they could give. She felt as if she was blossoming right now, like one of the roses on the wall, getting rounder and richer and, somehow, more rosy! And she'd give love back too. She knew she could, with practice.

She remembered Zippo's circus and the performing cats – that was what she wanted, to join the circus and have her own act with Scaramouch. She wanted to be with spitfyres and become a sky-rider too. She wanted . . . everything. She wanted to try everything, go everywhere, see everything . . . and now, perhaps, it would be possible.

Hettie was flourishing too. Straight away, something had sparked between Hilda and Hettie and they had hugged and

313

Hettie wanted Hilda to be her mother. She'd even thrown her arms around Gerta and sworn undying adoration for her.

The next morning, Gerta received a letter from Mr Pynch at the Knip and Pynch Home for Waifs and Strays. She read it at the breakfast table.

'Oh how dreadful!' Gerta said, after she'd glanced at the letter's contents. 'Listen to this. That woman, that Miss Knip, has vanished, believed dead! It says she never reached the Home after she visited us. The cart-driver said she vanished into thin air as they were travelling through the swamplands . . . She must have fallen out or something – how awful!'

It was on the tip of Sparrow's tongue to say *Serves her right*, but she held it back.

'And Mr Pynch is leaving the Home too!' Gerta continued. 'He's just writing to me to see if I know anything about Miss Knip's disappearance, as we were the last to see her. *What was her mental state?* he asks. Oh dear. I hope they don't think we were responsible?'

'But that's amazing!' Sparrow said, grabbing Hilda's hand. 'Because now *you* can take over the Home!'

Gerta let out a little shriek. '*What?*'

'Yes, all of you! You, Hilda and Bruno,' Sparrow said. 'You've all got so much to give and those girls need loving care so badly. It's a perfect solution. Just think, Hilda, not one new daughter, but forty-four of them – at least, that's how many there were at the last count. It will be forty-six with me and Hettie, and forty-seven when we find Glori, if she wants to come. You could include boys too, if you

314

wanted! Oh do say you will! It could be a *real* home. And think, Bruno, Tapper isn't going to be making any more spitfyres, so you'd have to reconsider the shop and the stock anyway and . . . It's a perfect, perfect plan.'

'It's an amazing idea,' Hilda said, grinning. 'Of course I'd still want to continue with my work on the committee. We must stop all Brightling production and sales. It's imperative!' She paused. 'But I do like the idea of running the Home. I like it very much.'

'We'll think about it,' Bruno said. 'My shop –'

'The shop! The shop's not important,' Hilda said. 'Oh yes, we will think about it,' she went on. 'Forty-four, did you say? Poor little things – no parents, no good food, no warmth.' She rubbed her hands together. 'Oh Bruno, what fine girls we could help make there!'

The doorbell sounded shrilly, making them all jump. Gerta went to answer it. She came back a moment later and ushered in a thin, short young woman, wearing a too-small black coat and a long green skirt. The girl's dark hair was plaited in a long rope that hung down her back to her waist. Spotting Sparrow, she licked her small, round teeth and broke into an enormous smile.

'Sparrow!' she cried, rushing to her. 'My little *Birdie*!'

'*Glori?*' Sparrow ran to her and they hugged and rocked from side to side. 'What happened to you? You smell of *oysters*! I'm so glad you've come. Why are you wearing these funny clothes?'

'Let Glori sit down,' Bruno said, vacating a chair. 'Let her have some space, dear girl. Then she can explain.'

Glori sat down and told them everything.

'After I left you, Miss Hilda,' Glori said, 'I met Tapper. He'd followed me. He took me to the river. Tapper meant to drown me,' she said.

'The rogue!' Hilda cried.

'Ah, you mustn't mind him,' Glori said. 'He couldn't help it. I mean, he was hurt bad when I let him down. I *did* let him down. Betrayed him. So he rowed me out into the river, only this old oyster-catching boat was coming and I'd seen it. So I let myself fall in before he could push me. I did think, I did wonder if he'd help me and, when he didn't, I knew for certain. Knew he didn't love me, not really; he couldn't. Or he loved me the best he could love anyone, and it were no good.

'I played dead – was real close to dead, it were that cold, but the oyster-catchers had seen me go in and they fished me out a few seconds later. I was sick as a dog. All my lovely clothes was ruined! This is all they had to dress me in – stuff what belonged to an oyster-catcher's daughter. Don't I look funny? But who cares? I'm back and aren't I so glad to find you alive and well, little Birdie!'

Later, Sparrow went into the garden with Bruno while he shook out the breakfast tablecloth so the birds could eat the crumbs. 'Well, it's wonderful to have Glori safe and sound,' Bruno said. 'She's a fine young lady and will be an asset to our growing family. And now we have our future all mapped out for us! What a little fixer you are, Sparrow dear,' he said. 'Just like your mother.'

'You don't mind, do you?'

'Not at all. I think it's a wonderful idea. Perhaps we could move the Home up to Sto'back so we don't have to negotiate the krackodyles every time we make a journey? Perhaps I can still keep on the toyshop, without the spitfyres? There are lots of possibilities and best of all, it will make my Hilda happy – might even make Gerta happy too.'

'I'm so glad you think so,' Sparrow said. 'Because that's what I think too.' She paused to watch a little robin come down to peck at the crumbs. 'You never forget to feed them, do you, Bruno?' she said. 'You are kind.'

'It was Mayra that started it,' he told her. 'She loved all animals, but the birds especially. Fed them every single day of her life. That's probably why she called you Sparrow.'

'And that's why Scaramouch doesn't eat birds,' Sparrow said. 'And I bet he was her cat at the circus too,' she said. 'Dear Scaramouch.'

'Yes . . .' Bruno said. 'I think you're right. And she placed him in charge of you.'

'Do you think so?'

She longed to tell him that she wanted to go back to the circus, take Scaramouch with her and be daring and adventurous like her mother, but she didn't want to hurt his feelings.

Bruno nodded. 'He is definitely a Sherbavian cat; there's no doubt about it. Even Gerta has to agree on that one!'

They laughed.

'So you're happy now, dear?' Bruno asked her. 'Content?'

Sparrow nodded.

'Promise?' Bruno said.

317

'Very content, thank you – but I *do* keep thinking of all those lonely girls back at the Knip and Pynch Home,' Sparrow said. She paused. 'And I *do* think I'd like to join the circus with Scaramouch!' she finished in a rush.

Bruno laughed. 'Later Sparrow, later; there's plenty of time for all of that when you're a bit older.'

Sparrow smiled. There was plenty of time for it all. She picked up Scaramouch and he pushed his head under her chin and purred.

Never abandon Sparrow. Never leave her alone, dear Scaramouch, were Mayra's words to him. *You are her protector. Care for her if ever I cannot.*

Scaramouch purred. He had done his very best.

HOME   AUTHORS   BOOKS   BLOG   EXTRAS   ABOUT   READING LIST   SEARCH

nlock the power of stories

15/5   BLOG   14/5   BLOG   @HOTKEYBOC

@HotKeyBooks Come & here from young p
talking about books and their own creative
at @LiftandPlatform next Tuesday 21st
platformislington.org.uk/express-yourse...

May 15, 2013 | 02:58 PM

@HotKeyBooks We are coo-ing over the la
Hot Key Baby (3rd so far since we were bo
see @saramoohead & little Drew

Discover more at hotkeybooks.com!

Living (rooms) through
history

Following on from Becca'
yesterday about history's
More

Now you've finished, why not delve into a whole new world of books online?

- Find out more about the author, and ask them that question you can't stop thinking about!

- Get recommendations for other brilliant books – you can even download excerpts and extra content!

- Make a reading list, or browse ours for inspiration – and look out for special guests' reading lists too...

- Follow our blog and sign up to our newsletter for sneak peeks into future Hot Key releases, tips for aspiring writers and exclusive cover reveals.

- Talk to us! We'd love to hear what you thought about the book.

And don't forget you can also find us online on
Twitter, Facebook, Instagram, Pinterest and YouTube!
Just search for Hot Key Books